FOR KING OR FOR COUNTRY

FOR KING
OR FOR
COUNTRY

A story of the English Civil War

Geoffrey Cloke

Troubador Publishing Ltd
Unit E2 Airfield Business Park,
Harrison Road, Market Harborough,
Leicestershire LE16 7UL
Tel: 0116 279 2299
Email: books@troubador.co.uk
Web: www.troubador.co.uk

ISBN 978-1-80514-450-2

British Library Cataloguing in Publication Data.
A catalogue record for this book is available from the British Library.

Printed by Printed and bound by CPI Group (UK) Ltd, Croydon, CR0 4YY
Typeset in 12pt Adobe Jenson Pro by Troubador Publishing Ltd, Leicester, UK

MIX
Paper | Supporting
responsible forestry
FSC
www.fsc.org
FSC® C013604

This book is for Su and Leo.

CONTENTS

CHIEF CHARACTERS

Robert Grey: Son of Lord Hugh Grey – an advisor (or courtier) to King Charles I

Olivia Grey: Daughter of Lord Hugh Grey, Robert's younger sister

Mark Green: Son of Sir Henry Green, local squire

Harriet Green: Daughter of Sir Henry Green, Mark's younger sister

Stephanie White: Daughter of local vicar, Reverend Thomas White

Luke White: Son of Thomas White, Stephanie's younger brother

Edward Brown: Son of John Brown, steward and housekeeper to Lord Grey

Lucy Brown: Daughter of John Brown, Edward's younger sister

Thanks to:
Susannah Lord-Cloke
Gillian Smith (née Cloke)
(proof reading and comments)

INTRODUCTION

In 1642, the English Civil War started. The history of this war is well documented, but most histories take little account of the effect of the war on 'everyday' people of no rank. Sometimes, books or programmes document the stories of the wealthy or influential characters, some fictitious, but few are about those of no importance. This is the story of eight young people from that period, their families (in part), their lives, loves and hates. All of the main characters were in their late teens in 1642 – old enough to be drawn into the events of the times but not necessarily mature enough to make sensible and considered decisions, or to be considered fully adults. Two of them were considered wealthy, others less so, and two were perhaps just 'ordinary' villagers. This is the story of the eight main characters, but also of their village, Helmdon in Northamptonshire, and how it fared in the war.

Stephanie, the vicar's daughter, loves Mark, the squire's son, at the start of the story. She can see his shortcomings but sees in him, too, the sense of purpose that will drive him onward. Mark wants wealth and power for himself. He considers the status quo (divine right of kings and wealthy powerful Church) unfair, and sees that change in the government of the country could be beneficial to him. He also wants his share of wealth and fame. He will join the Parliamentary forces in the war with the intent of attaining that wealth, status and power, and he sees the war as a great opportunity for him. Robert Grey is less ambitious and only sees that his duty is to follow his noble father, Lord Grey, in his support of the King.

He does what is expected of him. He does not realise that the ability to follow others and obey existing customs is what is driving others to want change, and that the military will also face changes in the way that it fights and wins a war.

Luke White wants a simpler church where each man is directly answerable to God. He sees the current church (in the person of his father, the vicar) as standing between each person and God – he says, "It is a bit like praying to my father." He, too, will join the Parliamentary forces. Edward Brown, the son of Lord Grey's steward, John, perhaps wrongly sees the Parliamentarian cause as likely to change the lot of the common man – and to give him more chance for advancement. He will risk the wrath of his father and his father's employer to join the Parliamentary cause. The women in our story, and of the village, see no place in the conflict for themselves, and resolve to take on responsibility for maintaining the home or village or place for the men to return to. They will, however, be drawn into events which will change their lives. Lucy Brown (sister of Edward) is our narrator. Everything is seen through her eyes. Essentially, this is Lucy's story. When our story starts, Lucy is eighteen years old. By the time the war is over, and the repercussions of it dealt with, she will be approaching thirty.

In the war, people will die. Some deaths will affect the emotions and opinions of our main characters. Those deaths will also remove the inner control on the younger generation's behaviour and allow them more freedom of choice. Some will die at Marston Moor and Naseby. Those left behind will find that their control of the village and the local estates will grow and they will become more important. Eventually, they will have to manage or control their houses and lands and make the decisions that their menfolk or parents used to. How will Luke's view of the Church be reconciled with that of his father, the Reverend Thomas White? He loves Harriet – but is unable to marry whilst he is away fighting. He will find that neither side of the war actually supports the Church he wants properly, and he needs to consider how to change his loyalties to a more honourable cause. This will affect his loyalties, his friendships, and in the end, it will affect his life.

King Charles I surrendered to the Scots in 1646. He was handed over to Parliament, and the 'first' civil war ended. In 1647, however, he started negotiations with the Scots, and in 1648, he escaped to start the 'second' civil war. The Battle of Preston, the last battle of the 'second' civil war, was in 1648. By the end of this phase of the war, some of our characters will have risen higher in status, and others will have fallen. Edward, for example – who has achieved his goal of rising through the ranks and has become a senior military commander. His rise has brought him a mature view of management of troops and (despite being a soldier) some humanity. He appreciates opposing points of view, and his rise in status has placed him outside of the class that he was born into. He is also a fair man.

Mark will become obsessed with his goals, and his obsession (and his behaviour) in pursuit of his goals will prevent his rise – when others see what he is capable of. He will meet several of the village folk, whom he knows, and will not allow his knowledge of them to dominate his wishes and desires, meaning that people will suffer at his hands. Some will be harmed or even killed. One of his victims will swear revenge on Mark, just as he in turn has sworn revenge on others. Who will die in battle? Who will die at home? What will happen to the village and its inhabitants as the war rages around it? Can it stay free from involvement in the war? What will happen at the end of the war? Can a country divided in half by war ever be truly reconciled? Do some of the stories come to an end immediately the war is over, or do some stories still have a course to run? How can the story be complete?

Helmdon is a real village in between Brackley and Towcester. The other places named in the story are real. None of the events in the village actually happened in Helmdon (or at least we don't know that they did), but all of it COULD have happened, in just the way that I have described it, and some of the events did happen in other villages and towns across an embattled England. Certain facts of what exactly happened in and just after that war have been documented quite well, but they tend to be those things that affected important people and large groups (as the book says). This doesn't mean that the events of these chapters are impossible. What happens in this book are the things that people wanted to happen – and history tells us that innumerable stories start because of people's wishes, not because they are likely, practical or realistic. This is the story of a range of 'normal' people, and it documents how the lives of them changed – temporarily or permanently – due to the Civil War.

PROLOGUE

I heard the sharp bark of the muskets, and then the roar of the attackers as they advanced up our lane. I heard, too, the screams of the wounded and dying as they were hit by the musket balls, or attacked with a sword.

I saw flashes from the muskets, but also as the sun caught the metal of musket and sword. Periodically, I saw the colour of a uniform as a soldier moved between hedge and field, and the shouts as the men called to each other.

The sounds of the battle made me sick, and I was only grateful that I was not close enough to see the blood on the road and the mutilated figures of the bodies. What on earth was I doing there as a civilian woman?

I could never kill someone in that way, and I could not understand the excitement of a lot of the men I knew as they had marched off to be a soldier – with the magical images of colours and victory in their minds.

The battle seemed to progress up the lane as the attacking force still outnumbered our men. Was I going to have to deliver the message to the village that we had failed to stop them? Were the residents going to have to flee into the woods and fields?

I was conscious of the beauty of the summer colours – the greens and browns, and the blue of the sky. There was gentle motion caused by a slight wind, and against that was the stillness of bodies. They assumed in my mind a darkness that contrasted with the colours.

ONE

PRELUDE

"Once upon a time," I would say if I was telling a fairy tale. Unfortunately, this is not one, and the times and events I tell of are real – even if, on occasion, they seem less than believable. For some, the ending was happy, for others, not happy. My story begins in the 1630s with a peaceful tale of village life in Helmdon – a village between Brackley and Towcester near the road from Oxford to Northampton. I am told that once, the main road came through our village – but I find that hard to believe as we are not important enough to warrant a main road. We have just the drovers' road – which does not run directly to the two closest towns. In the time that I speak of, our village was about two miles or so from the main road from Oxford to Northampton, and the nearest other villages were about the same distance from us either along this road, or on lanes that were parallel with it, or about a mile or two on the other side of the main road. Similar villages were located along the length of the main road, and it seemed to have been designed to just miss the villages.

The road had been laid out with the purpose of allowing more important people the chance to get from city to town, and not for the benefit of those of our villages to get to other villages. We used the main road to get to the markets in the towns. Not as often as we might – as we had most of what we needed in our village. Our village and the other villages and hamlets used the main road only when we needed to, but that was not often – and it felt as if it wasn't an important part of our world, before the war. If we were using the main road, it was out of the usual for us, so it felt like an adventure. Learning, most work, picnics or meals, dances or small music performances all took place within the parish, and as a result we all knew our area, welcomed the familiarity of it perhaps, or secretly envied those who brought back stories from the town and made us feel even more isolated by their exciting tales. Politics, scandals, perhaps hangings, or fights from the town – all seemed much more remote, especially when told about people we had never heard of, or met, or did not want to hear of, or did not want to meet! The road was important and we were not, so it was not really OUR road!

My father and us, his two children (and one or two aunts and their families or occasionally friends), would go to the town market at Brackley or Towcester perhaps once a month as a treat. Less frequently perhaps, once a year, we went to Oxford or Northampton. Although we could get ribbons from the tailor here, or pans repaired in the village, and food or drink, the stalls of the town market offered more excitement. There was usually music or drama on offer for a small donation in return, and part of the treat would be to have a cooked meal – that we had not had to make ourselves. Then there was the travel, itself – usually in a cart with seven or eight of us, and games or singing or jokes and tales whilst we journeyed. We would often arrive home after dark and tumble into the house with bags to store, and perhaps then heat up some soup that we had prepared before. It made a really nice day. I notice the seasons a lot. Often, the things that I remember get tangled up with the seasons in my mind. I remember our visits to town as happening in the summer. Perhaps they did. Perhaps we went to town when the days were longer and brighter. In my mind, though, happy days were summer days.

I start my story in the 1630s because I can't really remember anything much before then, and certainly nothing important happened to me. Our village was like many others. It had about four hundred people – but I don't think anyone had ever counted them accurately. We knew that officially we were counted every so often, but there were some people who were never mentioned. Every time I saw or heard of anyone counting, it was in the summer. A lot of folk in the summer worked from farm to farm. When folk in houses were counted, those sleeping in barns or in little camps round the farm were missed out. Some people deliberately avoided counts in case they led to higher taxes or because they had committed a crime and didn't want to be found. I knew one person who they say was counted in about 1600, and had avoided the count for forty years. I think the official figure for the village was about three hundred people, but everyone knew that was wrong. If they had counted in the winter, they would have found more people indoors, and the figure might have been more accurate. I don't remember being counted, but then I suspect they asked my father and he told them how many there were of us. He would not have lied, they would not have checked, and anyway, who cared if I knew!

Our village was bigger than most of the other villages in the area. Some village folk came to us rather than Brackley or Towcester for some of their goods. I think that sometimes caused a little resentment from other villages, but we had tailors, carpenters and shoemakers as well as the butcher, baker and blacksmith – so it made sense to get all of your things in our one place. We had the stone quarries not far out, too. A lot of really nice well-known houses had their stone from our quarries – and it meant that Helmdon needed more shops to supply the quarry workers and masons. It also meant that some of the people who lived in the village were rich – they got money from the quarries. We were proud of our stone! Some of our housing wasn't as good, though. Not much of it was stone. Some was timber framed and wattle and daub. Part of the reason for the variety in standard was that we actually had more than one manor in the village – and although we felt that we only had one 'squire', we also had some housing owned by those other manors whose owners were not as good at doing repairs and replacements. It didn't seem quite fair!

Our village also had the whole range of social classes. We had our own names, too – some I had not heard even in the next villages. We had Bragby and Harriatts, Emeley, Tue and Elkinton, for example, as well as

Brown or Browne and Greene or Grey or White. All in all, we felt that we were further away (in who we were) from other places than just the actual two miles or so. We could provide for ourselves well enough, but there was Brackley or Towcester or even Oxford or Northampton if we needed them. The thing about the bigger towns was the actual idea of the town itself, more than the reality. Towns felt like they had everything, and we felt that just going to one was excitement enough – although when you went, you ended up buying the same things that you did in the village – they just cost more, or were perhaps a more interesting colour! It also meant that some of our lads went away to work in the towns for the same reason – bigger and more exciting! Often, they ended up working in the towns for less wages, and they paid more for lodgings!

In our village, there were eight of us who made up a group. Eight children of similar age although not of the same social standing. The social standing, or 'rank', didn't matter to us as children. I can't remember when or how we first met. It felt as if we had always been together as a group, although I suppose that is not the case. We were just aware that we had played together since we were children. I suppose that we all felt a bit like brothers and sisters – and as a result some of our relationships were a bit like that. I suppose, too, that the isolation of our village helped form us into a group. If there had been other villages or towns a bit closer, then maybe we would have sought others for company – and then perhaps some of the stories and events that I will tell you would not have happened, or I would not know about them. In those days, people travelled around less than they do now, and I suppose that it was the war that started both the mobility that people see nowadays and started my story!

The eight of us that I talk about were all within two or three years of each other's age. We were all born in the middle or second half of the 1620s. We played tag, hide and seek, and other games when younger, and cards or other games, danced or played music when older. We passed on to each other the different things we learnt in our lessons (those of us who had lessons) – from worldly facts through history or perhaps languages to farming or business knowledge or management, and we did what all folks did, which was to spread the news (or gossip) – both local and from further afield – to each other and so on to our families. We learnt very quickly the local news – spread by eager tongues – although news from London or other areas could take a lot longer, and some events we would be shielded from completely, when it was felt that we did not need to know them – that is adults for you! Sometimes, we even had to go to the town to hear proclamations. It was the same for us as for most of the village folk, but our mixed group seemed to have more interest in the way the world worked.

By name, then, we were: Robert and Olivia Grey: the children of Lord Hugh Grey – an advisor (or courtier) to King Charles, who was the First of that name. Lord Hugh seemed to us a very important man, and like all of the village folk, we were expected by our parents to bow or touch our forelocks when he came past – or even on the rare occasions when he spoke to us. Robert and Olivia were not like that, and they amazed us by telling us that their father did not really value his importance too highly. He liked people, and he liked talking to people – but he happened to be in charge of most of the people he talked to. He was responsible not just for our village, and the villages around us, but for quite a large local area, and it just so happened that he and his family lived in a large house with gates and a wall around their house and its small park in Stuchbury, just on the edge of our village. Robert Grey was the oldest of our eight, and I think that meant he was expected to be in charge of us (or at least he felt that in himself). The estate was well run, and it occupied a large area around our village and others in the area. There were animals, extensive drops and woods – which contained birds and animals for hunting. This all meant that quite a large staff was required.

Lord Hugh Grey had the responsibility of raising any troops from not only the village but the surrounding area if he was required to support the King's wars, or even if he had to support the local civic authority in controlling malcontents or travellers. It meant that he was responsible for those men and women in the rural area between the towns (because although women did not fight, they were expected to support the men whose property they were seen as). You might think that this call to duty caused resentment amongst the villagers – the possibility of being told to take up arms and be taken away from their family – but the younger men often welcomed this as a change from the boredom of their day-to-day life, and sometimes their fathers would willingly let them take their own places – certainly if it just meant marching to Northampton and being seen in a line with a pike to show strength. Most householders kept a pike in an outhouse, and often a farmer had a few – so as to give out to labourers who lived on the farm. We used to like watching the labourers get them out, just to see if they could hold the pikes properly. Many couldn't!

Lord Hugh was often absent from our area. He was regularly required in London at the King's service, and his family had a townhouse there, as well as the large house and estate at Stuchbury. I think, perhaps, that if he had been at home more often, he might have spent more time in instructing Robert and Olivia in the ways of society and their rank, and then perhaps they might have had a higher opinion of their social status. Instead, their education was often left to his wife, and to the staff of the house. The staff of the house (at least) believed that Robert and Olivia befriending the rest of us made them more open to a wider range of views, and more tolerant of our status and our different opinions. It also meant that when they were instructed about the duties and responsibilities of the house, some of the instruction was about the feelings and concerns of other people. All of this made them both nicer people to know and to be with. Lord Hugh, though, actually spent more time in London (and travelling back and forward) than he did at Helmdon or with his family. It made him more distant and harder for the rest of us to know.

Every so often, His Lordship would think it important to show off his family to important friends or social contacts, and he would whisk them all off to London – or another 'important' place. I think he worried that he and his family would be seen as 'country cousins', lacking in manners and unaware of the correct protocols in life. As a result, Robert and Olivia travelled more than the rest of our group or even the rest of the village, had a wider grasp of the geography of our country, more knowledge of other places, events and people, and were possibly able to use their knowledge better to guide or inform the rest of us. Robert and Olivia were, in appearance, twins. In fact, there was two years between them, but they both had blond hair and blue eyes – which clearly marked them as siblings, and possibly of Norse heritage, I was told. There were many similarities in the way that they spoke or reacted to us or to events that emphasised their physical appearance. Olivia would often agree with Robert, and if he wasn't there to judge or decide, she would make the same sort of sensible (boring?) decisions as he often did.

Mark and Harriet Green were the son and daughter of Sir Henry Green, the local squire. Sir Henry owned one of the three manors in the village – the biggest and perhaps the most impressive of the three manors. His family had owned stone quarries for generations, and this meant that he was able to do better and longer-lasting repairs to his stone houses. Actually, he did more repairs to any of his houses – because it made him proud of them. As a result, he was more popular and held more influence in the village than those families who owned the other 'manors'. There was a village joke about them – 'the manners of the manors'. Sir Henry was the only one who was referred to (sometimes affectionately) as the 'Squire', whilst the other manor owners were just politely (or less politely) referred to by name, and just as often they were ignored. The quality of their housing was often complained about (as I have said) – and their tenants were generally unhappier!

Mark and Harriet's parentage put them slightly lower down the social scale than Robert and Olivia – but as I have said, I do not remember that social scale affecting our relationships as children, and I don't think until we became young adults that I heard any of us speak to each other in a way that suggested that this mattered. I think Mark was quite bossy, sometimes, and his instructions often had a hint of 'I know more than you', which could be interpreted as 'So you should do as I say' when he wanted things to happen. He was bossy, though, because he was Mark, not because he was the son of Sir Henry, and he didn't have very much respect for his father. On the other hand (and we joked about this, too), he certainly would argue with Robert – as to the course things should take – despite the fact that Robert knew more than Mark did. I haven't said much about Harriet – as most of my memories of her as a child consist of her agreeing with Mark. Luke liked Harriet a lot, and this meant that he tended to support Mark's opinions. Harriet liked Luke, too – but was reticent in showing it.

Sir Henry also took the role of the Squire, too, in important discussions which took place between the men of the village – and truth be told, very little went on in the village that was not submitted to him for his approval, or to his steward, because most village people 'knew their place' or often did not want to take responsibility for decisions about crops, or who actually did own 'that' field, or who paid for repairs to buildings that they did not own, or how a particular law applied to them, or which tax they had to pay. Sir Henry, too, often tried to be seen as an advisor to the village rather than a master, and he obtained a good deal of respect from villagers because of the wisdom of his decisions, and because he took the time and trouble to explain them and was careful with his wording – his tact, as they say. He, too, had the responsibility of supporting Lord Grey in any matter that required military support – perhaps military displays or even conflict.

Sir Henry, too, sometimes had duties that required him to leave the village – but he was considered the Squire of Helmdon, and that was where the centre of his importance lay – and he knew and felt that. Accordingly, he tried to make sure that he was at home most nights, and seen around the village most days – perhaps riding out on his hunter, or visiting outlying farms, or attending town meetings or church services. Sir Henry made it obvious to villagers and farmers that he was often there mainly to help or support them, and whilst there would always be issues of rent or tax that he had to deal with, he never appeared to visit people just to ferret out these matters or other problems. Often, he would leave getting involved until he was directly appealed to, and it was this approach to his involvement in village matters that also made him respected the most. He had discretion as well as tact. What was most important to Sir Henry, though, was his garden! He spent a lot of time directing how it was laid out and what was to be planted in it.

My father – John Brown – was Lord Hugh Grey's steward, and the only reason I have a proper understanding of Lord Hugh's role is that

Father would regularly tell Edward and me of his (and his master's) responsibilities in our village. He passed on tales of some of the disputes that took place, stories from the assizes where Lord Hugh sat as a magistrate on occasion and any other news or events that he had overheard at work ("but you mustn't tell anyone"). Father was also responsible for passing on instructions or decisions from his lord and ordering the estate workers or tradespeople about. Sometimes on minor matters, Father was allowed to make his own decision about what action to take, and obviously Father had to decide for himself if something was important enough to be passed on to Lord Hugh. This was not easy, and I think that it is a tribute to Father that he did it well, and wasn't treated so much a servant but more an advisor sometimes.

I don't think Father actually abused his position either, but I also think he didn't always ask the Lord about the decisions he made. He had enough sense to know what was not really important to the Lord, and what sometimes needed to be passed on to the Squire or even further down the line. My name is Lucy Brown – and my brother's name is Edward. Edward is older than I am. The fact that our father is the steward for Lord Grey goes a little way to ensuring that Mark and Harriet Green do (or did) not just dismiss us as servants or villagers. We are useful to them in that we can sometimes pass on information from the estate that we have heard (even if 'we mustn't tell anyone', or fill in details of what they have heard, and in return, we can pass back comments or facts from the others to Robert or Olivia, as regards what is being said or done around the village. I often saw my duty as a messenger – or sometimes helpmate. I helped where needed and passed on messages.

I have no mother, and have had no mother for as long as I can remember. I found out from listening to conversations around me that my mother died giving birth to me. My father did not tell me that – because I think he thought that I would feel guilty about this, but I overheard others in the village talking about it. Being called 'poor motherless waif' when you are young is quite useful – because often that statement was accompanied by the offer of a biscuit or a slice of freshly made bread. I am surprised that I was not made fatter, but then I did a lot of moving between houses of those people who looked after me when my father was at work. As I got older, I learnt to look after my father and brother, and learnt to run our house as well – because everyone told me that men are useless at that sort of thing, and I think my family proved that to me as well!

All of the villagers taught me some skill or another, and I became very useful around the village on that account. I was always running errands or helping out, and as I grew older, my advice was often asked for, and sometimes I was able to lead judgement or actions. My brother, Edward, fancied himself, too, as a bit of a leader. If we had teams in our games, Edward would often lead one team and Mark the other. Edward saw equality as important. Although he knows that the country will judge him as a steward's son, it was important to him that our group judged him on his merit and did not judge him on his lack of wealth. Robert often let Mark and Edward battle it out for being leader as I think he knew it was just play, and in real life he would be seen as one of life's leaders. Robert settled for being some sort of advisor in games, and a lot of time the others took his advice on what we should do. He phrased it as advice, though, not as leadership, and he was good at that.

Then we had Stephanie and Luke White (in our group), the children of the local vicar, the Reverend Thomas White. His stature as the vicar gave him the authority of God – in that he might not say who owned a field, but he could often comment on whether events were 'right' or as God would want them to be. He rarely said publicly that any decision of Lord Grey or Sir Henry was 'wrong' and often contented himself with quoting a relevant section of the Scriptures that supported them. I think it was Lord Grey that was responsible for the vicar's 'living', as it was called. I have never read the whole Bible, so I do not always know where the vicar's comments come from, just that the quotes usually did support the Squire or Lord. The vicar was respected, too, as someone who did not pontificate at length on unimportant matters. Even his sermons were direct, to the point, and only lengthy when a local matter threatened to disturb the harmony of the village.

His duties also included visiting the ill or infirm, not just in the village but in the area around it. The hamlets did not have a resident clergyman

– and the Revd White with help from some visiting clergy from the town or diocese would manage services on the Sabbath as well as weekday services for all of the churches. That meant that he had to do the visits to the sick, poor and elderly in those hamlets, too. Additionally, he would have to hold baptisms, weddings and funerals in our local church, and would be called to bless harvests or new houses or significant local events. Revd Thomas and our religion were a necessary part of our everyday lives. No one wanted to risk bad luck or God's displeasure caused by ignoring the Church, or God's word, especially when a blessing or a donation to the Church could avoid this. Everyone knew that God saw everything – but they sometimes thought that he wouldn't mind them missing the occasional service – even if the vicar did mind!

The vicar's Church of St Mary Magdalene was an attractive one, which had been added to and changed several times since its establishment – believed to be in the 13th century – although the vicar once told us that there had been earlier churches before that. We found it difficult to believe this as the church building looked like it had been there forever! It had a tower, but not a huge one, and then it seemed to have been built in two halves. The stone looked old, and the corners were rubbed a bit so that the edges were not completely sharp. It was a tribute, though, to Revd Thomas that the church was generally well looked-after. There were flowers most weeks, the grass round the graves was kept quite well trimmed, metal plaques and woodwork were regularly polished or repaired, and whilst the silver we had would not compare with a London church, at least the chalice and plate were real silver and not some lesser metal.

If the reverend wanted a new shelf in the vicarage, there would be several people who would willingly build it, and his wife never wanted for help whilst she was alive – although she died when I was quite young, and I didn't remember her. There were two murals in the church, which had survived the Restoration and which we were told was unusual (the survival of them – I mean), and some coloured glass in the windows. The church was generally light and airy, and when I thought of it in my mind's eye, it was as a nice place that people went to, was welcoming, and which they liked. I liked it. I have been in some churches that were much darker and less clean, and which seemed to exist as a breeding ground for spiders and insects. We didn't seem to get many of either in our church, and the cleanliness was a tribute to the village's support for their vicar and their respect for his hard work. He didn't have favourites – and perhaps kept people at more of a distance than he could have. This might also explain why he never remarried, and relied on the favours of the many.

Stephanie White – Thomas White's daughter – secretly loved Mark Green more as we got older and things like love started to be an option that we could consider. She appreciated the drive that made him make decisions or take a stand on ideas or actions, even when he just appeared opinionated to the rest of us. She said nothing, and I don't think that Mark knew how she felt about him. I flatter myself that, as a girl, I knew from her actions, the secret looks she gave him, the way she supported him in arguments and, in unguarded moments, the longing of her looks. I also think that men often miss looks and gestures from women. If Stephanie had been more obvious, then perhaps Mark might have taken more advantage of her. An idea such as their marriage would not be impossible, but as a woman, Stephanie was waiting for Mark to take the lead – perhaps ask her to sit next to her in a game or at a meal. Mark – tall, dark-haired, self-centred and tempestuous – remained oblivious to her love, and Stephanie remained alone.

Mark disliked the wealth and ostentation of the Church. He resented all the attention that was lavished on the local church – and appeared to dislike the loyalty. That was what he said, but I think that perhaps he wanted more wealth and ostentation for himself. That feeling against the Church perhaps influenced his disregard for Stephanie but definitely caused him to occasionally argue with Reverend Thomas. Mark rarely went to the church except for occasions like the Sunday services when his family had to be seen to be seated in the Squire's front pew. It was rumoured in gossip that Mark's views were even more extreme, and that he even disputed the divine right of the King! Perhaps Mark wanted divine right for himself when it came to the power and wealth of others? This was an unacceptable view in the son of the Squire – so no one mentioned it to the Squire himself. No one tried to discuss it with Mark, either, if they could avoid it!

Mark shared some opinions with Luke White – the vicar's son. Luke thought that the Church should be more separated from government and wealth. He thought that the vicars should not be decided (as they often were) by the local landowner – and they should not just be the younger son of the Lord. He thought, too, that churches and cathedrals should not display vast arrays of silver plates and sumptuous robes for the celebrants. I am not sure how much he had seen of this, but he seemed to know about it. He thought that the money should be shared with the poor or for good community causes. He also thought that the church ritual should be simpler, and that the people should clearly understand it. No Latin, no mumbling away behind a screen, and just plain dress and perhaps no music. He felt (or maybe his friends thought) that the high altar and screen separated the priest from his congregation, and that communion should be celebrated at a simple table placed in the centre of the church, and visible to all – after all, wasn't that what Jesus had done?

In our discussions as children and young adults, Mark would speak out for firm and solid government for all – possibly because he wanted to share in making it more fair (and he saw his part in that being at a higher level than his father had achieved). This inevitably caused arguments between him and Robert Grey – who accepted without question the status quo. Often, Luke would take Mark's side – because both of them had issues with the wealth of the country, and both agreed on more separation of the Church and government. Like the rest of us, though, they were not accepted as adults yet, and their views were not accepted as anything other than the ramblings of youths. By 1640, we were all over the age of fifteen and the boys could possibly have become soldiers and fought in the army – but their opinions were still not accepted as those of adults. Arguments with Mark rarely led to fights, because of the other side of Mark's character. Everything he started, he took through to the end. He was courageous, and helped us solve problems or strove to find solutions.

Finally, there was the issue of the colours. Our families were all named after colours. My father said that our surname came from the colour of our hair, that at some point someone had been named John the Brown or

Robert the Brown, and that the surname had stuck. White was similar, in that it meant 'of fair complexion' – and apparently also meant it was Norse or Danish in origin. It wasn't the same with the others, obviously – the Greens believed that Green was an abbreviation of Greenway – and this was linked to where they came from. The Greys could (obviously) trace their name back for generations, and whilst there had been Grey or Gray in the time of Richard the Lionheart, the name was originally Norman and may have meant something else. It wasn't really the best explanation – as the Greys looked more Norse than the Whites. Whatever the case, we, as a group, identified the link between our names quite quickly as children, and saw it as an identifying factor.

I haven't really said much about the village. It was well spaced out – with wide gaps between most houses or cottages. The church was a bit to the south, and the village stretched across a small river – more of a stream really. It had poorer streets or houses but no real rich or poor areas. Most people in the village knew most other people in the village. They didn't like everyone, but they didn't hate them much, either. The small river was the River Tove and it flowed through the middle of the village. There were low meadows either side, and sometimes the river flooded, which got in the way a bit of travelling to Stuchbury or Wappenham. We kept a couple of small boats maintained in the village for those occasions – although they weren't used very often. Most times, the floods didn't stop the waggons getting through with their large wheels; it was only grandmas or sometimes children that we put into the boats as the grandmas were less sure-footed, and the children didn't take enough care of themselves. The boats, though, also meant that we could travel up and down the river to other villages – sometimes carrying a small amount of goods as well, and they were used for fishing.

Folk didn't drink the river water unless it was boiled – but most used the streams that flowed into the river, and there were a couple of springs within the village site. I think that all of this detail is important if it shows a village that could look after itself, had resources and showed how well we could cope in England in the 1640s. We stayed the same people (as a rule), and the world changed around us. There had been large changes in the way that the country was governed, and in the way that we worshipped. Many people wanted peace in the country – because of the fight between the Catholics and Protestants and their kings and queens within the last hundred years. I knew one man in the village who remembered the Spanish Armada, and lots of men remembered when Queen Elizabeth died. There were lots of people around our country who shouted their dissatisfaction with king or government or church, and as we moved towards the 1640s, these voices of discontent seemed to get louder and more frequent. Those of us who wanted to get on with our lives peacefully were not listened to. No one ever shouts about peace loudly enough!

That is, or was, us, our lives and some detail of how we lived them. We all had families who dictated what we did and when we did it. We all had to share our family's responsibility for certain duties, and we were expected to behave as our parents wanted us and them to be seen. We all had to make sure that in our public behaviour or activities, we didn't let our parents down, and for a long time that is what we did. In return, we expected our parents not to let us down, and for a while they did not. For about ten to twelve years (I suppose), from about 1630 until the summer of 1642, we remained linked to each other by our games, discussions and our company. Our family lives changed little, our relationships to family or community stayed the same. If any of our group thought the other members unsuitable playfellows, I never heard it said or noticed it in look or gesture, and our lives remained the same, generally unaffected by the events of the wider world.

We were about to be tested. The whole country, its government and rule, the Church and its factions, our local government, the stature and content of our society would all change, and survive or be found wanting. Our morals and self-confidence, the way we usually behaved, or behaved in difficult circumstances, would be found acceptable, or found wanting. We would have to cope with others who disagreed with us, and it would matter to them what they did about it. Sometimes, we would worry that we were wrong. For nine years or so, we would have to find solutions to problems that we might never have considered problems, and we would have to find new ways of dealing with them. We would be deprived of the news that we would need, our relationships would be torn asunder, and we would still have to take the part of responsible members of society – whatever our age was, and to some extent whatever our status in society was. For all of us, our age would make a difference to the way we coped with nine years of war, and for some of us, our social status would change, too. Perhaps the rights and responsibilities of women might even change when their menfolk left for war!

TWO

1642 AND CONFLICT

Other people thought the same way about the country as Mark and Luke did. Some others stood against them and their loyalties were split. Individual conflicts tore groups apart. Villages and families, all of them, were hit by these differences of opinion. More and more people got drawn into opposing points of view. Brothers, sisters, friends; affected across the whole country. Where on earth would it all end? Some counties, even, wanted change; others did not and were happy with the status quo. Conflicts arose across borders, status and ranks. North argued with south, east with west. Noble or commoner were on both sides. Church disagreed with Church: Catholic, Protestant, Puritan – even the positioning within the church of the altar. or the decoration or simplicity of the church. The names of the faiths inspired the conflict of loyalties. Letters, proclamations or word of mouth spread the arguments. Taxing the country became an easy word or concept for the disaffected to rally behind – and provided a flashpoint amongst those who were already arguing.

In 1642, King Charles raised his standard. I laughed when they told me that. As a child, I had often been told to raise my own standards, and I thought that this meant that 'King Charles was going to behave himself better in the future' than he had done (according to rumour) in the past. I regretted my laughter when they told me what it really meant. King

Charles had rallied troops loyal to himself behind his Royal Standard. It meant that he was organising an army to fight against Parliament, and it was taken (by Parliament and the King's opponents) as a declaration of war by the King on his own country, and therefore as 'treason'. It immediately meant that troops loyal to Parliament (and possibly who felt that fairer government needed to be done by the people) would flock to their banner (assuming they had one). It did not mean, though, that everyone who fought shared the same views.

Lord Grey was responsible for raising a troop of soldiers for the King, and he would expect those in his troop to accept his word and flock to his side through personal loyalty, or through the threat of losing their livelihood or home when the war was over. Those who would not accept his word (and his loyalties) might have to leave secretly to fight for another cause, and they would need to find a secure home for their family. Generally, the country, though, was split into the areas controlled by those who allied with the King or those who allied with Parliament. If you had coloured in a map of the country, it is difficult to say whether there would be a larger area or number of people for the King, or for the country. In Helmdon – and a lot of the land around – we would be expected to side with Lord Grey, and Lord Grey would expect Sir Henry to loyally follow him with his smaller group of men.

It meant war. Thousands of people would be torn from their homes, families split asunder and perhaps starving, menfolk dispossessed and press-ganged into bloody pointless contact or separation when the tide of war moved back and forward across the country. Homes, goods and lives potentially destroyed, wives and children raped or beaten, men's livelihoods destroyed, and in the end, what would all this madness achieve? Who would ultimately benefit from this war? All of it was about controlling England, controlling England's money, and ultimately, controlling those about to die! In the end, the small number of those rich people in charge would still be in charge. What would be left to control, after all the senseless slaughter and after all those lives had ended? I, as a woman, could tell you that another man's voice would raise the taxes and tell us how to worship. War would solve nothing!

My father wanted to go with Lord Grey. He was actually slightly younger than Lord Grey, so he could not be told he was too old, and although he had two children in the village (although I no longer thought of myself as a child), so did some others of the men who would march with Lord Grey and Sir Henry to fight, as well as some of those whose consciences told them to join the Parliamentary army. In the end, it was pointed out to Father than he would need to be responsible for supplying Lord Grey and his troops with some foodstuffs and other resources from the estate. This meant that he would have to travel on the road with carts or waggons on a regular basis, maintain contact with the estate, and that until it was agreed that resources were needed and he was called for, he had best stay at the estate and help Olivia and her mother to run it. I can't be sure, but I think Lord Grey arranged this so that Father would feel valued but, as an older man, would not get in the way!

From Father's point of view, this meant that he would still feel useful, but it did also mean he would spend extra nights away from home on the road, and there was a risk to him and the supplies from marauding troops around the countryside. It meant, too, that he would have to know where Lord Grey's troops were moving to, to meet them, and it helped him to feel that he knew which way the war was going when he started to make these trips. I think that Father's self-image and his view of his role mattered to him. My role in communicating with the estate (and with Father) became more important, too, because messages needed to be sent more frequently to the village, and Father would not always be there to deliver them. It seemed to me that all of my family would be moving around at one time or another, and that we might never meet again.

Those of us who were friends met as a group of eight for the last time outside the Greens' manor house in their garden about a week after the declaration. Robert told us what we already knew and would have expected; that his father was raising a regiment to support the King. He told us what Mark and Harriet also knew; that Lord Grey had asked Sir Henry to act as his second-in- command. I could see Lord Grey as a commander, as that suited his demeanour and presence. Robert – with absolutely no military experience – would become one of the Royalists' captains, responsible for leading men who would accept his decisions because he 'was their lord's son'. He would play his part for the King's Flag, and imitate his father. Mark sneered at this: "I am told that it took a lot of argument to force my father to agree. Although he doesn't support Parliament, he is fat and lazy, and he wants to do nothing more than sit at home on his backside and cultivate his flowers." I had to admit that I, too, did not see the overweight Sir Henry at home on a horse, or as a leader.

"What will you do then, Mark?" asked Olivia.

"I intend to fight for reform in England," he said. "The King and the Church must change! Call me what you will, a scoundrel, fool or rebel, I won't join in with my father to support a king who believes he has a divine right to squander our money on foreign wars whilst his people starve. He ignores the advice of his ministers and he threatens them. The King's ministers have a much better knowledge of governing this country, but the King only calls Parliament when he needs money!"

"I, too, am for reform," said Luke White, "and I, too, intend to follow with you, Mark, although I mean to fight for a better church, one with less ritual! The people whose views I value about Church reform are those on the side of Parliament. I have some doubts about all of this, and I am certainly not a rebel, but if we don't fight for what we believe, nothing will ever change, and I think the country needs change!"

This was not really a great surprise to us – although Luke's general demeanour had not led us to believe that he would actually take up arms and fight. Before any of us could say anything else, my brother, Edward, had moved across to join them, saying that he, too, believed in reform.

"Edward, no!" I said. "Father will support Lord Grey, and you might end up fighting against Father!" Edward said that he thought it unlikely that father would fight. He said that this was not an unplanned thought, and that although he would not fight our father, he could not support the King or the King's men. He felt that in the King's army, the leaders would be the rich or the sons of the rich, and there would not be a fair chance for him. We tried to persuade the three of them – but they wouldn't really listen, and presumably they had been thinking about this for some while and had just told us their decision when it was made. I tried to persuade

Edward again that he might end up fighting against Father, or at least against Father's employer – but I could see that he didn't think he had much chance of rising up under the current system of rule in this country. Harriet was split, too. Should she waste time in talking to her obstinate brother, or Luke – who was more considerate of her opinions?

"Are you a Puritan?" Harriet said to Luke, not wishing to believe ill of the boy who had often supported her, but unwilling, too, to see criticism of the church that she attended weekly. "A Puritan dislikes the pomp and the ritual present today in the Church. I think they are a bit extreme, and I am not a Puritan, but praying in our church feels like praying through my father, and seeing God through his rich garments. I want a purer and simpler church, and I intend to fight for Parliament's side. None of that makes me a Puritan by name, but I see their view!" He stepped back, by Mark's side.

"All that I want," repeated my brother, "is a chance to be equal in the eyes of my fellow man. That does not make me Puritan, or a Parliamentarian, either, if you want a label, or if labels even matter to you, but I, too, intend to fight for Parliament's side."

Harriet made one final attempt at a plea. "Luke, you know that I care very much for you, but please think carefully before turning your back on your father." He held out his hand towards her but did not step forward – just waited for Mark.

Stephanie turned towards Mark, too, her plea clear in her eyes, and I towards Edward, my brother, and held out my hand to him again, but they both looked resolute in their decision and didn't meet our eyes. Our group split into three. Robert left in one direction to meet his father; Mark, Luke and Edward in another, and us four girls stayed in the middle, uncertain what to do next and where to go. Stephanie said, "What are those of us, who are left behind, supposed to do?"

"We are expected to follow the lead of our men," said Olivia. "Whilst they are gone, we will have to pray for them to be returned to us, but we can't do nothing – or there will be nothing left for them to come back to. I will take charge of the Grey estate whilst my father and brother are away from here. My mother does not have too much control over day-to-day matters. Nice though she is, the estate needs me in charge. I shall discuss it with your father, Lucy."

"My father has always relied on my help with his accounts," said Harriet. "I can keep looking after his affairs and mind the manor to make sure that it is kept as it should be, but I think that with Father and Mark gone, Mother should be able to look after the actual house and any servants that Father does not take with him to war, so that will not take up much of my time. I think that it will still be seen as a good thing if we are still able to help our tenants and see to our responsibilities. I will look to see if I can keep the quarries going – as there is always a need for stone, but I will need to see if the manager is staying. Olivia, I can help you, too, with the estate accounts or any paperwork if you need me?" Olivia remarked that she had my father, too, to help, but she was sure that he would probably welcome more help. The estate was largely to be denuded of male staff, and those remaining might well be transferred to more manual labour. I think that she also welcomed the idea of Harriet's company. It seemed there would be few other people that she could just chat or gossip to.

"I imagine I could help out a physician with nursing, because it seems to me that there may be a need for nurses!" said Stephanie. "I help my father a lot here, but there may be less for him to do, and I think I would feel more useful if I had something to do all of the time, and not just occasionally."

I told her that taking out food to the poor and needy was something I could help her father with. "If that does not fill my time, I can polish in the church, replace the flowers, maybe take messages and help out in the garden, but I expect that a lot of the women will help around the church. They do that at the moment anyway," I said. I knew what else I would do. I would run with messages and spread the news around. If we had friends and neighbours fighting on different sides of the war, it seemed to me that news of them would be welcome. I could act as a go-between and keep on helping out my family and my friends, or even between those families who had members on either side.

Our friends found the best ways they could to take their leave from our village. Edward sneaked into our house whilst Father was about his duties, collected his belongings and left to meet Mark at the manor again, unwilling to face Father's wrath or argue the merits of the cause with him. Father was not happy about Edward's decision, but he did not ban him from returning to our house, and when Edward was able to send letters, Father would write to him by return. Mark told his father face to face what he was about, and Sir Henry, torn between his loyalty to the Greys and his wish to 'sit at home on his backside and cultivate flowers', was not able to mount more than a token resistance to his son's demand. He had had enough arguments with Mark in the past to know that Mark would do in the end what he wanted, and he could not mount the energy to have another fight. He gave Mark some money but told him that in future he would be required to have him detained if he returned home, and then retired to his flowers and his garden to argue with his roses.

Possibly the most tempestuous argument in the village was had between the Reverend Thomas White and his son, Luke. This was told to me by Stephanie after Luke left. Although Thomas White was required to raise his voice in the pulpit to pontificate against his flock, none of us had ever heard him shout before quite like this. He clearly saw Luke's arguments as disloyal to his employers as well as a rejection of his (Thomas') worship of God, and once all of his rational statements had met with rejection or counter-argument, he tried to win the discussion with loud logic. Stephanie said that in the end he was reduced to pleading with his son not to go – unwilling to shun him or shut him out of his life but unable to agree with him or accept what he said. Although Thomas preached to his 'flock', he was able to plan in advance what he said, and didn't have to prepare for arguments against his sermon. When it came down to debating his religious beliefs with his son, he was unable to do it at all well. Those who saw Luke striding through the village on his way to meet Mark and Edward with a small bag of belongings said he was pale and shaken.

In my heart, it rained – but actually it didn't. Our friendships and our families divided on a nice crisp day when the wind blew the trees about, and there was a restless energy that matched our mood. A year passed.

At the start, it felt as if there was a large gap in our lives – but gradually we got more used to it. During that year, we had sporadic messages about our menfolk. Often not direct messages, but sometimes a letter delivered by a passing man. Sometimes, we saw nailed-up notices about battles in the town or village, but we all worried that we would not hear of deaths, and that we might wonder about the men for many years. We found that it was the battles that brought us the most news as the results were usually posted in the towns, often with information about the rich and powerful and how they had fared. We would not hear about the marches, the mud, the struggle to find food, the treatment of occupied villages and the treatment of people who did not welcome occupation well enough for their new captors or gaolers. We would also not hear much about the thousands of poor unknowns who die in battles. Sometimes, we would get a bundle – often from those who could write, but containing other notes for families in their village or town. We did not stop speaking to those whose menfolk were on the opposite side to ours, but we were cautious when we asked about them. We felt that if we gave them a chance to say how well their sons (or brothers or fathers) were doing, they would tell us something to the detriment of our sons, and, in turn, we were cautious not to do so much boasting about our sons' side of the conflict.

The seasons changed. Our yearly rituals were affected. Harvests – we needed to do the work that the menfolk did. In the autumn, we had to try to bring timber in for the fires. Some of us had to learn how to trim thatch, or even try to build a wall or a pigsty. Each time we did something like this, the work became a little better, and a little less shameful. Farming work, too, relied increasingly on the women folk or the elderly or our youngsters. Some youngsters decided what age they might want to join the army – because being a soldier is more exciting to a lad than a grown man with a family. We lost several fifteen- and sixteen-year-old boys. Sometimes, we heard stories of them later, sometimes not. One came home crippled – he had lost a leg – but that was a couple of years after he had run off. His mother was just glad to see him alive. Rituals like bonfire night were more subdued. Although we still had a village bonfire to commemorate the gunpowder plot of 1605, the children picked up on the mood and didn't run around getting as excited as they had the year before. All Hallows' Eve seemed to feel more like a premonition of doom and bad things to come.

Although Helmdon remained quiet, we heard tales of wholesale confiscation of horses, cattle and poultry in other towns and villages. We heard of the burning of houses – just to ensure that they could not be used by the other side. It appeared that if your village was furthest from the path of a march, or furthest from the overnight camping of the army, you were safe. If you lived on a main road, then you would probably lose everything as a troop went by, and if you were within a mile or two of a camp, you could lose crops, stored food, animals or birds, even children or wives. This supposes that you, yourself, were not of a military age – and could not be forced into the army, perhaps to serve without a weapon until you could pick one up on a battlefield. We were lucky in that we were several miles from the main road, and at least ten miles from the nearest town. Often, we heard of entire villages where only old people were left. I heard, too, that Silverstone on the main road had been raided several times, whilst we in Helmdon had no serious raids at all.

Cities and towns had it differently. They were often known to support one cause or another. Often, they had a wall, and if 'their' side approached, they would welcome it. It would camp outside the wall and strip the local villages for supplies. If it were 'the enemy', the gates would be shut – and often the town had enough notice to strip the local villages so that the enemy had nothing to live off, and a siege might be over quicker. Garrisons were left in most major towns or cities to protect them from smaller troops, and obviously they would survive on food and supplies from local villages. In short, the worst place to live in the first few years of the Civil War (as it came to be known) was in a village within about five to ten miles of a large town or city, one directly on a main road, and anywhere in an area controlled by the other side. When the large armies were not marching around, smaller groups would be raiding the countryside and 'recruiting' anyone who hadn't actually volunteered to join an army. There were stories of men being executed for refusing to join up, and the burning of villages that refused to give up supplies.

Christmas was quiet and subdued. Almost half of the village was not there to celebrate or take part, and those left behind were swamped with the memories of previous Christmases. Some groups in England did not believe that Christmas should be celebrated, and in some areas of the country, too, there were no real Christmas celebrations. In Helmdon, we observed the traditional services in the church. We went there to pray, to give thanks (often for no news), and we tried to eat and meet with the ones we loved. It seemed a bit of a relief, though, when we finished the festivities and the artificial sense of Good Will to all Men could stop. January and February are always hard months, and at the beginning of 1643, the elements sent Helmdon the message that they were in charge and we were not. On several occasions, we were cut off from the road by the snow and ice, and cut off, too, from any supplies that we might want to get from the town. Even the discovery of New Zealand in December 1642 had no impact, as we didn't hear about it for at least another year!

Bargaining for food and essentials and buying goods in the past had always been the responsibility of a few people – usually those who had learnt trades. For those of us left now, taking on these duties seemed dangerous. We were worried that we would be duped into buying bad produce or we would lose all of our money by robbery or cheating traders, who would take advantage of simple village women. In reality, the people left trading in the towns were not much better off than we were. They often had fewer goods than before to trade. Prices were higher, because no one could get enough of anything. As a village with our own milk, eggs and livestock, we had more than others, and I think we were lucky in our trading that we did not lose more to thieves and vagabonds. We did not need to buy 'pretties' – ornaments and the like – as we did not need them. Occasionally, we could make things that were less than essential purpose. Gradually, we organised the fields of our village, too, so that each farmer contributed to what the village needed. It meant that we had a little spare, too, to grow some crops that were less essential.

We were able to turn more fields over to maize and corn to grind in the village and make more bread. We grew potatoes and more vegetables in areas that had previously been just waste ground, and we discovered quickly that if we planned all this as a village and worked out what the village needed, we could sell the surplus for goods we needed – like fabrics to make more garments. The blacksmith's wife, Mrs Cartwright, knew how to use the forge, so we could shoe horses and do simple metalwork needed to repair pans and the like. We began to enjoy the freedom of making our own decisions to produce what we needed. Brackley was about ten miles away, and Towcester fifteen. In terms of travel, a light cart could do about five or six miles an hour, whilst a heavier waggon could do about three. There were fewer carts than waggons in the village – but most of them were still not used for large parts of the day. It made sense to make sure that there was a waggon each day going to Towcester and to Brackley, for the transport of goods and sometimes for passengers, too.

Sometimes, we would sell at those markets. Sometimes, we would buy. Sometimes, folk just needed to make contact with relatives or business contacts. We pulled together all of the waggon drivers and arranged a rota so that we could guarantee a waggon to each town each day (except Sunday, of course). If the owner of the waggon was unable to do the trip, we could find a lad to drive the waggon, and of course there were about forty horses in the village that could be used. It meant that we were using more waggons each day for the benefit of more of the villagers. The waggon to Towcester left each morning at 6am and usually took five hours to get there. It came back at around 4pm – which was a bit of a long day, but each driver would only do it once or twice a week. The Brackley waggon left at 7am and used the drovers' road, arriving at Brackley at 10am – then coming back at 3pm. This is a lot of detail, but it shows how centuries of individual organisation could be centralised into a village resource for the benefit of all. It seemed a completely logical step for us.

We set up a village council or committee. The villagers elected those who they knew had their best interests at heart, and they elected those people irrespective of sex or wealth. The Reverend was respected as a fair and just man, so he was on the committee. Harriet Green was the member of the Squire's family who was still in the village and displayed sound judgement, and everyone wanted one member of the Squire's family involved. Mrs Cartwright had shown in the past impartiality and generosity, and as she managed the forge in her husband's absence (Mr Cartwright was making horseshoes for Lord Grey's troops), she could guide us on the village's equipment. Mr Roland – an older farmer – was added to the list to represent the farmers' interests. It was important that the farmers were not brought to ruin by supporting the village. The farmers' representative would be 'rotated' each year, so that no one person's farm benefitted. Over the years, additional people could be added to the committee if they were important, and anyone could be removed if they died – or if it was considered that they had not placed the village interests first.

Much to my surprise, I was elected to the committee, too. The villagers knew that I knew them and understood them, but practically, too, I could list decisions made and take the messages or convey decisions to the villagers – who said that they trusted me. I was really flattered by that. It meant that I could also take messages to Father and to the Grey estates – small packages, revised instructions, news – and that those messages would be honestly conveyed. It meant that I was considered reliable. I could also run quite well, and I would not stop and gossip and waste time. The rest of the committee was to consist of three people who would serve for a period of a few months, and then they would be replaced by another group. In that way, all of the groups or areas of the village would have a chance to submit their representatives to the committee, and we in turn would listen to them all, so that decisions were fair. I even had to ask a neighbour's girl, Eve Bragby, to come into the house and help me. Father agreed to a little bit of money for her, but I found myself so busy that even if I was out all day, the house grew dusty, the fire was not on, and it was cold when I arrived back.

We knew that outside our safe haven the war went on. We had long periods where we heard nothing, and on the face of it we continued a normal existence (albeit with a number of our friends and family missing). Although the progress of the war was measured by the large battles, and by the areas of the country safely under the control of one faction, in reality there were lots of small 'skirmishes', I think the soldiers called them. We did see soldiers. We decided that if a troop came through the village, we would feed them as if they were our own menfolk. This surprised them. They expected to have to arrive and demand food from us. When we saw them coming, we would lay out any surplus on trestles and make big pans of soup for them. We gave that job to those of us who were keen, or the elderly or our youngsters – as we figured that soldiers might not only want food from us women. As a result of our care, we did not have any real trouble, except that occasionally a few of our girls decided to leave with the soldiers. There were several occasions when this happened.

On the 5th of July 1643, the Battle of Lansdowne took place. Few of us knew where Lansdowne was (and fewer cared), but the importance to us was that Mark Green had been in the battle, along with Luke, Edward and a few other of the village lads. The proportion of Helmdon villagers in a battle in Somerset was a significant number to a village of about three hundred people. I suppose, to a lot of us, it was a real surprise that some of our villagers had travelled that far. Most of us had been no further than Oxford! As significant to us, too, was the fact that Simon Watkiss from a farm on the edge of the valley had died – but we did not know how that had come about. Mark, Luke and Edward were all spared – God be praised! It was Mark that wrote to his mother about this battle – the first major one of the war – and included some of the details (to her) of the others from the village. Harriet passed Mark's letter on to me so that I could read some of the detail, and this was followed up by news at Towcester Market a week or so later.

There were actually fifteen 'battles' in 1643. Lansdowne may not have been the largest, and it certainly wasn't the closest – that being Middleton Cheney in May 1643 (or possibly Cropredy in 1644) – but as far as we knew, none of our village men were involved in that battle, and so Lansdowne of Somerset assumed more importance to us. We were told that the King's army had won. This seemed to be the general news, but what that meant was that they had forced the Parliamentarians to run away from their position but had lost lots of their own men in the process, so it wasn't really a real victory. It seemed to me that the least careless army could claim they had won the day – but what did I know about it? Mark wrote that it was a triumph for his side because it was an unimportant hill that they hadn't really needed, and that they had planned their movements so that the Royalist army lost lots of their soldiers in trying to win it. Mark's letter, although it contained news of Edward and Luke, showed, too, that Mark was only really interested in winning battles, and a lot of it was about what he had done and how long it took, and how clever he had been. I was also told by Olivia – who did not share this news with either Harriet or Stephanie – that Mark was getting a reputation as a leader who took his men into hazardous situations. It was said that he lost more soldiers than lots of other captains or troop leaders, so it was ironic that he criticised the Royalists for exactly the same thing!

Olivia also said that Edward was getting a name for himself as a leader. He had worked under Mark's patronage for a while, and had showed that he had a good grasp of tactics and was careful with his men. Mark had shown him how to look at the land and how to see the possible advantages of certain moves, but Edward was quicker to see all of the consequences of different options. Once again, Olivia did not share this news with Harriet or Stephanie, as it seemed to criticise Mark too much. I was not sure, either, how she had received news of Edward from 'The Other Side' as it must have been to her, but she summed it up by saying that Edward was now being given his own commands and was being marked down as someone to watch out for. I was very proud of Edward for this, but scared, too. I wanted him to come home, and many leaders didn't! Olivia didn't really say very much about her father and brother. I assumed that meant that they were doing what they were told but not seeking opportunities for brave and reckless actions – which might be a relief to her.

Luke wrote to Harriet – and she in turn shared his news with me. His letter came to her slightly after the others, and contained some information about him and some events after Lansdowne. As I had suspected, Luke – as a man of strict conscience and a strong Christian – had realised that the idea of killing another man was abhorrent to him. Although Lansdowne was his first battle, Luke had seen men killed before that – some in training and some in skirmishes. He realised that he was not going to be able to lead men into a battle or fight with them, and I think that fact became obvious to his commanders as well. Luke was the person that others turned to, to hear their fears. He didn't actually preach to the troops – as they had their own lay preachers – but he was respected as an advisor or counsellor by the men who talked to him. As such, he was valued more by his leaders and not simply placed in the front rank and told to fire his musket.

Accordingly, when they marched into camp ready for Lansdowne, Luke was detailed to pick a troop of men – of like mind – to take responsibility for retrieving the wounded and injured from the battle (those who could be saved) and to bring them back for treatment from the regiment's doctors, or even the local doctors of the area. Luke told Harriet that he and his men had to carry their weapons as they were expected to fight if needs be (or they might even be used just to swell the ranks so that the army looked bigger), but they also had to find, make and use additional equipment for their 'rescues'. They would bring injured men back from the battle on canvas 'stretchers' as the men usually could not walk unaided, and carrying a man on someone else's back, along with a pack, and carrying a weapon as well was not possible. It meant that they might have to shoot to save their own lives, but not just because authority needed them to kill another man for being on the wrong 'side'.

Luke and his men were also given packs with strips of cloths to act as bandages and to tie off wounds. Luke was made some sort of serjeant – which meant that the other men he picked had to do what he said. His group were laughed at, at first, by those who saw themselves as 'proper fighting men', but the laughter died away when it was seen what Luke and his men were doing. They wore strips of white cloth on their arms to show that they were not fighting – or at least that the strips might be seen as a 'parley' (Luke's word) – and so they might not be simply shot out of hand. The thing that impressed the other soldiers the most was that they were going out when the fighting or shooting was still happening, not ready to fight themselves, and they were bringing back injured men whilst the battle was still going on. Once the other soldiers saw this, they would direct their musket fire around Luke's men to avoid hitting them by accident.

Luke said that he had seen that the Royalists had the same sort of troop, and that quite quickly, he saw others carrying wounded men with the white strip on their arm. He said, though, too, that some of the men were still shot – and he thought, even, that some soldiers targeted the men who were helping the wounded. Some of the men on both sides of the war were very unpleasant, he said. Most of the troops had either a sense of loyalty, or a conscience, or a sense of duty, but there were others who seemed to take a positive pleasure in fighting or killing – they seemed to think it made them superior to others. Luke said that this path of others had separated him off from Mark and Edward. Whilst Edward still greeted him as a friend if they met, it was clear that Mark regarded men who would not fight as some sort of inferior beings. It was clear, too, that some men saw themselves as superior just by the act of killing others, and Luke thought that they jeopardised their immortal souls as a result.

Luke finally said that his troop was going to be recognised as a separate group or cohort or even a more structured unit. The army was already looking at ways of getting more men to help them, and they would have a waggon or two to carry their equipment – and possibly to transport wounded soldiers back to hospital or camp. The army had realised that just leaving every wounded man on the battlefield to take their chances was not popular. The army had realised, too, that they were not going to win the war without a lot of casualties – and this had come as something of a surprise to the army and its leaders. Fighting men wanted to know that their friends might receive some help – just as they themselves might need help at some point in the future. Getting help was seen as some sort of loyalty to those men by their commanders, and it meant that they in turn would fight better for those commanders. There was a final page of the letter which Harriet did not show me – and I guessed that page might contain some indication of Luke's feelings for Harriet or his wish to see her again.

THREE

SOLDIERS IN THE VILLAGE, 1643

There was a rise in the road towards our village from the main road. One lane ran past the church, and the church was on a higher level than the road. We posted a couple of children there most days to watch for strangers approaching us up the lane or the road. It was boring work, but if they had a companion and a game, they would be happy enough, and we never got them to do more than a couple of hours by the church clock. We had a rota of children or adults who could do this 'watching-out' duty, and it always meant that at the very least we would have a quarter or perhaps half an hour's notice, which was time enough to get a small greeting party to meet the visitors. Sometimes, the leader of a group would ask us if we favoured the King or were for the Country. Usually, if they put it that way, they were probably for the Parliamentary side – because it suggested that the King was not for the Country. If, however, they asked us if we were for Parliament or Fairness or Equality, or mentioned Roundheads or 'the Rebels', it meant that they would probably be on the King's side.

It didn't really matter. We always said the same: "There are three hundred souls in this village. If you wish, we can have a meal ready for your men in less than an hour. We can provide you with a place to sleep, and maybe a little beer!" Most of them realised that it was not worth fighting a village for something that was volunteered to them, and most of them had seen enough fighting, so they did not want the trouble of a bit more when it wasn't needed. From our point, we could also sing them a song or play a bit of music to entertain them, and we got news from them. Often, the news was about places we had never heard of. Sometimes, it was about places or people that we knew or knew of. Either way, we gained. Once or twice, we had a group of soldiers come back. They had been to us before, and rather than march on a bit to Towcester or Bicester, they would stop with us. We didn't talk to soldiers about other groups we had seen. We were deliberately vague – "Oh, I think we did see some a month ago – but I can't tell you who they were." We avoided involvement in discussions.

In 1643, this changed quite suddenly for a while. We had a regular troop of soldiers billeted on us, and they were in the village for about a year. It all started one day when our 'watching' children told us that there was a group of soldiers up towards the road (by which they meant the main road from Towcester and Northampton to Oxford). They said they seemed to have stopped there for a while, but they had not made camp. Perhaps they had stopped for a meal, but they had been there for an hour or so before we received the message in the village, so the children had come to tell us anyway, to warn us. I marshalled together members of the council – which sounds quite formal but actually means that I ran around to find them – and asked them to come with me and the children down towards the lane to watch. My father came, too. We stood and watched the little that we could see from our viewpoint. We were not unduly worried, but it was as well to make sure that we knew.

The children were right about the troop of soldiers. There was a camp fire we could see, and although we could not clearly see all of the figures there because hedges and bushes got in the way, we could see the occasional figure move. We guessed that there were others perhaps sitting or resting who were out of view. We sat down to wait and took it in turns to watch the soldiers. If they came to the village, there was not much we could do to prevent them, but we could hide some of our stores – we had done this before – and we could also send young men (who might be considered old enough to recruit) out to hide in local farms or in the undergrowth, and we could suggest to young unmarried girls that they might want to conceal themselves. In any case, we would offer hospitality as we usually did, and then perhaps we would find out what they wanted or were doing. Waiting is always boring and we played games with the children whilst we waited – always making sure that one or two of us watched the road.

The day warmed up. We were conscious of the heat, and although we were not panicking, we grew a bit more irritable at the flies, and we moved around so that the sun did not catch too much of the same side of us. It was about mid-afternoon when we saw the fires of the group being dowsed, and whilst we still couldn't see all of them, we saw more heads than we had before as the group rose up. After a few moments, they did what we had hoped they might not do, and we started to see a troop of soldiers in two files in the lane towards the village between the bushes. I and the children had the keenest eyes, and we could tell as they moved from the road that there were about thirty of them. Young William then said, "And some of them are wearing masks! Their heads are all black!" and as they moved steadily closer, I realised that he was right. There was something strange about the appearance of these soldiers that made them different to other soldiers that we had seen (not that we had seen many soldiers). We sent the two children back to the village with the usual messages about concealment for the young men and women and, as a committee, waited to greet our visitors. They walked closer as we waited in the road. There was no evidence of hostility or threat.

The uniforms of the soldiers identified them as Royalist troops. Most soldiers wore the same sort of clothes, but these had sashes of the Royalist army, and the officers were in quite smart uniforms. It would appear that there were three leaders – perhaps an officer and two subordinates – but as we had noticed, the rest of the troops were all apparently wearing some sort of black mask or headgear under their hats. It wasn't until they were within a couple of hundred yards, and unobscured by branches or bushes, that we realised that these were black-skinned men – the first like this that we had ever seen in the village, or anywhere, except (it turned out) for the vicar. The vicar said, "Goodness! They are Blackamoors! Africans, perhaps? I once saw one of them with a travelling fair at Northampton! Nice fellow he seemed to be – polite – but his appearance frightened some of the townsfolk because he was so different to them! I tried to talk to him properly, but the fair owner would not allow that. He was considered an exhibit or an act – and they didn't want me to talk to the exhibits. That was a few years ago, though. I haven't seen anyone like that since."

The vicar was obviously right about the nature of the men approaching (that they were Blackamoors), and perhaps he would also be right that they were nice fellows. Generally, though, soldiers are not known for being 'nice fellows'. As these men were so different to others we had seen before, though, we drew closer together around the vicar as a small tight group for protection, and awaited the advancing soldiers. It occurred to me that our usual tactic of offering food or drink to the group might not work with this group as they had just had a large rest and presumably had some food at the roadside. We knew that by now, our young folk would be in hiding – but we also didn't want to antagonise the soldiers, who might not believe that we had no folk of the right age in the village. If they were here for recruitment, they would resent us concealing our men. We could not see any real positives from our situation, and so we waited for their arrival in more trepidation than we usually felt. We didn't back away, but perhaps we drew a bit closer to each other than we had been.

About 10 feet from us, the troop leader raised his hand, and the troop of soldiers halted. The troop leader then moved forward to meet us. "Price," he said. "Thomas Price, officer for Cavendish, Earl of Newcastle in the army of His Majesty the King. I am commanded by the Earl to establish a base here, to prevent looting of supplies on the main road back there," and he pointed towards it. "There have been a lot of small raids recently, and we don't know whether these raids are organised by the rebel forces, or whether it is just outlaw gangs chancing their arm. We need to put patrols on the road, do some night patrols as well, and I am afraid that your village is where we will need to have a base, so that we may send patrols in both directions. We don't need to patrol past Towcester in the north, and we will agree a border with our Oxford troops somewhere near Bicester. We have been asked as a regiment to do this sort of duty in the areas north of Oxford – as it is a city important to His Majesty." This was not quite the news that we had been hoping for, but it did seem that they were not just here to recruit or steal our stores. We also didn't know that Oxford was important to King Charles – at that stage, I think we assumed (perhaps naively) that most of the country supported the King, and that all areas were important to him.

"It means that you will need to put up with us for a while here in your village, feed us and find billets for us. I can give you a little money for these inconveniences, but it does also mean that I am not here to raid all of your carefully hoarded supplies and drag all of your able young men off to war," he said, and a smile lit up his face. We appreciated his humour and the fact that he was aware of one or two of our worries – and he had dismissed them quite quickly from our minds. Perhaps he had been in this situation before in other villages.

"We have two barns that we have used for visitors in the past," I said. "They are warm and comfortable, and if you do not mind the occasional visitor sharing with you, I think they will suit you. We have firepits there too, so that we can feed travellers! I expect having a few soldiers in the village will be a bit of a change for our village. Perhaps they will want to watch what you do!" Thomas Price's face lit up. He was obviously expecting protest or denial or complaint, so our agreement was gratefully received by him, and it immediately established a better relationship between him and us.

"I thank you all," he said with a small bow.

Our vicar, though, had a question for him. "Tell me about your men, Officer Price," he demanded.

"Prior to the war, vicar, these men were servants or possibly slaves to His Grace the Earl of Newcastle, and some other nobles nearby. I don't know how long they had been servants, or whether their parents were also servants. I am told that some of these men probably had families, too – but it didn't seem to make much difference what they were defined as. They were just told to go and serve by their masters. When war was declared, many men from the estates of the nobles were told to follow their masters to the colours in exactly this way, and amongst them were these African servants. Sometimes, the Africans were sent so that family men from the villages could stay at home. Sometimes, they were just told to go so that His Grace had raised the number of men required. It was a question of who could be spared the easiest. They are nice enough men, but it means that we don't pass through villages that they know – and so they don't desert. They stay with us because it is a more secure existence for them. They all came from estates."

He also said that the life of a soldier was preferred by some of these men. Physical activities around the countryside, such as marching or military activities, were preferred by them instead of duties in a house, dressed in tight servants' costumes, often prevented from moving unless they were directed to move by the master of the house or by his designated senior servants. They were trained to fight and use weapons, to support each other, to scout the ground, report, advance as a unit, sometimes to chase or run, and to learn to construct temporary billets or to learn to live in different places. They were well fed, and regularly fed. Instructions were clear and could be easily followed, and in Price it would appear that they had an officer that cared to make their existence better. These aspects of soldiering were as attractive to the Africans as they were to the local farm lads in England, and they were extremely attractive when compared to their previous lives as servants. Their level of communication and feeling of community were much more genuine in this troop of the army, and they did their work very well.

"But they all ended up in the same troop?" asked the vicar.

"That was deliberate," said Price. "It was found that the black faces of these men unnerved some of the soldiers or volunteers that they were asked to serve with. It was decided that if Black Africans were to serve, they would be formed into a troop of similar men – and so far they have served well, and seem to get on well together. They came from different areas of Africa, so some of them do not speak the same African languages, but they have all served in England and are able to follow instructions in English. They listen well, ask questions when needed, and try to do their best. We also find that their appearance frightens troops from the other side, and that is useful to us. After all, there are cases in our past history of battles being won just by one side being afraid of the others. These men follow instructions well, fight well and work well as a troop. It also means that they are not asked to fight a battle in with other men who do not trust them because their appearance is different.

"Come here, Joseph," he said to one of the African soldiers behind him. The soldier walked quickly up to the officer, drew himself up smartly and gave a little bow to the officer. "Tell the vicar, here, who you are, Joseph," said Price.

"I am Joseph, known as Joseph Brown," said the African soldier to the vicar, and gave another little bow.

"Brown?" I said. "That is my name, too. I am Lucy Brown!"

"Good afternoon, Miss Brown," said Joseph to me.

"I am called Lucy," I said again, "not Miss Brown."

"Good afternoon, Miss Lucy," said Joseph, and smiled at me.

"Have you been taught about God, and Jesus?" said the vicar.

"Yes, sir," said Joseph. "We have been taught about Jesus, and the Holy Bible, and I have been given the name of Jesus' father, Joseph, by my Lord Cavendish." We were very impressed by Joseph's grasp of English and the nature of his reply – because we did not know what to expect. Also, I think that Joseph spoke English better than some of the men from the village. I think that the vicar had quite a lot of other questions for the soldiers – because he opened his mouth to speak again, but at that moment we had an interruption.

Young William and his friend came running back from the village to us. This was not expected, and we turned to face them. "Vicar, vicar, Mr Brown, there has been an accident," William gasped, short of breath from his running. "An axle broke on one of the big waggons. It has gone over on its side and one of the children is under it – Rory Stone – and we can't lift the waggon off him. We can hear him wailing from underneath so he ain't dead, but we can't get at him to free him! We need more men!"

"Take us there!" said Price – and I turned to run off with William and the other child towards the village. "Come on, men, follow me," said Price to his troop, and I heard the clatter as many boots started to run behind us. The soldiers all had heavy packs on their backs and carried muskets, but they kept pace with me and the children as we ran to the centre of the village. They were clearly very fit, and clearly very strong. Potentially, they could help us. A cloud of dust rose up as we ran along the road. There had not been rain for a few days, and I was conscious of the amount of dust that could be raised by a troop of soldiers. We had seen much of it along the main road in the past.

A group of some of the women – who had obviously been unloading vegetables from the waggon – were crowded around it, and the waggon bed was tilted over at an angle. We could hear the thin wailing of a child. The women drew back as they heard us and the soldiers running towards them, and they turned to watch what happened next. They retreated still further as they saw what sort of troops were advancing towards them, until we had a cordon of them standing at a safe distance from the soldiers and watching to see what would happen. Price knelt down, grasped the lowest corner of the waggon bed and asked his soldiers to join him. Whilst most of the men lifted the waggon bed to its normal position, two of them crawled underneath it and gently lifted and dragged young Rory clear of the waggon and into our sight. They laid him flat on the grass verge nearby, and then looked around to see who was there in the group who could examine him and check his injuries.

One of the women with a bit of nursing experience looked at Rory and checked his limbs. "Nothing broken," she said scornfully. "'E's just frightened," she said, and even as she spoke, Rory was struggling up, although he looked terrified by the black-skinned soldiers who had just carried him out and helped him to his feet.

Price and the soldiers had lowered the waggon bed back to the ground and Price looked at the axle. "Sheared through," he said. "Old." And the axle was taken away to Mrs Cartwright to be fixed by her at the forge.

"Where are all of your young men?" said Price. "Surely you have folk here who could have lifted that waggon for you?" We looked at each other a bit shamefacedly. "Oh, I see!" he said to us in sudden realisation. "When you saw us coming up the lane, they all went into hiding, so that we didn't take them with us?" I nodded and told him about our warning system.

Price continued: "And I suppose you have more young women here as well?" I nodded again. "And were they all going to come out after we leave?"

"That was the original intention," I said, "but if you are going to be staying here for a while, hiding them is not going to be possible! Eileen," I called to one of the women – and she gave a shrill whistle.

We waited for a few moments, and then doors started to open, and one by one our younger women and men started to appear from the houses, and some came around the corner from the direction of the church. After a few minutes, there was twice the number of people standing around the damaged waggon. Price started to laugh, and some of his soldiers joined in. We explained to the girls what had happened – and then who these soldiers were and why we had called them back. They looked at the soldiers with more interest, and Eileen said, "Whoever they are, they helped us get young Rory out from under that waggon, so they are welcome." I told the villagers that this troop of soldiers would be staying in the barn for a while. We walked them down to their new billet, and the village started to prepare food that would be served to them that evening.

There were a lot of advantages to us from the troop of soldiers being billeted in the village. They went out on patrols as we had been told – but a patrol was usually seven or eight soldiers, and that meant that the rest were often in the village. They seemed to work in three groups – one on patrol, one resting, and the other in drills or preparing equipment. They undertook exercises and drills on the green, and these were the object of fascination to our children, and often to our younger adults – when they thought they were not being seen to watch. Sometimes, they stood guard for us at the entries to the village – and word got around that we had a troop billeted here. People from other villages came to watch, and it was noticed that petty thieving in our village decreased now that we had soldiers. Our older adults – initially frightened of these younger, fitter adults, so strange of appearance – watched them in the evenings as they fed them food, lent them tobacco for their pipes, and listened to their stories. Gradually, the relationships between soldier and villager strengthened.

The soldiers all had Christian names. As well as Joseph, there was Jacob and Josiah, and James and John. All of the apostle names were present, and quite a lot of others from the Bible. I have mentioned just a few of them (and, in remembering, I have only mentioned the ones with a J – which apparently was done because one landowner picked names from an alphabetical list). Their culture was English. All of them had been either brought to England when very young, or they were the children of those brought as slaves in previous generations. They had been taught stories of Africa, but none of them had a clear memory of coming from another country. Ironically, the English saw them as African, but they had no other culture than England to relate to. Most of their own stories, their dress, customs and some art were English-inspired. They understood that they were different because of the colour of their skin, but did not understand why we found that strange. Some of them could read passages from the Bible, too, and they were very fond of the stories of the Israelites in captivity. These related to their own existence as captives in a foreign land. I didn't know if they had stories of their own history or heritage, too, or whether the Israelites filled a gap.

They sang and performed music, too, with pipes and drums. We sang with them – some of our old songs and we learnt some of theirs – and it started to be a ritual that once a week there would be a village meal together with some music, dancing and singing. They helped us, too. Once we realised that they would rather be active than laze around, they started to help us, cutting vegetation back, removing rotten timber, repairing our waggons, and on at least one occasion building new waggons. They even helped in the field on occasion – but less so as they needed to be within call if they were needed for their duties, and the fields were further away. They often helped replace thatch or slates on roofs, or repaired joints. At least we could teach them woodworking skills and joinery, even if it was their strength that carried out the work. They liked whittling as well with knives, so they took to woodwork very easily. On one occasion, they went up to one of the quarries with us in a waggon and loaded it up with stone for repairs to the houses in the village. They did all of the things that we had to do, but often did them better and quicker than we could do.

Price told us a lot of things about his troops, some interesting, some strange, and some unacceptable. Price told us that the appearance of the

Africans was seen as intolerable by a number of other regiments and other troops. They refused to serve with the Africans, behaved as if they were superior to the Africans, and whilst the Africans were still separated into different units, there was evidence of bullying, assaults on them, unfair allocation of duties and even accusations of theft and injury made against them – although subsequently these had been shown to be false. There had even been one allegation that a Black African soldier in a skirmish had been shot from behind – from his own ranks – but that could not be proved. It had been decided to put all of the Black Africans into one troop, and Price and his subordinates had been placed in charge of them as they had worked for Cavendish before the war, and it was judged that they could maintain discipline over the troops. It meant that the Africans had officers who knew them, who could be expected to listen to them and speak for them if there was a question of their fitness for duty.

Even when the troop was formed, some other troops in the army would not work with them, or avoided them. It was difficult for the troop to operate as part of a regiment or battalion, as other officers would not communicate properly with them, and in a battle they were at risk from their own side as well as from enemy action. The result of this was that they operated as a separate troop on duties, like the one in Helmdon. They engaged in skirmishes, or were sent to combat small opposition forces, or to do patrols where they would not be in regular contact with other forces. Price pointed out to us, wryly, that his troops invariably excelled in their duties, and one factor in this was the terror shown by Parliamentary troops upon seeing the Africans attacking them. The Africans encouraged this terror with loud war cries, relishing the fright they caused to the other side. They even made up dances to display before battle started, but they still did not really want to fight a battle if they were in front of their own troops who also did not like them. It showed that some people would not make an effort to find out if these Africans were human or good-natured, and that some people, even on the side that wanted 'change', would not change themselves to tolerate them.

We had something like this in the village. Some of our villagers would not speak to the Africans or associate with them because of the colour of their skin. Some ordered them around like servants. The officers would not allow this treatment of their soldiers if they knew about it, but I noticed several occasions when a villager arrived home with a soldier carrying bags for her. I asked the soldiers what they thought about this, and their reply was that if they could help folk, they would do, even if these were folk who considered themselves superior. It didn't do them any harm. To me, they were true Christians in their behaviour – but it really made me laugh with anger when I heard a fat toothless old man tell another that they could order these men around as 'they were superior to them' because of the colour of their skin. The idea of a fit young man of perhaps twenty years of age being inferior to these others was just stupid. It didn't seem to be the same with the women, though. Generally, those of us with a conscience tried to make the soldiers feel welcome, and valued.

There was another aspect to the Africans' presence in our village – which apparently had not been an issue before, and caused more arguments. Once our village had welcomed the soldiers in and had become used to their residence amongst us, then other, different, thoughts occurred to the women. The presence of around thirty fit young men became of interest to some of our young women – and even to some of our older women. Often in jobs that the Africans undertook for us, or their duties, they would strip to the waist for comfort. They would often find an audience, largely female, observing them in their physical activities with a pick or a saw or a hammer. This audience seemed to want to both check that the skin colour was the same down to the waist and also seemed fascinated by the effect of the activity on their muscles and bodies. They would comment in a favourable manner on the men, who were particularly noticeable in a village where most men between eighteen and thirty were absent! It seemed that 'watching the soldiers' became a routine.

I will not go into any further details about the number or type of relationships that started in this way, but the African troops were billeted in our village for more than a year, and in the second year of their occupation, and after they left us, a number of babies were born in our village – whose skin colour was darker than what we normally expected in a village child, and whose dark hair showed something of an African origin. These children grew up amongst us. They were all told that their fathers were heroes who had fought in the war, but there did not seem to be any other similar children in other villages, so this was a phenomenon that just seemed to affect us. Interestingly, it showed that some of the village women had no prejudice against African soldiers. Their children, though, suffered some of the prejudice that their fathers had experienced when living with us – from those same bigots. This prejudice and bigotry led to further arguments and even fights – because no one wanted their own children discriminated against. None of the Africans returned to us after the war – presumably, it was felt, because others had decided their future lives and where they were allowed to live and work. We heard nothing further of them or their troop. It was a chapter of the war which had no real end.

FOUR

THE BATTLE OF HELMDON

T
he African soldiers were to be with us in the village until early in 1644, but one event at that time affected us all dramatically, and hastened (if not caused) their departure from us. That event was the Battle of Helmdon in May of 1644. The Battle of Helmdon exists in no published written form, and is not known outside of our village, except by any members of those African troops who left us after the battle. Although we presume that they went on to take part in Marston Moor in July 1644, there is no recorded evidence of that, and we heard nothing further from them. None of them came back to visit us in the future, and we presume that they were made to return to the estates from whence they came, and presumably to continue their servitude – unless they died in the war. There are few references to them (apparently) in history books, and those that mention them do not make it clear what their role was in the war. It may be considered ingratitude on our part that we did not seek them out after the war, but then we did not seek out many others, either.

Technically, I suppose that the Battle of Helmdon was a skirmish rather than a battle. It was certainly not equal to the level of numbers of the thousands of people that took place in the major battles of the war – but it was equal in importance to those of us in the village of 300–400 people. A battle involving some 200 people (which was equivalent to more than half of the village) was one of the most memorable moments of the war for us, and it will be remembered here, until those of us who were present are all dead and gone. I always see a 'skirmish' as perhaps twenty to thirty soldiers, so perhaps Helmdon was a 'minor battle' – but the title doesn't really matter very much. The winter had ended, spring had clearly arrived, and the weather was beginning to show some promise of the summer to follow. We had had several days of warmer temperatures, and although there was still the freshness of the spring skies and the colour of the vegetation, we were starting to anticipate the warmth of June and to shed more garments.

Officer Price disappeared in the early morning with his usual patrol of eight soldiers. As usual, some of our children watched them go and waved. There was some activity on the green from exercises done by the other soldiers – but they didn't last more than an hour or two, and in the late morning on that day, it looked as if things were settling down for a lazy afternoon as well. Around lunchtime, though, we had another warning from our watchdogs on the lane to the road. Once again, some of us walked to the watch post, asked them about it, and started to look at what was happening. This time, I asked one of the troop's subordinate officers and a couple of his men to come with us, in case of trouble. We were starting to get used to involving them when trouble looked likely. Once again, we were told that there was another troop at rest on the road by the junction to our road, and cooking fires could be seen being lit. From the number of fires, it looked as if the troop on the main road was larger than the troop we already had in the village.

Two of 'our' soldiers were detailed by their officer to scout the land between us and the group, and to spy on the location and number of that group. They were told not to be seen but to report back to us alive on what they found, rather than take any risks and get captured. We made sure they understood and then we sent them off. Technically, it was the officer who sent them – but I helped! We watched as they walked down to the junction, but as the lanes and roads had hedges and bushes around them, we could not see our two clearly after the junction. The rest of us settled down to watch, wait and listen. I suppose it must have been an hour or so, but it did feel as if the two soldiers came back quite quickly and reported to their serjeant (if that is what rank he was – I am not very good with ranks and titles). They spoke quickly to him, and I was not used to military terms, but the information was then repeated back to us in simpler terms, and it was possibly as bad as it could have been – under the circumstances.

On the road was a group of perhaps one hundred men – known to be a renegade troop – who had fought on the side of the Parliamentarians earlier in the war, but who had then formed into a separate group who basically roamed the countryside, stealing, raping and killing. They were known to have decimated several villages, and although both sides of the war were on the lookout for them and determined to remove them, they had escaped detection so far, and continued with activities unacceptable to more reputable and regular troops. This group was now at rest on the main road at the junction of the lane to the village, and they had been recognised by one of the banners that they carried. We had no way of knowing (at that time) whether they would carry on moving up or down the road, or whether they were moving cross-country – in which case they would pass through the village or very close. It was possible that they would divert from their route and advance to our village just to see what lay here. We had to prepare for this – as the worst alternative.

We had several immediate imperatives. We needed to despatch two men to track down Officer Price. The soldiers knew where he would be patrolling, and could take another lane from the village down to the road (further up the road) to find him and deliver the message. We had no idea how long that message would take to arrive, so a runner was sent to the village to warn our friends as well, and the two men were sent off to Price immediately. The message to Officer Price stated that the renegade troop was paused at the bottom of the Syresham lane, that they outnumbered the serjeant's troop three to one, and asked, too, if Price could get a message to Towcester, telling Towcester that we needed their troops to come and support us. He was also asked very politely if he could return as soon as possible (it said 'at all speed') to help us. We waited, and whilst we waited, the subordinate officer told me what he thought might happen, and then we started to prepare.

The obvious (and sensible) military action would be for Officer Price's troop to withdraw from the village and hide out, should the renegades move towards the village. They could then avoid engaging a larger force – at least until possible reinforcements arrived from Towcester. With Price on patrol, there were a total of twenty-five soldiers in our village at that moment, and that was felt insufficient to engage the enemy. If they DID engage the enemy, there was a good chance that they would be wiped out. On the other hand, though, 'our' soldiers liked us very much and knew that if they withdrew, there was a strong chance of our village being stripped of resources, and possibly even of human lives. They actually wanted to stay in the village to protect us. It was impractical to try and evacuate a whole village – even if we could find them all where they were working. It was also felt that Price, too, would want to protect us in gratitude for our hospitality of his troop.

The subordinate officer present decided quite quickly – even without the support of Officer Price – to mobilise his troops and mount an ambush (if an ambush was needed) just at the village side of a junction, a mile or so south of the village. There was a lot of concealment around the junction, and often troops or normal people slowed at the junction either to check which way to go or to peer around the corner and check that the way was clear for a waggon. This new group or force would probably send scouts ahead at that point, but the main force would stop and start to wait for the scouts to report back (as they might do at each junction, or where there was concealment for other troops). The African troops showed a remarkable aptitude for concealment, and could hide in the vegetation until enough of the renegade soldiers were immediately in front of them, and then bring the front ranks of the renegades down with musket fire. I was told that because the muskets would only have one chance to fire (being slow to re-arm), the Africans would then have to leap down the bank and engage the other soldiers with swords.

This seemed to me only half a plan – which would almost certainly result in the death of all of the Africans, and might well leave enough renegades to then take the village. With the blood lust of the renegades up, they would want to take revenge on someone, and that someone would be our village. I voiced my reservations to the soldiers. "What else do you suggest we do then, miss?" I was asked – politely, as if my opinion mattered to the serjeant, but I detected a hint of 'what does she know about it?' in his voice.

I told them, "We have a better chance if we organise a further ambush, so that we can attack the renegades again before they get to the village. If they get this far as a whole group, their soldiers will be able to use our houses to shield them, and you will not be able to fight them properly in the village. We need to organise a second set of defenders down this lane somewhere before they get to the village."

I told the serjeant that there were ten muskets at Stuchbury Hall, another five or so in the village, and we could provide people to fire them. I suggested to him that his soldiers carry out his ambush as planned, but that instead of following up the muskets with a sword attack, they then run back up the field using the bushes and vegetation to shield them, and that also, our fifteen or so villagers push a waggon down the lane, overturn it, and then use it as a barricade to attack renegades coming up the lane. This would give the Africans the chance to reload, and they in turn could fire on any renegades who came up the fields instead of the lane. It meant that instead of just having twenty-five musket balls fired, perhaps this might make up fifty or sixty balls, before we had to consider whether any sword attack on the uninjured men left (with their muskets) was necessary. I don't think I really thought about this idea; it just seemed to occur to me – but then I knew the lanes.

"Cor, miss," he said in admiration. "How did you work all of this out?" I refrained from telling him that I had no idea (the idea had just occurred to me) and told him that we needed to get the messages to Stuchbury and the village at once, and our remaining men dutifully set out to tell the African soldiers, the village and Stuchbury Hall folk what was needed. Gradually, men started arriving – in a variety of states of dress – including some of the other soldiers who had not expected to be fighting and were only partly dressed in uniform. The Africans filed down the lane and into the bushes and fields either side, and then the villagers arrived with some muskets and a waggon, and later still the Stuchbury Hall men – all either quite old or youngsters – arrived. We decided not to overturn the waggon until we saw the renegades move, and we detailed several young lads to watch, report back, and take messages – but NOT to hang around to see the fighting. None of us wanted to be responsible for a lad taking a stray bullet or being in front of fighting men.

I ignored my own concerns and did exactly what I had told the youngsters not to do, by staying at the watch post. I took up a position with the serjeant and a couple of men about 50 yards behind the waggon. I knew that if the renegades got through all of our men there, then there needed to be a last-ditch message to warn any villagers left to run, or to tell them to conceal themselves better than they ever had before, and I felt that I needed to be the one who was to take that message. Again, we waited – as we had done on the afternoon that the Royalist soldiers had arrived. Again, it was hot and it was a frustrating wait. I can't think what it must have been like for the soldiers in those heavy uniforms. About four in the afternoon, we got a message back from the leaders to say that the renegades were packing up, and then another to say that they were coming our way – up our lane. They took about half an hour to approach the road junction, and although they had scouts in front with loaded muskets, most of their men had their guns slung over their backs. Either they expected no trouble or they were going to unsling and load those muskets when nearer the village.

At the moment that the renegades left the main road, we overturned the waggon across the lane and our men moved behind it. We overturned it early because we didn't want the renegades to hear the crash of the waggon and to be warned early of possible threat. They approached the road junction below the church and paused, as we had expected. Our African troops had been told to let the scouts through unharmed, and only to attack when the main body of men advanced as that would cause the maximum chaos. They had grinned and indicated that they understood before they quietly moved into place. We could not see them at the moment we overturned the waggon, but we knew that they were there. At just this moment in time, Officer Price and his eight men arrived and, having been warned, moved very quietly into place. Price and two of them stayed with us, and the other six went down to the waggon on its side in the lane.

"What is happening, Roberts?" he asked his serjeant. His subordinate told Price what the plan was, where everyone else was, and then he paused and looked at me.

I knew he was either going to lie to Price about whose plan this was or tell him that this was all my idea, so I interrupted, saying, "This was all the serjeant's idea, Mr Price. He had the really clever idea of the ambushes, and spreading out the forces, and so far it is working very well! I am very impressed with him!" I could see the serjeant behind Price with his mouth open at this lie, so I smiled at him.

"So, what are you doing here, miss?" said Price – who obviously did not like the idea of civilians being in a conflict, and maybe, even less, women being there.

"I sent the message to Stuchbury Hall and the village, telling them where to come when the serjeant told me," I said quickly, "but if something goes wrong, I am the one who will run to the village and tell them to run or hide. I am very quick at giving messages!"

Price looked at us. I suspected he knew that his serjeant had not worked this all out himself. The man was a good soldier but had not demonstrated great knowledge of strategy to me; nor had he (I suspected) demonstrated it to Price. Price, though, did not want to demonstrate suspicion of the plan, disrupt what was working, or show to his serjeant that he considered him incapable. He also did not know me well enough to suspect that I had done some of the planning. Instead, he put his hand on the serjeant's shoulder and said, "Excellent plan, Roberts, well done!" although he looked suspiciously at me and the serjeant gave me another dog-like look of gratitude. Price said that the message had been sent to Towcester, but he didn't see how they could arrive in time to help us in any useful way, so we would have to do this ourselves. He also indicated that Towcester was not known for the quickness of their response – although he did not say that they were lazy.

There was a volley of shots from the crossroads, quickly followed by a second one, and a few ragged answers. The Africans had obviously used the bushes both sides of the road, and each side had fired almost together on the renegades. I think the answering shots were the rear half of the renegade troop trying to fire back – perhaps over their own men. I saw across the fields the African men running back (I knew them from their uniforms), but instead of running all the way back to the waggon, they disappeared into the undergrowth halfway up the lane. There was silence for a few moments, and then some of the renegades appeared above the road in the field – having climbed the bank. They moved cautiously across the field in ones and twos, but then they were hit with another round of musket fire from the concealed Africans, who had a chance to reload their muskets. I saw men die – for the first time – and I felt sick, even seeing them die at a distance.

The day was clear, the skies were blue, the greens of the fields and the trees had not been around long enough that year to start to be dull or the fields faded, and against all of that clarity of colour and the beauty that I see in England in the spring and the early summer, men were dying. The last thing that a lot of them would be aware of would be the panic of the moment, the physical pain, and then possibly a few moments when they might be dimly aware of the colours and the peace of the surrounding area. They say that it often rains at funerals, and that is appropriate for the mood. When should battles be fought, then? When should men breathe their last? I was acutely aware of the dullness of the still figures contrasting with the movement of the trees and the grass from the slight breeze. There would be another flash of movement or of colour, and then there would be that gentleness of the countryside – but still those bodies. I knew that this image and this contrast would stay with me when the battle was over and done. I had chosen to stay here and I had to live with what I saw.

There was a roar – a battle cry perhaps – and the rest of the renegades advanced up the lane towards the waggon, only to be hit with fire from the village men behind it and Price's soldiers with them. As soon as they had fired, the Africans at the side of the lane were firing again, demonstrating that they had reloaded once again. A messenger came up to us. "They are retreating!" he said. "There are only about twenty or twenty-five of them left, and I think their officers are all dead!"

"Go after them, men," shouted Price, and some of the Africans ran across the field whilst those from the waggon moved slowly and cautiously down the lane. We couldn't see much after that, because of the shielding of the lane by the trees and bushes, but we heard more shots as our troops reloaded, and the screams from the lane as the Africans overran the retreating troops and used their swords to attack and kill them. It went on a bit longer than I had thought it might, but it was all over in less than an hour.

Price had been right. No troops arrived from Towcester, but thirty African troops and twenty village and hall men had defeated 110 renegades. The renegades were never heard of again. No one asked us about them, but we felt that we didn't want the village to be known as a place where we attacked soldiers, and Price felt that he did not want his Africans to be too well known as an attack force – in case it encouraged other commanders to put them at the front of larger battles. They were often disparaged because of their colour, and it would have been easy for others to place them in danger. They had been lucky in a small battle, but they would not survive regular large attacks in front of other troops on their own side who did not like them. Some of the villagers, too, were impressed by the increase in the stock of arms in the village when we added the renegade swords and muskets to the stock that we kept in the village, but nothing was said to anyone outside the village about the battle.

I had asked Price about prisoners after the battle. "Prisoners?" he said.

"Yes," I said. "There must have been some wounded men, or some who surrendered?"

Price told me that in the heat of battle, often the first shot or stroke injured a man, but this was usually followed up by a second stroke which was designed to incapacitate the opponent – because otherwise it was possible that they would rise to their feet again and attack their assailant from behind. On the second stroke (as he called it), it was almost impossible to judge it so that it, too, only wounded, and almost always that second stroke killed off an incapacitated opponent. He said, too, that in the heat of battle, it was not really possible to tell if someone put their hands up as a signal to other troops, or if they intended to surrender. He said that in most battles, surrender was only taken if a whole troop or force surrendered, and that was usually done with a white or parley flag, and then by negotiation. He said that none of his soldiers had seen any of the renegades make a move that indicated they wanted to stop the battle – probably because they thought they outnumbered 'our' troops. He also told me that in some battles in the war, prisoners who had surrendered had then been killed. He said that neither he nor his men had done that. In this 'skirmish', all of the renegades had died.

Accordingly, we (the men of the village, the hall, Price and I) took the decision to recover the bodies of the renegades using the village waggons, and to bury them in a field behind the village. There were no streams to be affected. The field was usually used for grazing, so we would not be growing crops in it. The soldiers collected the bodies that night and they were buried in the darkness. I am afraid I did not help – as I did not have the stomach for it. It was an unpleasant task, and the waggons needed to be cleaned and sanded afterwards. Perhaps half of the village knew for certain what had happened in general terms – but most had been sent to hide before the event, and whilst they had heard some shots, they had no idea of the full scale of the event. Our vicar insisted on blessing those men who had died, but he did this over the grave of them all rather than over each individual. We knew that they had chosen what might be described as a path of evil, over good, and there were none of them that had shown in the past (in other villages) that they regretted their choice.

There was one more 'lesson' that came out of our 'battle'. We knew that if a large army passed our village, there was a danger that we could be stripped of our resources to supply them. We could do nothing about that. We couldn't predict if there would be a battle nearby – and we could do nothing about that, either. If a battle was fought within about five miles of the village, there was a good chance that the village would be wiped out. If a battle was within twenty miles of Helmdon, there was a strong chance that we would be expected to contribute supplies to 20,000 or 30,000 men – and we could do nothing about that, either. The 'battle' had taught us, though, that forty to fifty muskets could take on a force twice their number and either deter an attack or repulse it completely.

We might expect the arrival of another small band later in the war. If they were part of a regular army group, we could expect to talk to their officers and arrange food or accommodation for them.

What we did not want – and there was still a possibility we might get it – was another unofficial or renegade band to attack us, intent on rape, pillage, robbery or just destruction. We had known from Officer Price that the African soldiers would be leaving within the next month anyway, and that we could not rely on having their support in the future. We did not know that we might have any other regular troops stationed with us. We decided to create our own militia – as a possible safeguard against small groups of marauders. We thought that if we were even able to put up just a small show of resistance, it might deter opponents or even persuade them to try their luck somewhere else. We did not relish the idea of sending marauders away to other villages – but at least we could try and protect ourselves, and we could always send warnings to others. If irregular troops got even the idea that they could not just walk into villages, they might negotiate first.

We spoke to Officer Price about this. I could see that he had doubts – but as he and his men would be leaving, they could do nothing about protecting us further, and in the normal course of things, a village our size would not warrant soldiers. His patrols were gradually being taken over by troops from Brackley and Towcester, and there was a chance – the way the war was going – that they would be fighting soon as part of a bigger army when they left us. In the meantime, they were likely to have less work to do for the next few weeks, and Price thought that they could possibly help us to organise our own defences a bit better. Accordingly, he did two things. The first was to walk round the village with us, showing how soldiers might be expected to attack the village, which routes they might take and what weak spots we had. He advised us on the possible use of permanent barricades – not to obstruct our activities but as possible defence positions with viewpoints. As part of this, he also advised us on our watch posts outside the village – and made some suggestions about improving those.

The other thing that Price did was totally unexpected. He borrowed one of our four-wheel waggons and two horses for a day, and set off quite early in the morning with two of his soldiers armed with muskets. He was gone overnight, and when he came back, there were four or five large wooden boxes in the back of the waggon. He stopped in the centre of the village, when he saw me, the vicar and one of the tailors talking. We were discussing the use of some fabric we had recently bought, but that is incidental, and we stopped anyway when we saw Price had come back. "Where shall we put these?" he asked. "It needs to be somewhere central, dry, preferably locked up, but they need to be somewhere that they can be accessible quickly in an emergency."

"What are they?" we asked him, mystified.

He gave us one of his grins. "I will show you when we get them stored safely," he said.

There were some houses halfway down Church Street, and one of them had a large storehouse – which I knew wasn't being used at that time. I directed the soldiers and the waggon down that road, and we walked down behind them. After a quick discussion with the owner of the storehouse, we were allowed to unload the boxes and use part of the store for them. Price unloaded all of the boxes with his soldiers, and left one just outside the storehouse. He then levered the top off the box, and inside were eight muskets – either new or in very good condition and wrapped in some sort of greaseproof material. I realised that the top of the box was stamped 'Ordnance'. If I had seen that earlier, I might have guessed.

"Oh my goodness!" exclaimed the vicar. "What are those for?"

"Officially for my troops," said Price. "Unofficially for your village. There is powder and ball in that box there, that is a different shape. Don't put it anywhere near heat, but don't get it damp, either!"

We told him that most of us had no idea how to use a musket, and that it was only luck, really, that we had been able to find enough men to use the Stuchbury ones. "There are thirty muskets in those boxes!" he said cheerfully. "We are going to have some classes on how to use them before we leave!"

"Who will you teach?" I asked.

"Anyone who wants to learn! The more, the better," he replied. "If we need more powder and balls, I think we can get them, but you won't be able to get any more muskets."

One week later, I found myself in a field with eight other women learning how to load and fire a musket. At the start of the day, the lesson was very hesitant, and the first time I fired a musket I thought that my shoulder was coming off – when it slammed back against me. By the end of the day, I was beginning to feel more confident, and I even hit the target once. Price took the line that the more people who could use them, the more chance we had of getting them all used. He and his men felt that leaving us able to defend ourselves was a good reward for the way we had treated them.

I didn't think myself capable of loading one of these things, pointing it at a man, and actually firing it, but I guessed that I wouldn't really know how I would feel when it was necessary. I thought that I might find things different if my friends or family were in danger of being attacked by renegades or marauders, but I also thought that if we could get the young and older men to use the muskets first, I might not be needed. I was right in that, as a lot of the men were just waiting for the chance to fire a musket, and insisted on having practice every week with targets. Price was right – we could get more powder. Balls were a bit more difficult, but we could get them in Northampton, and within a month, we had found a mould, and we were able to make balls at the forge. They were not the same quality, but they were certainly good enough for practice. Being hit with a musket ball made of an old plough was no different from one that had been made from new metal.

Whether or not people liked firing muskets, we were able to teach over one hundred people to use them before Officer Price and his men left. We found out that we could get thirty people armed with muskets out in position in half an hour or so from the time we started knocking on doors, but we suspected that it might be a little more time in the middle of the night. Like anything else, we had a rota drawn up, and we often did 'fake' alarms for each group so that they would not forget. We made sure that each group had a practice on the muskets once a month, and although I was never really comfortable with them, I at least achieved a level where I was not a danger to my friends!

Price and his Africans left in June. We lined the road when the soldiers left. Many of us were really sorry to see them go – as they had afforded us a level of protection that we had valued and had not expected. We would not see or hear from them again, and no questions were asked about the engagement at Helmdon. To us of the village, it was a battle of importance, but to the world and to history in general, it was an unknown minor event of no real consequence.

There is always an ethical issue with war. I know this, and I am a woman. Often, we have been told that we know less than the men, so how can this have escaped them? Perhaps men have the ability to ignore all sensible concerns so that they can take the cause of action they want. Anyway: how does one reconcile one's conscience as a Christian in a religion that talks about 'turning the other cheek' and befriending others with fighting in a war as a soldier? In this case (this war), we had two opposing armies, both 'fighting for a cause which was right' and both convinced that the worship of God – in one form or another – was a key part of their cause. A soldier needs to prepare for war and be ready to fight – but that means being prepared to kill. It is planned! We had equipped our village with muskets, trained our villagers to fire them, and we were planning (in that event) to kill other humans. The vicar took a pragmatic view of this – which was that having to fight and possibly kill those with an evil intent was just and right. I had a suspicion that he might feel differently about which side needed to be fought.

Some of the village, though, thought that using a weapon was wrong whoever was on the other end of the musket, and would not learn to shoot. The vicar thought this, too. He could not bring himself to damn those who wanted to protect the village or force them to discard arms. We did not want to make them do this, as forcing the issue could have led to a larger split in the village. There were already enough factions in the Church during this war, and we could not bear the thought of having two opposing churches in a small village like ours. Instead, the vicar stayed silent on the issue and resorted to platitudes about 'God's work'.

Practically, it worked out that those who wanted to learn to fire a musket did so; names were added to a list of those who could be called to fight if they were needed. Other folk did not add their names to the list but would accept being protected by those who did. Realistically, no one in the village would welcome those who they thought harboured evil intent, but all of us were prepared to try to welcome those who might just need food or shelter, or a small break from the discomfort, monotony or stress of the years of service in this war.

FIVE

1644: MARSTON MOOR – BEFORE AND AFTER

1643 had dragged on into 1644 the way that 1642 had dragged on into 1643. By which I mean slowly. We had prepared more foodstuffs, we had more hay for our animals, we had more animals, and we decided to have Christmas the way we had started to work – as a whole village working together. We had our Christmas meal all together in two barns on Farmer Lawson's farm – actually, to be totally honest, his wife's farm at that time as he was away with his lads fighting somewhere, and we had no idea where they were. Each family in the village was responsible for preparing space or places to sit or working on part of the meal or tidying or making the place look warm and welcoming. It meant that everyone had the same food, and there were no poor houses with nothing to eat. It brought us together, and petty squabbles were forgotten, at least for the day. We sat on hay bales, ate off a trestle table, put kegs of beer on stands, and cooked on very large spits. We had to cook food for a long time on these to make sure that it was done evenly and properly.

In the past, the church had encouraged us all to take food to the poor. Now, rich and poor worked together on producing all of the things we needed, and rich and poor alike shared them. This meant that we took the poor to the food. We even had music for singing and some dancing. We had trained our youngsters to hold a beat, or even a tune, and they accompanied the few proper musicians that we had amongst us, and the sounds they produced were completely acceptable to us. Some of what they did was Christmas hymns that we could sing along to, and some of it was dance tunes that we knew. We had storytelling, and we found that we did not really need what the menfolk always claimed was important – lots of alcohol. We were used to consuming less of this, and although care was taken to make sure that the vicar had a bottle of sherry for his Christmas, the rest of us were quite as happy with juices and the occasional glass of small beer! Apparently, Christmas Island was discovered that day, too – but once again, we didn't hear that until 1645!

Some things carried on, if not as normal then on a different level to our village Christmas. Olivia managed the Grey household – as she had promised. Their fields, crops and livestock were different to ours, managed by their estate workers (or their families), and they were usually sent on or sold. As Lord Hugh was in the King's army, it was expected that his estate would produce goods to support the King's soldiers. This put the estate at a bit more risk of being seized by the Parliamentary army, but the estate was further from the road than we were in the village, so it was at less risk of being found by accident. Olivia discussed with us in the village what we were doing, and we were sometimes able to change what we were growing so that we were not always raising the same crops as the estate. We found that we could regularly supply them with, perhaps, a pig, in exchange for vegetables that we had not grown, and they often needed help from our forge to repair ploughs, waggons and the like. We did a successful trade in goods and services.

Olivia would tell me about Robert, and about her father. Infrequently, she could tell me, too, about my father – for example, on the occasions when they sent him somewhere else and not just back to the village. She got regular letters from Hugh and Robert, but as they were part of one army group, the letters were usually about famous people that they had seen or met, or skirmishes, or those they had heard of. Once again, we would find out what had happened in Wilmington, or another village that we had never heard of – or more often, perhaps, there would be a comment about old friends of the Greys. With regard to my other friends, none of us had regular news from our soldier friends. Occasionally, the odd comment came – Mark was mentioned more than the others, as a hard and driven commander. His reputation was still tarnished by rumours of excessive discipline and hard raiding – but we did not get much information about Luke, or Edward, as they were of less importance then, and casual news bearers would not know their names. We shut it out of our minds. If we spent every day worrying, we became tense and fractious. If in our head we regarded them as 'away' or working somewhere else, it became easier to bear.

Harriet, too, helped to organise affairs for her mother – for example, her father's quarries had become one of her duties, and she ventured out to help out Olivia as well. I saw her more often than Olivia, because most days she was in the village to see her mother, to work with her sometimes, and to check that we were all also helping her if needed. Sometimes, I was delivering messages to or for Harriet and Olivia as well. In our village, the work of the vicar went on as it had done before, and I had kept my promise to help out around the church a bit when I could, although I seemed to get busier, and there were any number of people to help with the church. Stephanie had originally gone to Towcester to see if she was required to help as a nurse with any of the doctors, but it had become clear in the first year of the war that individual isolated doctors' practices were not going to be able to deal with the numbers of wounded after a large battle, and that those who had already been treated were also going to need places to go, to recover more or get completely better.

Someone sensible in the King's army (one of the few) had realised that if lightly injured soldiers were looked after properly, then they could return to a standard of health where they might be able to rejoin the army and serve the King further. If they were not cared for after their initial treatment, and even sent home, they were more likely to get some further infection, or reopen wounds. Many who were sent straight home never even managed to get there, and it had apparently become common for soldiers to die weeks or months after sustaining an injury in battle. Some even went mad – and although there was nothing to be done with them, it was felt that they should be kept in some place – perhaps working on the land so that they could be watched – rather than going home and making it clear to their family and friends what a bad place or thing the army was. This was pragmatic – the army would keep needing recruits, and they would not come if they saw bad results of army service.

From what I had heard, this idea of treatment for soldiers seemed to be better organised on the Parliamentary side, but as it was, the King's army established a place for their soldiers to be looked after on an estate in Blakesley near Towcester, and Stephanie, with other women who had asked to help out, were asked (also) to live on the estate and work as nurses full time to help soldiers recover. This was not the only recovery place – but it was the only one in our area. Stephanie told us that they spent some time teaching soldiers how to use sticks or crutches, or learn to use their left arm if they had lost their right arm. She said that soldiers who had some hope or a purpose recovered quicker than those who had nothing to look forward to. Occasionally, when Stephanie had a break, she would come and spend a day with us in the village, to see her father. She still talked about Mark when she spoke to me – but she didn't seem to see any contradiction in helping the King's soldiers and her love for a man fighting in the Parliamentary army. I didn't say anything to her about this, either, but I didn't think that Mark would necessarily share her views. Then again, I had not seen any evidence that Mark returned any of the feelings that she had for him anyway.

January and February were better months for us, too, this year. Not only were we more prepared to withstand the isolation caused by snow and winter storms, we took more time and pleasure to organise meals together – so we could share stories of our battles against the weather. We dug out our lanes together (and so we dug them out quicker), we broke the ice in more places (and fished together), we had more wood cut and stored and we had better fires as a result. Winter meant fewer visitors for us, too. It seemed to me that the armies retreated to garrisons in or near the cities for longer periods, and just sometimes they sent out waggons to look for supplies. Perhaps we were lucky, but we were even offered money for supplies for them. Whatever the case, we generally saw fewer people and were left to our own devices. Doing all of the things that we normally did, but doing them as a collective group, not just as a collection of individuals, made most of us happier and made the work less onerous. The winter of 1643 was quite a lot easier than the year before, as a result.

I think that there were seventeen battles in 1644 before Marston Moor in July. Once again, either none of our menfolk were in those battles (which seems unlikely) or we had no letters or news about them or from them, which I suppose is more likely. Only one of them was in our area – Cropredy Bridge, but we didn't hear it, and I didn't hear of it or speak to anyone about it afterwards. The spring of 1644 was taken up with the same sort of things that spring usually is, and I am not even sure in my memory of anything that made that year different. We had lambing, we had the usual lookout for the first spring flowers. March started hard and warmed up towards the end. We had the usual Easter services in the church, and the main thing that I remember about that Easter was my idea about what we could do at the Easter of 1645. I had an idea about doing an Easter pageant, but as this was going to take a long time to organise, I will go into more detail about it when I reach 1645 in my recollections, and not now where I am talking about the spring and summer of 1644.

The Battle of Marston Moor was fought on the 2nd of July 1644. Once again, I noticed – a July battle. The armies seemed to spend the winter holed up, the spring marching around and preparing, and then they met to fight in the summer. War by calendar! It seemed to happen regularly. Mind you, there were other battles (again) in 1644. It just seemed to me that the larger battles were in the summer – and again, we were more interested in the battles that affected people we knew. Marston Moor, it turned out, was in Yorkshire, and was a Parliamentary victory. This meant less to us than it might have, as we had men on both sides of the battle. Once again, we waited for news of the menfolk from Helmdon, and how they had fared. News arrived slowly – possibly due to our distance from the battle, but when news did arrive, we had quite a lot of it – from different sources, and with different opinions (as with

Lansdowne) as to what was good, what was bad (depending on who you talked to), whose fault it was and how it happened.

Sir Henry Green was dead! That was the first important thing for our village. He had been a major figure in our village life for so long (all of my life) that it was difficult to accept the fact that we would no longer see him again. It didn't seem to matter what side people were on; the death of Sir Henry was seen as a bad thing that had happened to someone who was probably too old to contribute much to an army, and who probably shouldn't have been there anyway. For most of us, the image of Sir Henry the gardener was the picture that stayed in our mind. Because Sir Henry the squire was a landowner – although of dubious importance – his body was to be returned to our church to be buried, and actually within the church, within the family crypt under the imposing tomb at the side aisle. In death, Sir Henry was to be accorded the respect that most of us had not quite shown enough of to him whilst he was alive. I would not say this aloud, but it seemed a long way to bring him from Yorkshire!

Sir Henry had died heading a small squad of Lord Grey's troops to capture an outpost of the opposing army. Effectively ambushed by reinforcements who were concealed, his small squad was cut down to a man. Opinions were divided on this. Edward told me that when Sir Henry was asked to surrender, he made some sort of speech along the lines of 'better to die in glory' and charged at them. Olivia told me that actually no attempt had been made to ask him to surrender, and perhaps no one had realised that the 'fat old man' on a horse was worthy of any sort of attempt at negotiation. Mark, although fighting on the other side, was convinced that Lord Grey or the Royalist commanders had deserted his father – as that gave him justification to continue to fight them. Mark always had to have someone to blame for the things that were wrong in his life. I was just left with an image of the Sir Henry I knew, as a fat old man on a horse. I said a prayer for him and apologised to him (and also to God) when I did pray – for the slightly unflattering memories that I had of Sir Henry.

Ironically, the men of Helmdon who were able to get back to the village for Sir Henry's funeral were all those who were fighting for the

Parliamentary Army; Mark, Edward and Luke. There was obviously some attempt at chivalry made by the Royalist side, to get the news to Mark, and then some agreement made by the Parliamentary army that Mark should be allowed leave to return his father's body to the village – with an honour guard consisting of other men from the village. Once again, honour in death for Sir Henry exceeded that given to him in life. A series of discreet negotiations took place with Olivia – whereby she was allowed to attend Sir Henry's funeral, but she was kept out of sight of Mark – not to protect his feelings but to stop him arguing with her. This was one of a dwindling number of occasions when a body would be brought home, although not actually the very last. The numbers of the dead in the war were going to become so large that even the bodies of important figures would not be returned much in the future. It rained. It did rain! I recall the sombre ranks of the villagers and the soldiers were made more sombre by the dark cloaks they wore over their uniforms. I don't know if Mark or anyone other than me cried, as the rain streamed down their cheeks. Someone held an extra cloak over the vicar to protect him and his robes as he walked to the church.

Mark left Helmdon a few days later, swearing loudly within earshot of the villagers that he would 'have revenge on the Grey family, and all those who supported or thought like them'. This statement and his emotions did not endear him to the villagers, who found it more difficult to see Mark as the replacement for their beloved old 'squire'. I thought, privately, that this was 'bravado'. I didn't think that Mark was feeling a deep inner seething hatred, but more that he was displaying what might be expected from him. I was able to have a talk with my brother, Edward, before he and Luke left with Mark, when I told Edward all of the things that I had heard about his prowess as a commander. He in turn told me about Mark's reputation amongst the troops as one who was careless with their lives, and that Mark was beginning to be seen as reckless from the army's leaders. He said it was ironic that Mark thought the army had been careless with his father's life, when Mark was so careless himself. We all kept some of the worst stories from Harriet, out of deference to her feelings, but the villagers rallied round her a bit to show that they still valued her and her work.

Edward told me, too, that the last two years had consisted of two armies led by men not really suited to leading, wandering around the country looking for battles that they had not planned properly. He told me that a new leader was emerging – the first time I had heard the name Cromwell – and that he and others like him were changing the way that their army was trained and operated. Edward said that he was now operating in a separate regiment from Mark, and that whilst he had learnt a lot about practical soldiering from Mark, he was glad to be away from him, and he intended to try and follow Cromwell's leadership examples where possible. He said that men of ability were more likely to rise in the Parliamentary army than in the Royalist forces, where leadership seemed to be passed down to the sons of the traditional leaders of the country, and that would be another reason why they would win. The men who would lead their troops would do so with ability, not heredity.

Edward had a lot of respect for me – because many men would not have shared this information with their sister – as a woman, and he correctly judged that it would not inform my opinions on his character. He did not, though, go and see Father, and Father, too, stayed away from the funeral, anticipating correctly that our family's business had no place at that event. Father actually had to leave before Edward, but he did, though, give me a note for Edward – saying that although their opinions differed, he still loved his son, and that if Edward was able or needed to return home at any other time, he was still welcome in our household. Edward showed me the note and said that he would write to Father, but asked me in the meantime (when Father returned) to tell Father that he, Edward, would write back, and to say to Father that he had appreciated the note from him very much. It was a complicated family relationship that I hadn't imagined a poor family like ours would have.

Luke White was quieter than I expected or remembered. I thought that he did not seem as vituperative as Mark, or as analytical as Edward. It was certainly difficult for him returning to his father's church for the funeral, and although I think he attempted to talk to his father, I thought (watching them from a distance) that it was his father who was the unforgiving man – this was strange for a vicar – and it was Luke's father who ended the conversation and then walked away from Luke. I also experienced another feeling that I had had before, because as the groups separated and people walked in their different directions, it was Harriet Green who walked after Luke, who grasped him by the hand and then walked off with him, talking. Happily, this interesting sight seemed to have escaped Mark's notice – as Mark was quite unpredictable, and I didn't think that he would approve of the vicar's son walking away with his sister, whatever he thought about social status. Maybe I was wrong.

Our menfolk left the village very soon after the funeral. They stayed together as a group, and stayed in the same house as each other until the following day. They left as quickly as they could, because that was the condition of their leave of absence from the army. Privately, I thought that if they had returned to their individual homes or slept in their own beds, it would have made it more difficult for them to leave as their emotions would have been tested still further. After they had gone, I awaited my chance to speak to Harriet. For a few days, I did not see her, and I later learnt that was because she had avoided me whilst she marshalled her feelings and decided what to tell me. She had seen me watching her and Luke, and although she had known me for many years and trusted me, she had to decide whether or not to tell me the truth, and how much of it. She took her time as a result, and then came to me when she thought she knew what to say.

Luke and Harriet had been walking out together even before the start of the war, and had developed a fondness for each other (as I had surmised). They had not told the rest of us, because they were uncertain of the depth of their feelings for each other, and they had worried that if they started walking out together, they might split our friendship group up. When Luke had stated his feelings about the war, and what he believed he needed to fight for, that had put Harriet in a difficult position – with Mark and Sir Henry on different sides. She had written to Luke telling him all of this, but of course he had not received her letter, and it was not until his return to the village that she had managed to tell him that she still felt the same way about him, and would wait for him. Luke was important to her, and however the war ended, she thought that they might have a future together. This made one thing clearer for Luke. Although his conscience and the situation with his father made things difficult, he could rely on some sort of future with Harriet. She cared little for class distinctions, and all Luke needed to do was to come home safely from the war.

She told him of all the things that we had done in the village. She told him that the villagers worked together as one force, and that this meant that we had achieved a much more equal society than we had had before the war. She said, too, that people like herself and Olivia were acting much more as managers of the affairs of others, such as her father and Lord Grey. This meant that they were continually speaking to others about the same matters, and it meant they felt less like owners or the traditional aristocracy but more like partners in some greater endeavour. She knew that if Luke returned home to Helmdon, they could have the same sort of partnership if they got married, and she thought that there would be less objection to her marrying the son of a clergyman than there might have been before the war. She said to him that in the village, the sort of worship people wanted had split them less than it had the country. They tolerated the views of others – and the nature of our church made people feel more welcome. She thought of me when she said that.

Luke had told her, in his turn, that he was planning to leave the Parliamentary side, that the army (and Mark and Edward) didn't know this yet, and that once he had retrieved his belongings, he would abscond from them. Harriet asked me not to pass this on to Edward. Luke said that he had joined their army mainly for religious reasons, but the reasons had failed to match up in reality to what his expectations had been. He said that although he wanted a simpler form of religion, all that he had witnessed was what seemed to be the desecration or destruction of churches. Soldiers tore up altar rails, or removed altars and replaced them with tables, destroyed religious statues and whitewashed over murals. "But they don't even pray," he said. "It is as if they are just obeying instructions, but they don't have anything to believe in. They just want the silver candlesticks to melt down, and they use the Church to complain about the privileges of the rich." He had even seen churchmen being beaten by soldiers when they had protested about the desecration of their churches.

He had failed to understand that when people don't have something, they are much more likely to want to take and possess the things that they complain about. The Parliamentary soldiers often complained about the richness of the Church's belongings, and then 'confiscated' things like silver candlesticks – which were then sold on to dealers in the local towns. Often, too, these things would then end up being sold on to rich folk – who were also seen as part of the hatred of the common folk. The chalices and plates that were seen by those poor folk in churches ended up being used as part of the dining services of the rich. There was no justice in this, just greed. The Royalist army was not fighting to change the Church or religious practices or to strip the wealth of the Church, and therefore often respected it more and left it alone. Increasingly, this attitude was seen as more popular – even with those, like Luke, who had joined the army to change things. The trouble was that although the attitude in the Royalist army might be more popular, the evidence was that they did not fight as well or as consistently as the Parliamentarians – and there was beginning to be a rise in the fortunes of the latter, based on their ability and the ability of their officers to change tactics.

Luke said he didn't see that either side of the war was actually fighting for the Church he believed in, and that he had become aware that he was fighting against some of the people he liked – like the Greys and Sir Henry – and was on the same side as some that he no longer respected (although he didn't mention who these were). He said to Harriet, "I know that your brother and Lucy's brother both believe in what they fight for, but I don't, and I have alienated my father by criticising him and his church for a cause I no longer believe in. I tried to talk to Father, but he put on his public 'I forgive you' face and didn't really listen. If I join the Royalist army, it may convince him more. I don't think the Royalists are right, either – I mean, who really believes that the King has a 'divine right' to rule – but they show more signs of respect for the different types of churches that I have seen." It had become more important to Luke to side or fight with people that he knew and respected, or whose views he respected, than to fight with those who did not 'practise what they preached'.

He had witnessed other issues in his work rescuing other soldiers – and he had seen more evidence of cruelty on the part of the Parliamentarians than on the Royalist side. It appeared that the Royalists fought for what had previously been important but believed less in the necessity to kill and maim to maintain it. The Parliamentarians that Luke had often seen felt that to change society, some elements needed to be removed from it, and that often meant killing more of those who they felt obstructed them. It also meant that on occasion they had killed the wounded or injured that Luke felt his duty to help, and in some cases they killed those who worked to help the wounded (like Luke). It would appear that the same attitudes to candlesticks, chalices and plates also extended to human lives, and on balance, Luke felt that he needed to protect life more than property. Both sides killed more people than they should, but in general he felt that the Royalists were better than the Parliamentarians.

He was obviously confused about his religious preferences, but Harriet said that one other thing was clear. He still had strong feelings for her, and he felt that if he was on the Royalist side, he may not be actually fighting for Harriet and their future, but he would no longer feel that he would be fighting against her. He had left to return to the army, afraid but determined, and she (and now I) would just have to wait and see what happened to Luke White. Like many other soldiers, the fighting had eroded the reasons for him joining the army – and this lack of faith in a cause was going to make things harder for Luke. Luke spent a lot of time in the first few years of the war considering his faith, its direction and how to live so that he stayed true to his principles and to his faith. We didn't know, in 1644, that it might be another two or three years before we heard much more from him, and that the gaps in communication with several of our friends would widen, along with the differences in our loyalties and our attitudes, even in our village.

We didn't know, either, that this sort of doubt was regularly felt by men on both sides of the war. I suppose we had simplistic ideas about what they all thought. At the start of the war, to me, a soldier was someone who might look good in a uniform, but he was expected to do as he was told, have no thoughts, make no suggestions and do what was expected. The army encouraged that, because if you want your soldiers to advance against the enemy, you don't want them thinking, *Wait a minute, is this a good idea?* I didn't want my brother to not think, though, and if he did think – he might take better care of himself and come home safely. As it was, though, it would turn out that he did think of ways of making soldiering better for himself and others, and would make suggestions to his officers. In Edward and in lots of others – including Cromwell – the distinction between those who were seen as natural leaders of the country and those who were seen as the common rank and file would change. Potentially, it would change the country, too.

SIX

WORK AND THE PEOPLE WHO WORK

The Helmdon stone quarries were failing. They were known for producing good stone for good houses, and during the war good houses were not being built. We had even been asked about stone for houses in Blenheim and Stowe, but these had not been started yet. Those building projects that were started before the war had stopped – as often the person behind the project was away fighting, and there was little interest in continuing the build until he returned. Even on the builds organised by some great lady, there was no labour to build or to deliver materials. The quarries would be needed after the war, but there seemed no way that they could be kept open that long, and once a quarry of a business shuts, others move in to take its place, and the cost of clearing it starts to make it unworkable. This was happening elsewhere, but this is about Helmdon. We had five quarries open at the start of the war to the north of the village, and after the first couple of years, we had three, and two quarries were on the point of shutting down.

The quarries were owned by three leading citizens in Helmdon, of which Sir Henry Green was one. When he left for the war, Harriet took over the administration of her father's business and had seen the gradual decline of the work. When Sir Henry died, Harriet became, for all intents and purposes, the owner of the quarry until Mark – the male heir – returned. The other two quarry owners had not left for the war – and indeed had tried to make sure that the fewest possible number of their employees had left, too. If an employee was not being forced into service in the war, they were told bluntly that their families would be out on the street if they left – and that was enough to deter some of them until they could make alternative arrangements. When the quarries started to lose money, these 'upright citizens' told their workforce that the quarries would close in a month – and the only delay was so that they had time to remove existing stocks of stone and tools.

Harriet knew that the village was short of labour, and that if some of the quarry workforce joined up, that would not seriously affect the village – but she knew that some of the skills would leave perhaps forever, and if she followed suit and shut Sir Henry's quarries, the village might never produce stone again. She also knew that when she paid her masons and cutters, they spent their money in the village, and paid her rent. If she didn't pay them a wage, they couldn't pay her rent, or buy goods in the shops, some of which were also rented, or buy goods from the estate, or pay others to have the goods shipped in. There was a strong possibility that more people would leave for the towns – or simply become destitute in the village. In a village of 300 or 400, we couldn't afford to lose perhaps fifty people. Harriet, though, also needed a project to occupy her after her father died, and the quarries seemed able to provide her with one.

Harriet came to Olivia and me, and we sat round a table whilst she explained all of this to us. We then asked her if we could bring in the vicar and the other committee members – as this was a village problem, not just one for individuals. When that had been organised, we reconvened. We realised that the future of the village might lie in keeping the quarries open, and that the way we had organised food produce, transport of goods, protection, etc., centrally, was something that needed to be done for the village. We as a village were not working for profit; we were working (and sharing duties) to maintain our way of life, and to ensure the survival of our village in a reasonable state. We therefore came up with an immediate proposal and some subsequent courses of action that we thought might give us a chance to keep the quarries going.

We went (as a delegation) to see the other quarry owners. We asked them if they had any intention of opening the quarries before the war ended, and they told us that they hadn't. We told them that we wanted to run the quarries as a village concern for the duration of the war. We would not take ownership of the quarries unless they wanted to give them up, but we would have control over the quarries until the end of the war, because we considered that they were needed to make the village work properly. We pointed out to these owners that if the quarries were unused for any length of time they would become unsafe and perhaps become impossible to reopen. We said that whilst we would want to use stone from them, they would be in a state in which they could be taken back by the owners at the end of the war. Finally, we threatened them that if they did not do this, we would effectively 'shun' them in the village – and levy additional taxes on them to pay for the upkeep and housing of their workers. Perhaps not surprisingly they agreed to our terms. We were not sure that this was all legal, but they didn't have anyone really to complain to.

We went to see the quarry workers and told them what we had agreed with the owners, and that they, too, had a choice. They could either cease work and join the army or find another trade, or they could remain as quarry workers for the village – in which case some of their pay would be in the form of foodstuffs to feed their families, and what else they got might depend on what stone we could sell, where we could sell it and how much for. We also saw the quarry workers of Harriet's quarry, because we knew that Harriet's quarry, too, was at risk, and we wanted our plans to be open and above board, and fair for all. Over the three quarries, we lost ten fit men who wanted to join the army and were only waiting to make sure that their families were safe. We assured them that their families would not be forced out of the village and left to starve. We then put in the second part of our plan, which was to find ways to keep producing stone in our quarries.

We found that there were (on the face of it) three ways by which we could keep producing stone, and none of them were traditional ways that the village had used in the past. One of the most obvious was in military fortifications. Essentially, that meant providing massive shaped pieces of stone, one at a time, for very large buildings – castles and the like – to either repair damage from cannons, etc., or for new buildings. It was clear that for the duration of the war these would replace the need for new mansions, and it was something we could do, although perhaps not on a large scale, and it might be that these were best supplied by quarries nearer to the buildings. But we could see about this. The second way of using stone was to repair buildings in the village and in the nearby towns. We were already repairing some village housing with stone (where the houses were not wood or another material) and could continue this, but there was not much money for this, and it would be better to ship more stone to Brackley, Towcester, Northampton and Oxford.

The third and final way that we could see to make money was in repairing roads. The roads across the country were in a dreadful state, full of potholes and ruts, and we could see that using a lot of small pieces of stone would help tremendously. We could do this in our area, but it would be difficult to transfer enough stone far enough to do this anywhere else in the country. It would seem that the two main problems we had, therefore, were transport and finding markets for our stone. We went to have a look at the quarries. As we had expected, Harriet's quarry was in a better state than the others. Tools were secured safely, trestles and wooden scaffolds were well built and maintained, and there was an air of neatness. In the others, stone was piled untidily, and mounds of stone were in danger of toppling. There was more of an air of haphazardness (if that is a word), which didn't seem safe in a dangerous area. We were told that accidents had happened there regularly in the past, and some of the workforce were still not working because of injuries they had received.

We took Harriet's quarry manager, Anthony Ellis, with us. He was a mature man of about forty-five, and he was settled in his life and happy in his work. Not surprisingly, he was quite appalled by the state of things in the other quarries, and as he walked around he kept tutting, and frowning in disapproval. The men in the other quarries understood this, knew Mr

Ellis, and were often at pains to tell him that they had not had the chance to tidy up or had not been instructed on how to do things by their managers. The managers in turn told us of poor finance, not enough workers, and pressure to keep up work rates, which had not left them the chance to sort things out properly. Ellis didn't really believe them, but it was difficult to sort out the tales of incompetence and allocate responsibilities. Early in the afternoon, he called the managers to a meeting with us and told them that they could either relinquish their roles as managers or they could tidy the place up and sort out the dangerous areas by the end of the week.

He said at that point (the end of the week) he would return and make another inspection. The managers opted to tidy up the sites and make them safe rather than lose face by demotion, and Ellis arranged with us to return later that week. He then sat down with us in an office and told us that all three quarries could produce stone safely but that reaching that point could not be rushed. He said that getting ready might be a slower procedure than we wanted but that most quarries seemed to be idle at the moment, and if we were producing stone, then we had a chance of taking over some work from other quarries. We could therefore take our time. We needed to solve (as we had already thought we needed to) the problem of transport, and we needed to know what sort of stone we were providing for which places. We also needed to consider which of the three quarries was best for the three types of stone that we thought we had a market for.

We went back to the quarries at the end of the week. In one quarry, there had been an acceptable level of work to tidy up and make things safer, and although it was not completely sorted out, the manager and his men had done significant work – and we let them carry on with it. In the other quarry, the manager and two of his men were dead. They had tried to sort out some stacks of stone without taking proper precautions, and now they lay dead under the pile of stone. It was tempting to leave them there (technically buried), but we could not use the quarry efficiently unless we moved the stone, so we had to move it and rebury the men. Funerals were arranged for the men by us, and we went to see the men's families to see that they were able to survive, that they had food, and to reassure them that they could stay in their houses and would not be forced out. I was a bit worried about this. The quarry had been visited, they had been told to improve matters, and a week later their men were dead! Would they blame or hate us in some way for this? In fact, they seemed to show little surprise or strong feeling. One of them told us that the quarry had been a dangerous place for so long that death was seen as a regular hazard. It was like being soldiers. If you die as a soldier, who is surprised?

There was little else we could do for them, so we went back to tidying up and solving our problems. We were aware that in some towns, stone was loaded onto barges and taken along the river, but the river at Helmdon was in no way wide or deep enough for that, so this idea was impractical. We had to use the roads to move stone, and we had to use them better than before, and the roads had to be better than before, too. It felt like a circular argument. On the other hand, the land around the quarries was fairly flat, and this aided transporting the stone out of Helmdon on the roads. We built waggons. We built them with more wheels so that the load on each axle was less. We built smaller wheels on them which meant that the load was lower, and easier to put on the waggon. On those that we loaded with crushed stone for the roads, the sides had to be made higher so that the stone did not overflow. On those with the biggest stones, the sides needed to be lower to get the stone on and off, and somewhere in the middle were those waggons with stone for the houses.

We made contacts in all of the towns and villages within about thirty miles of Helmdon. We worried that the length of transport over thirty miles was possible but maybe too difficult for us to manage. We repaired the roads between Helmdon and the main road, and then showed those roads to the town and county officials as an attempt to show them what they could expect. They were impressed, as we meant them to be, and stumped up some cash to help redo the roads in a wider area. We also managed to get money out of the county authorities for the main roads – but we couldn't get the army to part with any money. The army disliked the roads that they had to march or gallop along or drag guns over, but they were not going to pay money for a road that might also be used for the opposition. If we wanted money from them or the two main political factions, it would be after they won the war and were more secure in their domain.

We succeeded in our overall goals. In one more way, we had made Helmdon the centre of business between Brackley and Towcester, and restarted a failing industry that might cause harm to our village if it collapsed. We did, eventually, supply stone for major military rebuilding and the repair of major civic centres, and we put in place a stone industry that would exist after the war. Then it would be able to return to civilian projects, and another generation of mansions would be built. Harriet had her project in her own quarry, was assisting in running the others, and was to be busier than the rest of us for the rest of the war. She knew that her father would be proud of what she had achieved, and she hoped that Mark, too, would appreciate the way that she had extended the family influence and secured its fortunes. If the other quarries came to be as well run as Sir Henry's, then the village would owe her a debt as well in its fortunes.

Olivia Grey was in the habit of riding out each morning. Although her father and brother had taken most of the estate's horses to war with them, they had deliberately left her two horses that she liked as well as some of the heavier breeds that were used for hauling ploughs and waggons around the estate. Recently, Olivia had taken possession of a third horse. It was a beautiful dark brown horse with a white forehead marking. It came from an estate some twenty miles away, and it had been left behind when the owner of that estate had ridden away to war. I have almost no knowledge of horses, so I cannot give any detail of size or breed or any more detail about the horse. Lord Roger had not taken this horse to war as it was quite new to him and was considered a bit too nervous to ride near guns, and so it had stayed at the estate. It had been ridden regularly by one of their lads, but he had now left to go to fight, being fifteen and old enough – as he thought – to go.

Lady Helen, left in charge, thought the horse too skittish for her to ride, preferring as she did an old grey mare on which she could visit friends on occasion and amble down the lanes at a relaxed pace. She was not known as a horsewoman, and her old mare often decided when it would stop and snatch a few mouthfuls of grass before being persuaded to move on. Helen had asked Olivia if she would take the mare for her – at least until Sir Roger came back – and exercise the horse properly, and get it used to being ridden regularly again. Olivia had happily agreed to this and tried to make a point of riding each of the three horses every day, or at least every other day. Her wishes in this matter were often frustrated by matters at the estate which required her to work from the office, or other duties which made it unsuitable for her to ride. Her horses were not suited to pulling carts, so when she had to ride with others in a cart, it restricted her use of them still further.

She had no official need to visit the quarries as Harriet had nominally taken charge of them – but she was aware that Harriet had become much busier – arranging contracts for the quarries – and as a result Olivia had not only allowed her to reduce the amount of time that she spent helping at the estate but had also taken it upon herself to visit and tour the village and the quarries more when Harriet was away or 'in town' so to speak. She also often rode around the areas where she knew that Harriet wasn't, so that some evidence of her presence was seen. She felt – and this was part of her personality – that a 'supervisory' presence was helpful, although it often wasn't. Harriet had the gift of being able to watch from a distance and ascertain what was going on, whilst Olivia – less experienced – would often ride up to ask what was going on, and this meant that others would stop what they were doing to greet her. They would then happily give her chapter and verse on events, Olivia would ride away happy that she was being useful, and her men would feel happy that they had been able to tell her, but unfortunately it meant that less work would get done.

About six months from when we started the quarries going, Olivia visited the one where the men had died, to see what work was being done there. I think she thought that this would be the most difficult quarry to get working again, and that she should see how it was going. As it was, things were fine at the quarry. The manager who had died had been replaced by a senior foreman from Harriet's quarry. He was liked and respected locally, and he had quickly started customs of work which improved the efficiency of this other quarry whilst retaining the safe practices that he had grown up with. As a result, when Olivia arrived, the work was moving at a reasonable pace. Stone was being moved from one of the faces of the quarry, was clearly and safely cordoned off, and waggons were waiting for loading in the designated area. The manager stopped work to politely talk to the daughter of Lord and Lady Grey but made sure that his foremen were in control of the various operations, and he kept one eye on them whilst he talked to Olivia. She in turn saw a busy, efficient and safe quarry in action.

Olivia rode away from this quarry with a feeling of happiness. She had been necessary, had shown 'presence' and was sure that she had made useful and informative comments on the men's work which did not show her to be ignorant or just fussy. If this visit had an unfortunate side effect, it was that Olivia felt completely safe in the quarry environment and well able to handle any problems that might arise. Unfortunately, this was not always the case, and she was soon to find this out. Another month later, she visited the same quarry, but there were two main differences in this visit. On this occasion, she was riding the newer horse – which she was sure, by now, was safe to ride – and the quarry was doing some 'blasting'. In this process, small amounts of powder were pushed into holes in the face of the rock, so that lumps of rock of approximately the size required were removed from the cliff when the powder was ignited and exploded.

To ensure safety in and out of the quarry, a rope barrier with wooden uprights was pushed across the entrance to the quarry, with a notice saying 'Strictly No Entry' dangling from it. This barrier would stop anyone coming into the quarry from the road. Just down the road and around a bend, a waggon was waiting at a safe distance so that it could come in and load up any stone that needed to be moved. It had to be at a distance so that the horses did not panic at the explosions. Then a whistle would be blown, to indicate that blasting was imminent, and the men of the quarry would walk to a 'safe area' away from the cliff where they could shelter behind stone barriers until the stone had come down and the dust had cleared. Accordingly – on this occasion – the whistle blew, the workforce moved to the barrier, the fuses were lit for the powder holes, and at that moment Olivia arrived on her new horse, carefully directing it past the barrier with its notice – which couldn't possibly apply to her as she was a sort of owner – and she walked her horse into the quarry.

One of the foremen saw Olivia arrive on her horse and pass the barrier. Although she was not near the cliff face, he ran towards her to stop her moving any further, although a mate of his then tried to stop the foreman moving as well. There were several sharp loud cracks as the powder ignited, followed by a rumble as the rock started to move downwards, and a rapidly expanding cloud of dust. Olivia's horse whinnied and lifted its front legs in the air, and then with Olivia still in the saddle, took off at a gallop, leaping the rope barrier as it headed out of the quarry. The poor man who had run to warn Olivia was hit by two small pieces of rock which had been fired from the powder as it exploded, and he collapsed to the ground, insensible. His mate ran to him and blew his own whistle for help. When the other foremen and their gangs arrived, he told them of Olivia's arrival and what his friend had tried to do to help her. Unfortunately, his friend was now dead – one of the rocks having hit him with some force on the head.

Another man appeared at a run from outside the quarry, requested help and told him that one of the quarry men needed to ride for a doctor. "What for? He's dead!" said the manager, indicating the man on the ground.

"Not for him, for her!" said the new arrival, indicating the road. Olivia's horse in its panic had taken the clearest route out of the quarry, gone down the lane and run straight into the waggon around the bend that was waiting to load the stone. Perhaps it had been partially blinded by dust from the road or the sunlight in its eyes. It went straight into the solid waggon, injuring one of the waggon horses and crushing Olivia between her own horse and the drawbars of the waggon. Olivia had been knocked unconscious by this impact and was lying motionless on the ground surrounded by the waggon team, whilst her horse was rolling on the ground with a broken leg and impaled by a wooden splinter from the drawbar. The other waggon horse was tangled in the wreckage and unable to be freed for the moment. The waggon driver was standing guard over Olivia whilst his mate ran to fetch help.

The gang set off at a run from the quarry, fetching a stretcher for Olivia, a gun for the horse and sending another man off on another horse for a doctor. "Tell him to come to the big house!" shouted the foreman. "We'll take her there." Olivia's horse was dispatched, and Olivia was lifted on the stretcher, unconscious, onto a cart. With one horse at the front, the cart was dispatched to Stuchbury Hall with two men and Olivia – in the hope of meeting the doctor there. With hindsight, Olivia's unconsciousness was very useful to her. She did not have to endure being lifted onto the stretcher then lifted onto the cart, and then that awful slow ride back to the hall. We had done a lot to the roads by then, but there is a difference between a suitable road surface for a stone waggon and one for an injured person in a cart. By the time that Olivia woke up in her own bed in Stuchbury Hall some hours later, they had managed to give her laudanum to reduce her pain, and to carry out an examination on her injuries, all without her being aware of it.

She had a broken hip, broken fingers, concussion, lacerations to her face and body, and a lot of bruising. It was also possible that the impact had caused her internal injuries, and no one knew what they might be. I don't know all of the rest of the details, but I believe that she was lucky. She had not fractured her skull and she was lucky that the timber had not impaled her – any more than a few splinters. She was also tremendously lucky not to be dead, like the horse was now. I think that if she hadn't been so hurt, there would have been a lot more resentment about the death of the quarryman – but as it was, the attitude seemed to be that it was his fault, and that if he hadn't moved, Olivia might have died but he would be alive, so in one way it was nature's balance of things and it was his fault. As it was, there was not exactly understanding but possibly more sympathy for the 'Lady of the Hall' who lost her poor horse and was nearly killed by 'those quarrymen'. At least, that was the feeling of those in the village who knew nothing about safe working practices at the quarry.

For a while, no one knew if Olivia would live – as internal injuries were very difficult to treat. She would have to remain immobile for a long time so that she didn't damage herself further. Then they didn't know how well she would be able to walk; with a stick perhaps, or crutches, or even one of those chairs with wheels. No one mentioned riding to her for weeks. In the end, Olivia would confound them all. She would overcome the stiffness caused by the immobility and the wasted muscles. She would walk, and although she always had a slight limp, she was able to limit it enough so that it was not uncomfortable to watch, and yes, she would eventually ride again – although she confided to me at one point that riding a walking horse was a bit uncomfortable, and trotting more so – but she didn't think she would ever be able to canter or gallop again. She did visit the quarries again, and they appreciated that – sometimes, they felt 'out of sight, out of mind' – but she usually rode there in a cart. Eventually, she would walk down the aisle on her wedding day, too.

Olivia's injuries made her more sympathetic to those whom she saw around the estate and the village who had injuries. I think before the war that we had tended to see villagers as fit to work or not fit to work. If they were not fit to work, they were given food sometimes, and perhaps helped to go to church or helped with errands – but they had started to be given jobs when most fit and able men had gone off to war. Olivia's injuries, and her slow recovery from them, gave her time to think about how others with injuries could work. They could tend some livestock – if it was penned – and feed it. They could sort or chop vegetables for meals. They could do some cleaning jobs. They could work on carpentry or some joinery, tend the furnace in the forge and even make some things there. One of the biggest things that Olivia did whilst she was ill was to start reading and writing classes for adults. It meant that she had more help on the estate for written records. It meant that the vicar had help in copying church records, and more letters could be written to the armies requesting information.

Whilst Olivia recovered, she had to find ways to help herself move around more, and she quickly realised that what she was doing for herself could be used for others. Estate workers learnt to make walking sticks and crutches, to design particular furniture for those who couldn't use traditional chairs or stools or tables or work surfaces, and in time, we had those who had some sort of physical problem themselves making items for others. One of the estate outbuildings was turned into a 'workshop' to make wooden items. It was equipped with pedal lathes, chisels, hammers and the like so that wood could be properly worked there. The forge expanded its area and the range of tools there, too. Those in the village who had felt useless started to realise that they had some involvement in our future and our daily life. Some of them were able to teach youngsters some of their skills, and that meant that they would not have to make as many mistakes in learning. The Bible taught us that good things could come out of trouble or misadventure, and we started to see this happen more in Helmdon.

SEVEN

RELATIONSHIPS AND DEMOGRAPHICS

S omeone once taught me what the word demographic means. Unless I misunderstood it (and that is quite possible), it describes how a population is built up of different age groups. In our village, the population make-up changed quite a lot during the war, and the difference in the age groups affected the way that people of the village behaved and acted. For a lot of us, it felt as if we were now responsible for ourselves, and that we didn't have someone older to make our decisions. Most of the men in the village who were aged between sixteen and forty in 1642 left the village – either in the first few months of the war when becoming a soldier seemed brave and adventurous, or after that as more of a trickle of men. Young men who had stayed would become fourteen or fifteen or sixteen, and then would feel that the world was more of an adventurous place to try their luck. Some youngsters were actually worried that the war would be over before they had a chance to fight in it.

No one checked the age of the recruits; they just judged them by their physical size as an indication of whether they could hold a weapon and fight. No one thought, *He's a big man, he will have trouble crawling or fitting through holes in a hedge*, for example, just, *He will be good with a pike!*

Fewer men left the village, though, after they saw the dead or wounded or maimed return in some form or another. Although the stories some of these old soldiers told were of adventure and overcoming danger, the person telling the story did not look as if he had overcome it very well. In the end, it didn't matter. Those who tried to stay behind were taken by recruiting squads anyway. We had several gaps in the ages and sexes of those left behind. We had children of both sexes – and roughly equal in number, and then from about the age of fourteen or fifteen there started (and continued) to be more girls than boys, and this difference between male and female went up to the older folk, from forty upwards, where the balance started to become more normal.

The war went on for nine or ten years, and so if a man left when he was forty to fight, he would be fifty when he came back home. It seemed to me that men of that age were exhausted when they returned, and went straight from being a soldier to being an old man in a smock sitting outside the house all day. I know that there were older soldiers than that, but I didn't think there were that many. I think that a quarter of our village men did not come back, and some who were to return were still absent until 1651 or 1652. It meant that the younger men who had not left, or wounded men who had returned, or overnight visitors, were much more attractive to our women and older girls than they might have been before. I had a cousin, Peter, and he was popular with the girls. Between the age of fifteen and sixteen, he fathered three children in the village, and then he left for the army. He never returned. There were, inevitably, a few men of military age who refused to join up and serve – but often they were hidden away and seemed to have less opportunity to make attachments. From 1643 or so, there were far more 'quick attachments' or 'furtive fumblings', and, gradually, we became used to seeing more and more children who only seemed to have one parent.

When the vicar asked (as he was formally required to do by the Church) for the name of the father of a child, the name of an absent husband or sweetheart was usually given – even if that person had not been seen for two years or more. No woman wanted to tell the vicar that "It was young Tom Perkins" if he was only fifteen at the time, or

"I didn't catch his name, there wasn't time" when those two messengers came through on their way to Northampton, or "It was Dan who was wounded" and had perhaps since died or deserted, or committed a crime and was being looked for by the soldiers or the magistrate. Especially, the mothers did not want to admit to a liaison with a man who had refused to join up. Men who refused to join up seemed less attractive – and you could not admit to a relationship with a man who was not supposed to be there, because the authorities were looking for him! Those women who had had children following a relationship with an African soldier could really say nothing about the supposed parentage of their children – as the colour of their skin made it completely obvious which group the father was from.

Some men came home from the war to find that they had a child – or even more than one child – in their house that couldn't have been theirs, and it depended on the man's age, or state of health, or even their temperament whether this child was accepted by them, or the man (or even the child) moved out and into another house. Many men accepted that they still loved their wife and wanted to stay in the marriage. I suspect, though, that some of the birth records of that time show less children overall (due to the absence of men) – but those children born have dishonest records. There were also one or two cases of very small children who moved to live in another house just before 'Father' came home, as well as just after. Some women or families wanted a child but could not have one, and the chance to adopt a child that 'Father' didn't want was also a great opportunity for them to fill that gap in their lives. There was no real difference between the treatment of the children if they were dark-skinned. It all apparently came down to the attitude of the parents.

Then there were the soldiers. I think there were two periods when we had troops stationed with us for more than a week or two, but whenever soldiers DID appear, there would be a major effect on the women of the village. Soldiers would parade, and so would the women. It was not as if soldiers arrived in wonderful uniforms with polished brass and wonderful colours – as they had sometimes done before the war. Most of the time their clothes were drab, only livened by a coloured banner or a neckerchief or some such – but they were men, and if fighting a war, it suggested they were fit and active. They carried arms – which were scary to a lot of us, but it meant that all of our boys started to imagine carrying THAT pike or musket or sword, and to the women, the soldier was an exotic foreign object that a lot of them immediately wanted to investigate to see if the reality lived up to the potential, or to their imagination. When the soldiers were here, there were more dances or singing evenings – even the chance to hold fetes or fairs.

I knew a lot of women who did not believe that one quick, torrid scramble would result in a child, and a lot who believed that if a child was possible, they could ask for help from old Mother Crabtree in the hut at the end of the village (the woman with the chickens, cats and a lot of 'herbal' lotions). What was believed almost universally by the women was that there was a man here, he might not be here tomorrow, there might not be any other men for months or years, and the feeling of the arms holding a man was suddenly desperately missed. If travellers or soldiers arrived in the village, then the village put on a show of hospitality in the evening with food and some music or dancing. This was then followed by a less official demonstration of hospitality all over the village in the night (or nights) that followed, and the departure of the visitors was usually accompanied by a small parade of women saying goodbye to them. Once or twice, there were men in the parade, too!

Some women (or girls) left with the soldiers when they left the village. Camp followers were permitted by the army, and for some of the younger women, the potential excitement of this life matched the excitement that the men had felt in 1642–43. The older women were not as keen to desert a warm or comfortable family home for the possibility of a billy can over a fire, and a bed in a waggon or a tent. I know of no women, either, who deserted their children or a parent who they were looking after, and the need to care for others was a big factor in women staying in Helmdon. For a younger sister or an older daughter, with little prospect of their own man or their own home, the idea of winning the loyalty and hand of the soldier that they fancied was too much, and off they went. Like a lot of the men, we never heard from a lot of them again. We had fanciful ideas that they had found a better life in a town or as a servant in a good house, but secretly we feared that they had been unable to cope with childbirth in a field somewhere or had died of disease or cold.

Relationships started younger than before the war. Girls of fifteen to eighteen, who would in the past have been approached by a slightly older man (or boy) would instead themselves (now) approach boys of their age or even younger, anxious to secure 'their' man even if he was only a boy. Further, it was not unknown for older women, perhaps in their twenties, to find an excuse to ask a boy to do some work for them, and then call him in for a drink – and perhaps another type of reward to follow. It was also known for several women – perhaps of a certain age – to share young men between them, and I once heard one call out to her neighbour, "When you've finished, pass him on." Some of the youngsters took advantage of this and made fools of the older women. Some of the older men took advantage of this opportunity, too, and there was at least one occasion when there was a fire in the village and several men 'of an age' appeared from completely the wrong direction (to where they lived) to help others put out the flames!

There were several arguments between women of the village over 'whose man' someone was. Some of the arguments were over quite quickly, whilst some lasted for years. This is not to say that the majority of women in the village behaved like harlots or harridans. Most behaved very well, waiting for their man to come home. Many of them waited in vain, some for many years. Some women lost their sanity or their desire to live when they lost their man. Our vicar was very tolerant in all of these situations. He evidently did not think that he should use God as a weapon to make folk feel guilty. If they had made a mistake in any way, God (and the vicar) should be someone who helped them rather than just blamed them. 'Let he who is perfect…' was one of his favourite mottos, and it was regularly proclaimed from the pulpit. This happened less with the soldiers, oddly enough. There didn't seem to be the same competition for them.

I never seemed to have time to look for a partner or to start a relationship, even if there had been someone in the village who was available. I did not fancy a quick relationship with a boy! My role in the village was to communicate information, allocate tasks, and to then take information back or change the instructions based on new information I received as I went round. Usually, I could make sure that all groups involved in a task had the information they needed, updated hourly if needs be. I was aware that I had started to expect conversations to be short and to the point – but it took some time before I realised that I was seen by friends and family as a woman of few words. I learnt this in a variety of ways. I overheard someone say that she 'never wastes a word' – which was meant in a kind way, that I never stood around and gossiped, or wasted people's time with meaningless chat, but it made me think more about the way that I communicated.

I didn't stand and discuss the weather, for example, as most people did. Whilst I did pass on information about other folk, it was usually part of my task. "Oh, Giles won't be here today as he has hurt his leg," or "Mistress Ward is expecting the baby shortly, so your linen will need to be done by the girls." I knew what was happening all over the village, and often repeated it several times a day to different people – but not just uselessly as gossip. I saw a lot of others who would stand and talk between jobs, and I knew that this was to take a break from work, but I knew that they had to make up the time later to get the work done. When we had social events, or provided hospitality, I made sure that I had a job to do – as it sat uncomfortably with me to sit and jaw for too long. There was some of this at home. If Father was there, I would bustle around him doing things for him as he rested. If he was not to be there, I would spend more time doing tasks for others.

I became aware that when I was hearing of gatherings or groups, I wanted to be with them as a part of the group, but when I was actually with them, I felt I needed to be doing something – cooking or washing or helping or even directing people. It set me aside as I felt in control, but it was obviously difficult for others to talk to me properly. The Reverend saw a need to fight this constant activity for my own good, and when I arrived to see him with messages or to tell him that he was needed, he would stop what he was doing, lead me to a seat and, with the excuse of a drink or a bite to eat, he would sit me down and talk to me properly, and before I was aware of it, half of an hour had passed, or even more – but I always left him feeling somehow refreshed and relaxed. Physically, I was very fit – in all the exercise I was doing – but mentally, as soon as I woke up, I was calculating what to do next. I seemed to work long hours most days.

I saw quite a lot of men. I saw renegades, deserters, travellers, merchants and stall holders at the markets, waggoners, some farm labourers, nobles, etc., but I am willing to swear that in almost every case, I spoke no more than two sentences to most of them, and was away from them in five minutes or less. As the activities around the village settled into a pattern and were better organised, I didn't need to spend quite so much time walking or running or messaging, and I was able to engage more in work that others did as their normal day – cooking, cleaning, some helping on farms – and this in turn often meant that I would be with others more – harvesting or helping with animals – and gradually my life started to return to some sort of balance, but I had had no relationship. I didn't know what would happen for the rest of the war or after, but at this time, I did not imagine myself having a normal relationship – like so many others I saw.

With so many away, the jobs that the village needed doing – hoeing, drilling, seeding, collecting firewood, harvesting, storing, animal tending, milking and repairs – had to be taken on by those of us in the village. Pregnant women could not be expected to do heavy or prolonged manual labour. When the women had given birth, though, they were expected to share with their childcare. We brought the babies into one house, and the mothers shared the care of the children so that two of them could look after eight babies for two to three hours, and that in turn meant that six women could gradually return to doing light work for the village such as knitting and sewing or helping cook food for others to work. The village had never had this sort of shared childcare before, and it not only benefitted the village but it helped the mothers to talk to others about childcare, and it meant that they had less time alone to soothe a crying child and to get frustrated or angry about it. The babies did not really notice which mother was feeding them; they just got the attention!

The effect of the men away, the imbalance of the age groups, the change in births, marriages, deaths, and (dare I say it) the number of illegitimate children would change the make-up of the village for much longer than the war. I did not know how long it would be before we expected the village to return to normal, but it turned out that it would be years after the war ended. Most folk in our village lived to around the age of sixty to seventy years old. As most of the older men left in 1642 were over forty, I think it meant that a quarter of them had died by the time the war ended, and there were fewer older men for several years after that. There were generally less children for several years. Some soldiers never came home because they found new places to live whilst they were away, and some just stayed where they were stationed when the war was over as the easiest option. Helmdon had become a bit of a dream for some of them, and they were unable to return to it.

We didn't forget our 'lost' men, either. The vicar kept a list with the parish records of all of the men who had left to go to war. It gave names, jobs, ages and, in some cases, their families – if they were the householder. There was a final column left for 'Return to Helmdon'. I saw this document once after the war, and half of the last column was blank. A quarter of that last column was labelled 'Died' or 'Believed Dead', and this seemed to be based on how reliable the information was. Another quarter of that last column consisted of those who returned, either whole or wounded. I don't think that anyone other than Sir Henry had returned dead. After the first couple of years, no one had the time or inclination to return bodies to their hometown. We heard nothing at all from or about half of the men who had left our village. It was suggested that we put some sort of plaque on the church wall – but that never happened, and in time it was forgotten. Just the records remained.

I don't know what happened over the rest of the country, either, but I suspect what I have said about our inhabitants and the changes we experienced were similar in other towns and villages. I suppose that someone worked it out, and someone worked out the effect of all of those disappeared men. I don't know if anyone added up the illegitimate children or the ages of marriages, or the number of old men and women over fifty in the years following. I can say with some certainty, though, that because we shared and pooled resources, the effect of the war on our crops, animal numbers and food produced was much less than we might have expected. We repaired houses for our people to live in. They had enough food even if they shared eating it in community meals with others. We just had a gap in men between certain ages, and that gap continued after the war.

Strangely, or perhaps not so strangely, the obsession with relationships in the village did not affect me and my friends. I had never committed to a relationship – I think mainly because I was afraid of the length of such a commitment. I imagined finding a man but then being disappointed by him and not wanting to see him further, or horror, having sex and children. In my twenties, I was not ready for children – although most women seemed to be, and more, they seemed to worry that if they weren't married in their twenties with children, they were heading for spinsterhood and lonely old age. I quite like my own company, and I like having the time to think when I am doing things on my own. Somehow, it clears my head, and when I plan things, it makes me more optimistic about them. I hate last-minute changes of plan – although I often deal with them very well.

Harriet was in love with Luke White. That was the feeling I had when we were younger. It was maintained when they parted, and she showed no signs of interest in anyone else. If she had not been set on Luke, I would have expected to see signs of other interests in the last few years, and there were none yet. Likewise with Stephanie. Mark still seemed to be in her thoughts, even if he showed no response to her and her affections. Mind you, if she was nursing soldiers, she might have had a dozen men and I would have had no idea! That is an unworthy thought, and I am sorry for it – but it was also true of the men. Robert, Mark, Luke and Edward could all be married by now and we would have no idea. I didn't think that they would, though. Robert would have too much idea of his station, Edward would (I think) have told me, Luke cared for Harriet, but I was not sure about Mark.

Some of the women I talked to in the village seemed to expect young men 'to sow their wild oats' and some seemed to positively welcome it. I knew that there were married women who did not want any more children and were quite happy for their man to seek pleasure elsewhere as long as he came home. There were also single women in the village who had not made a family but wanted some sort of physical pleasure, even at the risk of having a child – because, after all, they didn't want a man in their house bossing them around and 'bringing in dirt'. The war just seemed to have emphasised people's natural tendencies or caused them to have a wider focus. Furthermore, the war caused others to criticise less and permit more 'transgressions'. I digress. This did not seem to have any effect on me and my friends, and our priorities lay in our lives and that of the village.

In the next generation, neither I nor the Whites had a mother. Harriet's mother was at home but showed no signs (as she approached fifty) of being interested in men after Sir Henry died, and Lady Grey's husband had been away so much before the war that his service in the army must just have seemed like an extended absence to his wife. No one would believe, though, that she had any 'interests' elsewhere apart from her husband. She was too much a lady. I thought, privately, that if she had any interest in another man, it would have to be someone of her own station – but most of them were fighting, and there were no sudden trips or disappearances for several days. To the contrary, it seemed to take a lot to get her to want to leave the estate – with her books and her pastimes. She was happy there, and the evidence was that she just waited for Hugh Grey to return.

Out of our immediate circle, that left the vicar – who was very absorbed in his work and seemed to relish the competitive element that the village women brought to looking after him and keeping his house. I thought, too, that they would all prevent one of their number attaching herself to the vicar, and perhaps they would not want to live with a man who was regularly out at all hours of the day and night. That left my father… My father was approaching his fifties, too. He had been a widower for twenty years, and to all eyes, he seemed to have accepted that. He was not in the 'rippling muscles' school, even if he had taken his shirt off to work (and I never would believe he did). He was happy to come home to my ministrations most nights, although hall duties occasionally required him to stay overnight. If that happened, they would find him a bed, and he would eat his meals with the other staff. With the war, and more trips away, he seemed more grateful for the attention when he returned, and again, I thought that he was settled. This was until Olivia came to see me one day.

Olivia told me that my father (who was away for a few days at the time of Olivia's visit) had been having (in Olivia's words) a 'thing'. Olivia found it very difficult to explain this 'thing', but it would seem that Father had had a relationship with one of the housekeepers at the hall. Because the housekeepers were often required at unusual hours, the two of them had separate bedrooms. One of them was aged about forty-five, and she was married to a man who worked on the estate. Nominally, they should perhaps have lived separately, but they shared quarters and no one minded. The other housekeeper, though, Susan by name, was in her early thirties, and until the war, she had had an 'understanding' with Richard, a man who was a sort of cross between a footman and second dresser to His Lordship – in other words, he did what was required when it was needed. What was needed in 1642 was that Richard followed Lord Grey to war.

With Father coming back late from trips to the army with the waggons, and Susan being one of those designated to look after him on his nights in the hall, a relationship had developed over the last year or so. "And to put it frankly," said Olivia, "she is now pregnant, and your father, John, is the father of Susan's baby!" I had mixed emotions at this moment. Shock was indeed one of them, but I was also quite amused. I didn't think I had better show my amusement to Olivia – as she looked so appalled – so I put my hand to my mouth, raised my eyebrows, and tried to make the shock look like the dominant emotion that I felt. This seemed to work better than I expected, and Olivia patted my hand in sympathy. She carried on speaking to explain to me how, in fact, the situation was actually more complicated than she had already said. My father – according to Olivia – had expressed to Susan his intention to marry her. There was a pause at this point where I really did enter a state of shock. Olivia might have carried on talking for a minute, but she had to repeat what she said when I stopped kicking the chair.

"He certainly has not mentioned anything of the sort to me," I finally spluttered.

"Susan does not want to marry him!" replied Olivia, "and she told him that last week!"

Olivia explained that Susan still thought she had a chance of marrying Richard after the war. When Richard had left, he had said something of the sort to her, and he had written one letter to her saying that he wished they had married before the war had started. He was not a great letter writer, so only receiving one letter from him was not a surprise, but it did give Susan renewed hope. She was now hoping that when the child was born, it might potentially be fostered or adopted, and that perhaps Richard would not know about it. Whilst she found my father fun company, she would not marry him. Father had not received this news as well as he might have done. He had driven himself to consider that marriage to Susan might be a good thing. She was younger than him and could look after him. He thought at some point that I would marry and leave him – even though there was no sign of this yet – and he persuaded himself that his future lay with Susan on the estate.

He had confessed all of this to Olivia and then disappeared off on yet another trip, when she had told him that she would talk to me about it all. I think he was avoiding telling me himself because he was worried (rightly) about what I would feel or say. I told Olivia that if anyone suggested I should take on and look after my foster brother, I certainly would not! If I were married and had a family, it might be different, but I was certainly not going to give up my interesting role in helping the village to spend all hours with a baby – even if it was my half-brother or sister! I felt guilty in telling Olivia this in the way I did, but I was not prepared to be the solution to this problem, and to be fair to Olivia, she had not thought of me taking the baby, either. In her mind, the baby would be looked after by one of the village women who had children already and could cope with one more. The estate might make a small 'gesture' of supplies to that household, as the baby was in some small way the result of activities by the estate staff, and she did not feel that this would be a problem. She did think, though, knowing villages, that it would be unlikely Richard would find out – and that perhaps Susan needed to 'go away' for a bit to have her baby before Richard returned. Perhaps she could use the age-old excuse that 'an aunt needed help' for a bit – and perhaps the gossips would not learn the truth, but she was doubtful about this. Susan was not known for her ability to keep her mouth shut for long.

Father came back off his trip. He had managed to convince himself that he no longer wanted to marry Susan, and that whilst he had a responsibility to the child and should contribute to it, marriage to a bride who didn't want him was not the solution. He and I had the sort of chat where we sat in opposite corners of the room, and when he suggested I might think about taking on the baby, and after I had thrown half of the pots and pans at him, and after he had apologised profusely to me, and I to him, we went back to see Olivia again. For the moment – the next month or so – it was decided that things would stay as they were, but then Susan would move to another estate near Newport Pagnell, owned by relatives of Olivia, unless she could find her own place to go and have the child. By the time she came back, Olivia would have found somewhere for the child to be brought up. I think that Father hoped that 'somewhere' would be close by, so that he could look at the child sometimes – but I think that would have raised further suspicions.

In the end, part of the plan came to fruition, and part of it did not. Susan stayed for a month at Stuchbury, and then left for a 'stay in the country'. Unfortunately for Susan, whilst she was away, we received a message that Richard had died. It was one of those stupid deaths that accompanied the injuries and deaths from battle. He had died of cholera, in a minor epidemic that had carried off a couple of hundred people. It was only really the fact that several more of the estate workers had also died that caused the deaths to be notated down and sent back to Olivia in the hand of Robert Grey. He knew that the news would be wanted and thus arranged for the transport of it to Stuchbury, with my father and his waggons. Father, of course, did not know the news he bore, and under the circumstances, he had deliberately stayed away from fighting troops from the Grey estate, in case rumour had spread and he was faced with confrontation about Susan.

As it was, he was given the news of Richard's death by Olivia, who also had the task of giving the news to Susan – at the estate where she was 'resting' or 'staying' or 'helping out' – whatever the story was. Olivia went over to Newport Pagnell in the cart, in the end, to deliver the news personally and to find out what Susan wanted to do. Susan decided that she would have her baby there and would then return with it, and said that she wanted to keep the baby – but she still didn't want to marry my father. This was acceptable to my father – in his present state of mind – and it was better for him in that he might have a bit more access to his child if it was brought up by Susan at Stuchbury than if it had been adopted by one of our villagers. Olivia agreed to the baby being looked after – partly at Stuchbury and partly with carers in the village.

Susan gave birth several months later to a beautiful baby boy. Olivia drove me over in the cart to see my half-brother – who was to be called Richard. I have to say that for someone who had no interest in babies, I thought Richard was a beautiful baby boy and I enjoyed meeting him and holding him. Susan, once she was sure that I was not trying to 'claim' him from her, was perfectly happy for me to hold him and make stupid smiles at him to try and make him laugh. Father was not allowed to go with us (much to his annoyance) as there was no good reason why he should go and visit a baby that Susan – who was a 'friend' and 'had not' had a baby – was to look after, and we did not wish to start stories circulating. In fact, Olivia forbade him to see the baby until Susan brought it back in some triumph to the estate – nearly a year after the news had first broken.

The story then became (for circulation) that Susan had helped out at an estate where a cousin of hers had had a baby and had then died, and Susan had agreed 'out of the kindness of her heart' to look after the child, and this had generously been agreed to by Lady Olivia – knowing that the care of the child could be shared out between the workers of the estate and some villagers. I lost all idea of who knew what story at some point. I said nothing about the fact that my father spent a lot of his time making gurgling noises at Susan's 'poor orphan cousin' or whether anyone on the estate knew that she had really had a baby, or thought it was Richard's, or whether any of the village knew anything at all about this child that appeared from the estate periodically and was looked after. I am sure some of them thought it was really Olivia's baby. In time, Richard would grow up and learn the truth, but for the moment, this was just one of the stories that were not told.

EIGHT

PAGEANT 1: CONCEPT

I think I usually come across as someone who doesn't think or care very much about people or things. I think that I describe things in a 'matter–of-fact' way that encourages people to think this. The doctor says that I am 'analytical', and if I were not a woman, I would be a good scientist. I have seen him more over the last few months for various reasons, and I listen to what he says. To look at this in a good way, it makes me a good person to deliver messages and tell news as I am able to relate the 'bare bones' of a story without getting stuck on too much detail or becoming overcome with emotions when I tell the story. It meant that I could do my 'job' very well in the first three years of our war. On the bad side, though, it meant that I sometimes bottle things up to the point where I need to explode to let things out – and I don't do that well. Other folk see me mostly as the factual person who doesn't really care very much about them, and that makes me unhappy.

There are certain things I believe very much in, and care very deeply about. I believe in the God that Jesus taught us about, I believe that Jesus was sent by God to teach us how to worship properly, and I care very deeply for his Church. That makes me a Christian, but that doesn't simply mean that I am a Royalist – as I am quite happy to discuss ways of changing the way services are delivered, and the location of the altar or table – but it does mean that in my heart I also like the trappings of the church – particularly OUR church. I like to look at the pictures and the statues and the things in the church in Helmdon. I think that they call this the fabric of the church, but whatever it is called, it makes me happy to be there and happy to take part in the services and the life of the church – although some would argue that my concentration on 'material things' makes me a bad Christian!

My religion caused me to have an idea. I don't know how I arrived at this particular thought, but we had endured about two years of war by 1644, and it seemed as if it was going on forever. There seemed no let-up in it, and nothing of real importance to look forward to. Granted, there were moments of lightness in each week, and they often outweighed the drudgery of chores and regular responsibilities. When overlaid with the constant fear of the death or injury of loved ones away at war, and the holes in our lives that such news would cause, and the fact that we would then live with that despair or regret for months, perhaps years after the moment, it did seem that life was gradually weighing us down. I had an idea that I thought would give us all something to look forward to. I first had my idea (and I do claim it was my idea) at Easter in 1644, and then I wasted perhaps a month telling myself that it was stupid, I was stupid, it could never happen, I would waste everyone else's time by mentioning it when it was impossible.

In the end, I decided that a lot of this was a lack of belief in myself, and that if I didn't at least mention it, I would chastise myself more. I realised, too, that what I was proposing was an immense amount of effort that would take most of the following year for the whole committee to organise, the village to carry out the committee's instructions, and that we had to get started on it soon. If we left it much longer, I thought we would have to take another year, and it might go 'stale'. If I suggested it and it was turned down, at least I would have tried, and I would stop analysing my idea just to myself. I asked to address the committee towards the end of April. They agreed quite happily to listen to me – as usually my ideas were light ones that were easy to do and agree on. The actual content of my idea, though, in this case surprised them tremendously, and it surprised me that I had mentioned it to them, and indeed, actually put it to them quite well.

So although I had planned this conversation, they must have felt a bit that I sprang it on them. "I think we should do a pageant!"

"A what?" said Farmer Grant from his corner.

"A pageant," I said. "More particularly, I mean an Easter pageant!"

"That sounds interesting!" said the vicar. I had thought that a pageant tied to a major religious event would be of interest to him. It would raise the profile of the church and remind people of their faith. It wasn't why I had had the idea, but it did occur to me afterwards that the approval of the vicar would be helpful. "Tell us more," he said. So I did. I told them all of the ideas that had gone round in my head, since the first night when I had woken up at 3am with the idea, and after that had not been able to sleep. I watched their faces as I listed all of my thoughts, and although their expressions grew more and more surprised, was I wrong, or was there a degree of interest or approval as I spoke? I was aware that with each new level of detail, I might be making the whole thing more unrealistic, or frighteningly large and unwieldy. I had to know.

I started with the idea that had come to me first (and which I have mentioned before). I wanted us all (by which I meant all of the village) to organise, prepare and take part in an Easter pageant, which would take place at Easter 1645 – a year ahead. If we did what I had thought out so far, it would take the whole village, and it would draw most of the village together – and involve them all in the planning, organising and carrying out of my 'daft' idea. I used the word daft – as a defence. It gave them the opportunity to join in the criticism without feeling they had trampled on something important to me. I said that in my mind, I saw five or six or seven scenes from the Holy week story played by actors from the village in front of an audience. I said that the audience would be those in the village who didn't want to act but who would be involved in getting the pageant ready, and would want to watch it. I said we would need food for performers, costumes, some sort of backdrop or scenery, and we would probably want music, too.

There were a few minutes of silence after that, during which I wished

I could disappear down a hole, and then Mrs Cartwright from the forge (bless her) said, "It is not a 'daft' idea. It will take a lot of making, but I'd like to try it, and the forge can help make your things! Where do you think we would put on your scenes, Lucy?" and that was it. We were all drawn into a discussion, and I don't remember anyone asking for a vote. They all seemed to agree to the idea. It was how much we could do and what we could make it into that seemed to be all that mattered. The discussion was how we could make it work rather than whether we would do it.

"I want the stages to move," I said hesitantly. "I want to put each scene on one of the large quarry waggons that we have built. Then we can move them through the village. I think that if each scene is shown in perhaps three different places, that will be enough for the actors, and everyone can see it. Some people might even want to follow the waggons and see some scenes more than once!"

"Those waggons are used for stone," said Mr Ellis – the manager of the quarry. He had been on the committee since the quarries had been organised properly, and because the village was responsible for two of them. "The quarries are used six days a week. Some of your villagers complain about that! They say we should reduce the number of days we use them, but at the moment they are open six days of each week, except Christmas, and those waggons are very busy!"

"It will be Easter," I said. "They will not be used for three or four days anyway, and I thought we could get them ready for two or three days before Good Friday. No one will want to actually do the pageant on Good Friday! They will all be in church!" I added virtuously for the vicar's benefit – and he nodded vigorously. "I think we will need between five and seven waggons, for a week, but they would not normally be used for stone for four of those days anyway. It would be like the old mystery plays in the cities. They used waggons, too, for scenes!" I finished off.

That led to another discussion. The waggons had low beds for loading. They would be high enough to put things on so that people around them could see them, but low enough for the actors to get on them and so that other people could carry things and lift them up onto the waggons easily. We could even build some sort of stage on each waggon so that each scene would be easily visible (each scene could be seen!). I think Mr Ellis agreed to the waggons quite early on, but then we had to agree a route for them, where the performances would be, how many horses we would need and what route the waggons would take through the village. Some of our committee were more interested in the route than they turned out to be when we discussed the scenes and actors and content. I think they didn't see themselves as acting sort of people, but they wanted to say where the waggons should go!

We suggested – and this suggestion would also turn out to be the final outcome – that our scenes would play firstly at the Green, and then at the junction with the Stuchbury road, and finally at the top end of the village, where Cross Lane came into the Wappenham road. The advantage of the junctions was that they were widely laid out, and there would be room for people, horses and carts to pass each other whilst we were setting up. They were all on the main road, so the waggons would be able to do one straight trip through the village. It didn't really matter how many houses were around them; it was the room for the crowd that was important. Once we had started the whole thing, anyone could walk up and down the roads, but we would need to stop any other carts moving down the main road, and for the day of the pageant we would probably need to make sure that they parked carts in agreed places – sort of a 'cart park'!

"People will want to come from the smaller villages around here," said Mr Watts. He was a tailor, and he travelled to some of the villages and had a better idea of what people were like in them. "Greatworth, Astwell, Wappenham, even the Weston area. I can see that people will want to come and watch this. How long will it all last?" We were not sure that he was right, but we discussed the timing. We worked out that if one of our 'scenes' lasted perhaps half an hour, and we had seven of them, that would be three and a half hours. There needed to be perhaps half an hour between each scene for the waggons to move, and folk might want to get something to eat, or to relieve themselves, or even just to move around. That would mean another three hours, bringing the whole thing to a whole day's programme of about seven hours! If we started at ten o'clock, we would finish at five.

It was beginning to grow into a big undertaking. I always knew that it would, but I had underestimated how far it would go. We recognised even at this first meeting that we would need teams of people, and each team would have to have a leader. We would need someone to take overall charge of actors, even if each team of actors – those doing one scene – had a team leader as well. We would need someone to take charge of building all of the 'scenery' and 'properties', which were the words for the things that actors sat on or hid behind, or even what was seen behind them. Mrs Cartwright bagged that job straight away. It turned out that she was a secret lover of plays and the like, and whilst she did not want to act, the chance of organising all of the physical objects was wonderful to her! She even suggested that if we overran on time, there might be ways of using candles to light scenes. She was ideally placed, too, in the forge to supervise building of a lot of things.

Mr Watts suggested we would need costumes. I hadn't considered this, as I had no real idea what Jesus and the disciples wore. The only pictures of them I had seen were two in Stuchbury Hall and the murals that we had in the church. I don't know if any of them were exactly right, but Jesus either dressed in long flowing robes and wore sandals or he dressed in a style similar to Good Queen Bess' court. Mr Watts, though, had seen more pictures in the towns, and as this was his trade, he wanted to organise our three tailors and take charge before anybody else did. I thought the robes were simpler, but I knew we would end up with whatever costumes Mr Watts wanted. The vicar was going to HAVE to take charge overall of the acting scenes. He loved the idea anyway, but he also had to make sure that no word was spoken that would be blasphemous, or contradict the gospels, or be inappropriate in the circumstances. It would be difficult to do that well.

At some time in the past, the vicar had actually seen a play – as had Mrs Cartwright – and so they knew that someone would need to show the actors how they moved or how to say their words so that they sounded convincing. They said that what looked convincing on the stage was not what looked real in normal life. They tried to demonstrate what they meant. It all sounded a bit unreal to me and the others, and as we could not sort it out then and there, we decided to leave it for the moment – and discuss it again when we had more people that we could see doing it. It was also getting on for eight o'clock in the evening at this point. None of us wanted to stop discussing it, but we had a brief pause whilst we lit candles, and I went off to see if I could find some provisions for our group. Having a meeting whilst actually eating food and drink was a new experience for us, but we could see a great future in it, especially for longer meetings in the future.

The vicar was going to have to have overall say in this project as well as doing the words. We could not organise something like this without his approval, and it all had to be done (not just the words) so that it didn't offend God. The vicar agreed to all of this but said that he would need to have some help with the writing as we would need to make copies of it for those who could read, and they would need to teach it to those who couldn't read – so that they could practise it. With the idea of teams of people, each having a team leader, someone witty – and I think it was Mr Bragby, the butcher – used the phrase 'the vicar and his disciples', which was immediately dismissed by the vicar as irreverent and suggested disloyalty to our Lord. He promptly banned the phrase, which meant that it was adopted by everyone else in the village forever but was not used when the vicar could hear it.

The vicar mentioned, though, that what we were about was probably going to be unacceptable to Puritans, and anyone on that purer side of the church – established or otherwise. It could be seen as idolatrous – and would be disapproved of in the same way that murals or pictures or statues sometimes were in the Church. We, in our village, had grown up with these as a normal part of our worship, but we knew that some folk in the larger towns were much more plain and simple in their worship, and often much more critical of those who didn't follow their persuasions. It seemed to be more prevalent in the larger towns, because there was more room for groups to bond together than in the villages – which tended to laugh at minorities that they saw as different. Strongly Royalist towns, too (Oxford, perhaps), we thought were less tolerant of the reformists. The vicar warned us that we might be subjected to interference and criticism from external groups, and we would have to show complete committal to the pageant and be prepared to adjust it or alter it to avoid any problems.

Certain things could not be done at the meeting. We thought that we should have three groups of musicians – one for each performance place. We could have had the musicians travel around with the actors, but then we would have needed six or seven groups, whereas if they stayed in one place, we might only need three groups, and they could entertain the audience whilst the waggons moved on. They could play little tunes at the start and end of the scene, but most importantly, they could play music for the hymns. If the audience could sing hymns that they were likely to know, and that were proper Easter hymns, they were much more likely to enjoy the event, and to enjoy taking part. It seemed logical, too, that if we only had three musical groups, they would be better.

There was a little issue about asking the musicians to perhaps play for up to seven hours, but this was what we were asking the actors to do, and if the musicians only played between scenes, they would only actually play for half of the time. We would have to see how many musicians we actually had in Helmdon, what sort of music they could play and whether they were able to do what we wanted. We couldn't have them making their own little ditties and playing them at the wrong moment. Imagine a dance tune playing whilst Our Lord was on the cross! Most importantly of all, they had to see what we wanted to do with our pageant and to agree with it – the musicians had to act in union with our intentions. Without the musicians in union, we might have no suitable music. Accordingly, I agreed to make contact with musicians initially in Helmdon and to see who we had available.

We had to find actors, and test those people who wanted to be actors and who thought they would be good. If we had seven separate scenes, then we needed seven people to play Jesus, and the disciples, and Mary, and Pilate and the crowds. The vicar said he was sorry, but no women would be allowed to play Jesus, although it might be possible to use them as disciples who didn't say much, or as part of the crowd. He said, too, that he thought it might be still against the law to use women in a stage play (or even possibly to put on a play at all), but he did not want a young boy to act the role of Mary, mother of Jesus, or even Mary Magdalene. We decided to avoid discussing this in front of others, but the vicar agreed to start telling villagers that we were looking for actors to perform in a religious pageant, and to start looking for those who might lead them.

Mr Bragby volunteered to organise the food, and Mrs Harriatts would do that also. We knew that we would have to feed people throughout the day, whether they were actors or musicians, whether they had built 'scenery' or made costumes, whether they were leading horses that pulled the waggons, whether they were directing folks into the 'cart parks' or whether they were helping visitors in a myriad of other ways. We didn't think that we could charge our own villagers for food in this project if they had given up a lot of their time. We would have to provide food free for them, but also charge those who came to the village just for the day. We might have to have as many as twenty or thirty places where people could get food. The vicar referred to this all as 'the feeding of the five thousand', although he stopped short of suggesting we ask Jesus for help.

We decided that we would give a coloured armband to everyone who helped us out on the pageant, so that on the day it happened they could produce it as evidence and get free food for themselves. We would not tell them this yet, as we did not want folk stealing armbands, or even making them. We knew that if we had long days of practising or building, we would also need to feed the workers in the weeks before the pageant, but then we often did that with workers on other projects, too, so that would probably work out, somehow. On the day, we would have every food stall that we could manage, on site, and be ready to provide food for any people who wanted it. We would have to arrange to stockpile some foods – for example, potatoes – so that we could bake or cook them to provide a hot meal. We would have to make hundreds of gallons of soup, but if we did cook a large amount of vegetable broth, it could last for several days, and then perhaps we could cook meat on the day to add to it, or we could use it after the pageant.

We would need a lot of water in containers to drink. We didn't think it would be good just to get everyone to drink from the river – especially if others were 'relieving' themselves close by! People might bring their own food, and that would be good – but we thought that we should also make the effort to make sure that everyone could have something to eat and drink. If an actor was Jesus, it was probably not fitting that he should be rushing home for a bite to eat between shows, and for that matter, 'Jesus' should not be seen to be relieving himself, either, so the actors would need private places or privies to do that. We knew also, because the vicar and Mrs Cartwright told us so, that some folk really believed that the plays they saw were real – and that they were seeing real people in real stories. They got very upset when something spoiled the 'realness' for them, so we needed to be aware of doing anything that would trigger an upset!

I was to be in charge of running and delivering messages. Not only that, I was to recruit a team of messengers as I could not cope with what I was already doing and the amount of messages that would be generated by my pageant. Each team would have a messenger, and every time a message was to be delivered by them, it would be shown to me on the way, so that I could say if it interfered with or contradicted other messages, plans or instructions. I had to keep a list. Actually, I had to keep lots of lists – one for each team. I couldn't possibly keep a record of the content of each message, but I would put a number and a sentence of the main thrust of the content. I had to ask everyone to restrict each message to one main subject – which caused more messages, but there was no way of keeping a record of a message with four or five important subjects and making sure that we didn't contradict them or confuse them later. If only someone could have invented a machine to do this…

The most important thing to me about the whole pageant was the actual scenes from the Holy Book that we would actually portray in our scenes. We listed the possibilities and how they would work. I had had the idea that the pageant should take place on the Saturday between Good Friday and Easter Sunday, which would mean that all of our scenes would have taken place – but as it would be before the Sunday, we would have to be careful as we might be suggesting in the pageant that 'Jesus' was arising from the dead before the Sunday – and for those who believed in drama as reality, this would be a bit too much. The risen Christ should appear on the Sunday, but we didn't think that we could do the pageant on two days – especially if the second day was Easter Sunday, so we had to find some way to finish the pageant on the Saturday that was a) believable, b) permitted, and c) optimistic. So, we finally settled on the following scenes as suitable for our pageant.

1. Jesus fetching and riding a donkey through Helmdon – as mentioned above. This wasn't really a scene, but it needed a bit of planning – and perhaps Roman guards could 'clear the way' into Jerusalem for Jesus. We also wanted to separate this out from Number 2.

2. The triumphal entry into Jerusalem. This would be the biblical crowds following Jesus on the donkey. We would give the audience flower petals to strew in front of him, because Helmdon was not known for its 'palm trees', but we thought that in the spring we could find and spread a fair amount of petals around. Jesus would lead a small group of 'disciples' behind him on the waggon, and they could greet the crowds as they went. We would perhaps build part of Jerusalem on the waggon. It would provide a big opening scene.

3. On Monday, Jesus cleared the temple. This earned him the hatred of a lot of important people who might not otherwise have called for him to be crucified. We could even have our actors discussing this as part of the scene. We would build part of the temple as a background. We were not all sure what the moneylenders did – but the vicar said that there were also people who sold animals as sacrifice, and we all knew where we could get animals from!

4. On Tuesday, Jesus went to the Mount of Olives. This had potential for nice scenery on the waggons, and the vicar thought he could detail the events and words of Our Lord for this. The discussion about building a real mountain on a waggon took some time! We also discussed whether the crowds would be there at the start of the scene or whether Jesus would appear, 'climb' the mount on the waggon, and the crowds follow him.

5. Nothing much happened on the Wednesday, even though that is when the Tenebrae service is, so the next scene would be on the Thursday. This needed to include the Last Supper and the arrest of Jesus – betrayed by Judas. It also needed to include the disciples following him, Peter's denial of Jesus three times, and the cock crow. This raised the horrible suggestion that this waggon should contain a cockerel in a cage – which would be poked with a stick to make it crow. This was replaced quite quickly by an actor who was to make a crowing noise. It was possible, too, in this scene that we might have some bits around the waggon or before or after it – so that all of the actors would not be squashed into the same space.

6. The trial of Jesus and the Crucifixion. It surprised me that this was all on the same day, but it is according to the Holy Week timetable, so we would have to have a trial where Jesus was then taken out and hauled up onto some sort of cross – although roped in our pageant and not nailed up – and then quickly taken down once the waggon moved – perhaps drapes could be drawn when this happened. Like the previous scene, it might not all take place on the waggon. We could consider whether Jesus walked with the cross on his back, for example.

7. The last scene should be the garden on Easter day, where the risen Christ reveals himself in the garden. This needed discussion, as I have said. The vicar was happy with the discussions between Mary and the angels, and her running to find the disciples, but he felt that the final tableau would be acceptable if no dialogue took place at the point where Jesus appeared fully risen. Instead, the actors would fall to their knees, before a clothed figure. Candles would be lit along the waggon, and at that point the musicians would play several Easter hymns – in which the audience would join in.

So, six waggons then. Six great scenes (developed over a lot of discussion on that night, and actually finalised several times over the next six months – because of arguments about what was allowed). These would follow the first short scene. Six sets of actors, six sets of costumes, six sets of horses to pull the waggons, and men to lead and guide the horses. Possibly reliefs for any horses that got tired, and perhaps we would need duplicate actors to learn the lines in case any of the main actors became ill. Mr Ellis said that we would be using the entire set of quarry horses and the entire set of quarry waggons, if he had calculated this right. He also said that we would need those for the entire time of the pageant – because moving them in and out of the quarry would not be practical. Mr Watts had already listed the number of costumes, and Mrs Cartwright started to list what she would have to design and build. It started to show us how big this was all going to be. At some point, we would have to decide if the pageant took precedence over everything (like the use of the quarry horses and waggons), or whether anything else would be more important. This was a decision that we would have to make and remake several times in the next year. Officially – although we had said nothing – I had already seen the vicar making writing words.

In my eyes, it then all got a bit silly. The vicar's comment about 'feeding the five thousand' caused Mr Ellis also to suggest that townspeople from as far as Brackley or Towcester might want to come and watch the pageant – if we put up bills or notices to say it was on. The downside might be that we might attract religious protesters, whilst the positive side would be that we could take lots of money on the food stalls from visitors. He had a suggestion that I was even more uncertain about. Our village had a lot of standard waggons – like those ones we used to take people and goods to Brackley or Towcester. How would it be (he said) if we took perhaps twenty of the village waggons to each town very early, and used them to bring folk to the village for a small charge, which included a ride back after the show? That would use those waggons and horses that we had in the village but which weren't being used in the pageant. It might mean that we had less people bringing their own carts coming into the village, and we could make more money by selling them a ride. The alternative, he said, was that if they arrived in a cart or their own waggon, we could find a place for them to park or store that waggon, and we could charge them a groat or a farthing to do that for them!

Mr Ellis also said that some people would want to come for a night before the pageant (not afterwards – because that would go into Easter Sunday) and stay over, either in houses or our hospitality barns, or perhaps even that we could put up a lot of tents in two or three fields, and people could stay in them. This was considered and eventually agreed, although it was suggested that charging people for food, transport and a tent was a little greedy, and perhaps we were trying to make too much money for a religious festival. Mr Ellis said he could contact other quarries – because some of them had small tents – so that when their men delivered stone, they had somewhere to sleep if a delivery took more than a day. Mr Watts said he would talk to Mr Ellis – because if there were not enough tents, Mr Watts knew people who could make them. We decided to drop the charge for transport – as the drivers probably wouldn't do too well on that anyway – but folk who were not from the village would be asked to pay for food and for a tent overnight Friday to Saturday, which would include straw to sleep on. Water would be free. No one felt right about charging for water. If we supplied water that we knew was safe to drink, it should stop people drinking the river water.

NINE

PAGEANT 2: REALISATION

By the time we finished that evening's meeting, I think we had agreed a rough timetable for starting the whole project. We had agreed that we needed at least six months to pick and rehearse actors, probably the same amount of time to build scenery for the scenes. We had to recruit everyone in the village who might want to take part, and we had to find a way of telling and convincing everyone what we were going to do. We decided that we should start as soon as possible – because if everything (by some miracle) was finished early, then we could store it, or rest it, or go over it, or improve it. None of us had heard of overdoing things, and if we had, I don't think we would have changed our timetable for this anyway. In the spirit of 'as soon as possible', we therefore called a village meeting early in May – after we had consulted all of the important village people – to see if we had overlooked anything important in our discussion.

At this meeting, we told all of the villagers what we planned to do, when, how, and that they would all need to be involved. We told them of the timescale for this, the steps that we needed to take, and what we hoped would come out of this. We told them that this was a plan to involve everyone in a pageant that would make us all feel better by having something to do that was positive and involved everyone. Like the committee meeting, the more we said, the more their jaws dropped open, and then we waited for questions or objections. We waited a few minutes for someone to say something, and then we asked them, "Have you any questions?"

A voice said, "When do we start?" and then there were literally hundreds of questions – but they were all about how to audition, which team could they join, what we meant by 'scenery', etc. They were all questions about how they could be involved, and NONE of them were "Sorry, but I don't want to...." sort of comments. Two years of war meant that they wanted to do something positive with everyone else – and to do it for a long time!

That year went very quickly. Some things I remember as standing out, for no particular reason. We had to audition Jesuses. I think that thirty village folk wanted to be Jesus. We had to ask ten to leave because the vicar refused to have a female Jesus, although we asked them to come back for Mary and Mary Magdalene – both of whom were in at least two scenes. That left twenty potential disciples, of whom the youngest was ten and the oldest was sixty. When we asked the youngest one why he was here (meaning why did he want to be Jesus?), he replied, "My mother told me to come."

When we asked the oldest one the same question, he said, "My daughter told me to come." Both of them had been told to audition in the hope it would get them out of the house for a bit. Besides them we had Singing Jesus, Dancing Jesus (yes, a young man wanted to be a Dancing Jesus), Big Brutish Jesus, Young and Graceful Jesus, and even Drunken Jesus! In the end, we managed to get five Jesus actors, and we found another two later on.

We had around ten complaints from more austere Church groups, Puritans, Episcopal Groups and the like every week! For some reason, our idea had been circulated not just to the local towns, where we intended to put up posters looking for audiences within the surrounding county, but further afield – even as far as Scotland. There were obviously religious groups with chapters or affiliations who were in regular communication with their groups. We replied to all of the communications that we had, answering their concerns. 'No, this is not a puppet show...' 'No, it is not heretical...' 'No, we are not actually going to hang Judas for real...' 'No, there will be no women Jesuses...' 'No, we are not going to sacrifice anything...' fifteen complaints, '...whether it be chickens, goats or children...' 'No, there will be no dance groups in the pageant...' (Although, to be honest, two Brackley groups turned up on the actual day to entertain the audience – and whilst we let them dance, they didn't do it anywhere near the pageant scenes – or the vicar, as we thought he might not approve.)

The vast majority of complaints, though, alleged that some form of idolatry was involved, and that what we were doing was in some way against their interpretation of what Our Lord wanted. Answering them was a problem. In most cases, there was no way they would accept that their beliefs were faulty or flawed, and we did not want to suggest that they were flawed, even if they were not our beliefs. Perhaps the Church that King Henry had separated from Rome had started to allow too many different forms. We were fairly sure that a lot of the groups would not have been allowed to flourish under him, or his children. All we could do was to answer specific questions that they had, and to ignore the insults and threats that some of them hurled at us – which I am sure were not Christian in intent or origin. "What is a dog-faced maggot-eating son of Beelzebub anyway?" I asked the vicar.

"I think it is some form of mongrel," he replied – as his shoulders started to shake with laughter. We had to console ourselves with the fact that most of these groups were far from Helmdon.

By Christmas, the amount of scenery that had been built was starting to dominate some areas of the village. In some ways, this was interesting. I heard one person telling a visitor, "Oh yes, that is the Mount of Olives, and over there is the dining table for the Last Supper." We had scenery in barns, we had palm trees in sheds, we even had something called a 'cactus', but I couldn't really believe that was right. We had costumes everywhere. If a role had been allocated and the costume made, it went to the actor's house. We sometimes had to stop actors wearing their costumes around the village and whilst doing their jobs. We couldn't have a Saint Peter serving ale, or Mary, Mother of Jesus, milking a cow, or Judas reading a lesson in church, although we would have had if we had not interfered. We didn't want the costumes wearing out before the event. We had an imitation Judas who we were going to hang from a constructed tree, so that he could be seen dangling in the background.

I also had reservations about the dialogue – but I have to say that very quietly in case I am overheard. Mrs Cartwright said that the vicar had a gift for writing speeches – and that they were just the sort of speeches that you would have heard in a play, but I worried about how some of them would have gone over. I accepted that characters had to introduce themselves, because otherwise our audience would have no idea who the actor was, but "I am your Roman governor! Listen carefully because this is your Pilate speaking!" seemed a bit unusually phrased (to me at any rate).

"I am full of awe. Truly this man was the son of God!" was another. Mind you, the original Bible story was full of unusual wording, and the vicar was the man who knew how it was translated, what was allowed and what wasn't allowed, so there it was. We had planned someone to be on each waggon who could say the words if the actors forgot them – which seemed to happen most days.

We had goblets, wine bottles, plates and a table for the Last Supper, mock trees and bushes, a sword for Peter, a brazier for him to warm his hands at and a stuffed cockerel, Roman guard uniforms, robes for the disciples and Jesus, a crucifix, plants for the Garden of Gethsemane, bits of the temple – so it looked authentic. Sadly, our scenes would not let us tear the veil of the temple – but we had money for the moneylenders and stools for them to sit on. We even had a basin for 'our' Pilate to wash his hands in. Pilate was going to ask the audience who they wanted released, and we had to plant people in the audience to shout "Barabbas," because it wouldn't work if they shouted "Jesus," as some people might prefer to! The big properties or sceneries were the Mount of Olives and the base of the garden, and the hill for the Crucifixion, although we avoided having the city wall that He was crucified outside of. We had part of Jerusalem for the first scene, but we couldn't use it for two scenes. We had a sort of tomb – and plants to go outside of it. Wings for the angels, the list was endless. Somewhere, it became expected that my team would list where everything went on the days before the event – so that it would all end up in the right place.

By the week before the pageant, we had become a little alarmed by the number of letters that we had from Christian groups questioning our pageant. As I have said, some of them had quite offensive content – but paradoxically were well written. They would say things like 'You will burn in hell for all eternity for this blasphemy' and were signed, 'Yours faithfully' or even on one occasion, 'With best wishes for your continued health', from the Brotherhood of the Seven in Colchester (wherever that is). We had not even asked in the cities whether a religious pageant or mystery play was allowed – because we worried that they would find a reason why it wasn't. Because of the religious letters, though, we started to take precautions in the spring. We had so many rosters of people for the pageant that we just added one – which was guarding the scenery and properties and equipment that we had made, or acquired – and in one case I think 'borrowed' without proper permission. Anyone who volunteered for this duty probably just wanted their chance to be involved or just to look at what we were doing – without getting in the way.

One night in March, Jenny Pearce and Olive Tue were patrolling – when they saw furtive figures running in and out of one of the fenced-off yards where we had put a waggon so that we could try the various scenes out for size in the next few days. Mr Ellis had grumbled a bit about this, but he was so involved in the pageant that even he recognised this was necessary. Jenny and Olive were two of the girls who we had trained on the muskets, and taking a duty was all the excuse they needed to retrieve a musket from the store, and a pouch with powder and ball. Once they had decided that the furtive figures were up to no good, they loaded the muskets with the light of a nearby window, banged on a nearby door and told them to send help 'as we had robbers' and then marched into the yard and pointed the muskets at a gang of four elderly men – who were trying without much success to damage our waggon, and with more success, demolish part of the 'Garden of Gethsemane'. Jenny said that she didn't know who the men were, but they were dressed in simple black clothing that we associated with Puritans, and they immediately lined up and dropped their implements when faced with two young girls with muskets. Two more figures emerged from behind a smaller waggon and joined them.

Olive said later that the men started off by making wild accusations of idolatry and God's law – but as they kept shouting over each other, it was difficult to tell what they were saying. As she and Jenny were joined by more village figures, armed with more easily accessible implements like large hammers and swords, the 'robbers' gradually grew quieter and stopped speaking. "Where are you from?" demanded Jenny in a loud and angry voice.

"Don't tell them, brother Pike," said one of the robbers to another, who had looked as if he was about to speak. "We will answer to God, and not to you!" continued the same man.

"Get the council," said Jenny to one of our villagers – and in a short period of time, I and two other council people had been summoned – from our beds by furious knocking – and were standing there, looking at the group of vandals.

"Go and have a look," I said to William Young – one of the young lads from the group. "They will have a cart or waggon hidden somewhere nearby, unless they walked here from Brackley."

"Not Brackley," said one of our vandals. "Den of iniquity, that place is!"

"Towcester, then," I said, and the group shut up for fear of revealing further information. William went off with a friend to do this.

We talked about what to do next. We could easily repair the damage that had been done, and it was just a bit annoying. What was probably more important was to send a message to other groups, saying what would happen to other groups if they tried to emulate this sort of behaviour. None of us wanted any sort of physical harm to come to this group – with the exception of Jenny, who wanted to take them to the target practice field and try her hand at a live target. She offered to give them a ten-second head start, but we still felt that was an unacceptable way to treat our trespassers. In the end, William returned to the yard with the group's waggon – with two horses still attached – and a young lad who had been guarding them.

This young lad was now attached firmly to the fist of William's companion. Mrs Cartwright – who was one of the council members who came with me to the yard – had an idea! We stripped the group, including the lad, of their outer clothing, and by physical numbers dressed them in a few of our most garish costumes. These costumes were meant for actors in the pageant, but we thought that we could replace a few.

We painted their waggon, again with the most garish paints we could find in the yard, and without worrying too much if it was dry, made them climb into the waggon and shackled them to the railings – each on one long chain, and each with a pair of manacles on their wrists, which we just happened to have. This was not quick – and it took most of the rest of the night – finishing around three in the morning. Then William and Jenny and Olive found an extra horse and led the waggon and horses and the load of bitterly complaining vandals to Towcester (which was quite a distance), arriving in the centre of Towcester at around eight in the morning – just as it was getting busy. They tied the waggon and horses up as close to the middle of the town as they could (in the marketplace, I believe), and then they came back – taking it in turns to ride as a pair on the horse, with the other one walking beside it. They could not of course undo the manacles – which were secured with a metal pin hammering the chain into the waggon. We had no more visits from groups in Towcester – although we had a smaller group from Brackley. In the end, we had to make ten extra costumes in all. Jenny and William started walking out together, so that was nice!

Then came Easter 1645. We did it! I don't think I can say anything more about the event than those three words can say. I have a confused memory of the day, with thousands of people. Everywhere I needed to be I had to jostle people. Every time a message arrived or departed, it felt as if hundreds of people had to be jostled. We had a central message point where we were all based, and we delivered messages from it. Scenes on waggons went past – but we had no time to watch them. Every so often, someone would arrive with soup or rolls or water, and we ate or drank whilst we worked. Money came in and went to be hidden in the church safe. Each delivery of money was accompanied by several villagers as guards for it, so that it would not be stolen on the way. My greatest idea ever was happening, and I had no moment to watch, absorb, enjoy, notice good things or correct bad things. I was in a morass of things happening, and I felt as if I were drowning in a sea of people and messages. I think that three whole days disappeared from my life. Why oh why…?

No one had really slept for the two or three days before the pageant, or if they did, they only had brief naps. Those people in the village who were working stopped proper work on the Tuesday or the Wednesday and just did urgent jobs on the Wednesday or Thursday. Mr Ellis stopped the quarries on the Tuesday at 5pm, and then he sat all of the quarry workers down to a trestle meal in one of the quarry basins. They all had a chicken meal, some beer, a choice of puddings, and then they were carried down to the village on a few waggons. On the Wednesday morning, they were all up at the quarries at the usual time to pick up seven heavy stone waggons (six needed and one spare) which they then drove down to the village with their teams of horses. They were delivered to the agreed points, and then the horses were taken to a meadow where they could spend the next few days. Swarms of people descended on the waggons, and by the end of the Wednesday we had a complete fleet of them, in the right position for the Saturday.

Every actor had all-day practices on the Wednesday and the Thursday, and almost everyone else in the village was involved in problem solving, or cooking (either for the pageant or for the teams of others working for it), or putting up tents in the meadow, or organising the waggons to be used for transport, or painting something, or banging a nail in. We had a list of names at our message centre, and I think that on those two days we knew where almost everyone in the village was working and what they were doing. We had messages going out every few seconds as it became clear that Mr Watts needed twenty-five costumes delivered to scenes one, two and three, or a large amount of soup and rolls needed to go to scenes four and five, or a 'palm tree' had been delivered and could Robert and Harry go there with hammers, nails and a saw. Could scene four have an extra five people as the 'Mount of Olives' had got stuck in the gateway to the yard and was threatening to come apart.

We stopped work around ten at night at all points. Some had finished that day's work a bit earlier, but they were being diverted to other points so that all work could stop at ten. A last small meal was served to everyone around eight, and then the kitchens doused their fires until the Saturday morning – making sure that they had enough fuel for the Saturday, and that the fires would start well and were not clogged with ash or clinker. The intention was that everyone would be free to go to church for the Good Friday service on Friday morning, and could have the rest of that day for relaxation with loved ones or friends, or for prayer or merely for rest. More people came to the church than I had ever seen at one time. Some who were known to avoid church services went to pray for the Saturday's endeavours, some went to pray for loved ones far away, and I think that some just went there to be part of the village. All of the pews were full, and folk were standing at the back. Some swapped seats so that others were not standing all the way through, and I realised that some pews were seated in the teams that they had been working in for all of those months.

The village was nearly silent for the rest of the day. There was the laughter of children playing – and sometimes that of the adults telling stories of their work for the pageant. I went for a walk in the afternoon, but I don't think I saw more than ten people. All the rest were taking time on what proved to be a lovely afternoon to sit indoors or sit in a field; some were even splashing in the river. The village was completely quiet by about nine in the evening, and I saw no lights across the street. Everyone was preparing for an early start the next morning, which began at around five or six. The first hint of how large this was to become was when we went down to the tent field and saw several hundred people had arrived the previous evening or during the course of the night, and had rested for the night in one of our tents. Moreover, we had people already walking down the lanes, having left the closer villages to be sure of getting to us on time and, as they put it, 'being sure of a seat'. As I left to go to the message centre, the kitchens were starting to serve breakfast, the waggons had already left for the towns, and the food stalls that we set up along the road were starting to work.

I did not see anything for the next three hours – my sense of control was tested to the limit as message came, message went, boys came, girls went. We could not write messages down any longer, and for each new message that went out we already had ten waiting. If anyone in the village became available – such as the drivers of the waggons – they were sent off with a message, or with a waggon to deliver equipment or food, or just to go somewhere and help someone do something 'and then return here as quickly as possible' so that we could give them something else to do. Without any form of signal, all work started to slow and halt at around nine-thirty in the morning. With an event this large due to start at ten, we knew that everyone would be watching ten to fifteen minutes before that to see what would happen at ten, and how the event would actually start. At ten minutes to ten, all four bells of the church started to ring. I stepped out of my message centre to see a solid line of people as far as my eyes could see, watching and listening. Behind them, there was constant movement as others arrived or moved or worked, but they were almost all silent in what they did.

I looked across to the green and saw the vicar dressed in his best robes, surrounded by members of the committee and team leaders. He saw me and waved at me to come and join them. I realised that getting there would be difficult, and getting back to my message team after 10am would be nigh on impossible, so I waved back and shook my head at him. We counted down, and the bells stopped at 10am. There was a solitary bell that sounded ten times. The vicar stepped forward and gave one of his best speeches ever. It was one line long, and all he said was "Good people of Helmdon, and good visitors, the first pageant of this village will start now!" There was a great cheer from the crowd, and a loud whistle. The first cart appeared around the bend the other side of the green in response to the whistle, drew forward and the driver stopped the team when it was level with the vicar. I realised that the actors and the scene could be viewed from both sides of the road. I waited with the crowd to see the start of this first scene. I heard a short fanfare on some sort of hunting horn, and then a member of my team tugged at my sleeve and told me that I was needed urgently. I went back to my messages.

I saw none of the rest of my pageant. I was told an awful lot of it by other people, usually starting with "Oh, and did you see when…"

To which I would reply "No, tell me..." and I got chapter and verse on some really important event. After a while, I realised that getting information this way meant that I found out more than I would have done by standing in a crowd of a thousand or more. My messengers and other folk were giving me a complete picture of the whole event, and often they had come to tell me because so many of them knew that I was involved in running it – even if they did not know that it was my idea! I felt very much a part of the whole event from hearing all about it, and I lost all feelings of resentment at being stuck in a message centre. I heard about accidents, losses, unintended jokes or funny incidents. I heard about lines delivered wrongly, lines that managed to convey the wrong meaning, sudden emergencies dealt with quickly and efficiently. I knew when the wind had blown a costume high and the audience had seen more of that actor than was intended, and I heard when someone had needed a little alcohol before acting. I loved every minute of it, and true to my nature, I also relished the fact that I was in control of it!

People did what had once been suggested. They watched some of the scenes on the waggon and then picked up their belongings and followed the waggon to the next performance so that they could see it again. People are more complicated than we had anticipated. They applauded the scenes. The applause took time – and the actors needed to see the applause they got. The time between each performance of each scene took longer, and it meant that not only could some people watch a scene twice but they also had time to walk back and watch the next one the first time, and then walk with it to watch it again. I think that also meant that they only watched some scenes once, but they could walk back to the next one, and some of the fitter younger members of the audience could even get all the way back to the first performance from the place of the last one without missing a scene. Gradually, the audience moved with the waggons, so that by the time the last scene played in the third place, we had everybody there in one massive grouping. The pageant was expected to last seven hours. By my count, it ended up as about ten hours. We started at about ten o'clock and finished around eight!

The vicar had referred to 'the feeding of the 5,000'. In the end, some of us believed that we had actually had 5,000 people in Helmdon that day. Others argued the numbers, but no one believed that we had less than about 3,000 – although no one had actually managed to count everyone there on that day, and the figures resulted from counts of different sites at different times. Whatever the actual figure was, we had around ten times the usual population during that period of the war. It was a huge number. We picked up rose and flower petals from the road for weeks. The crowd enthusiastically threw them at Jesus and the disciples and each other, and even brought their own. I don't know about the 5,000 leaving twelve baskets of leftovers, but our audience left several hundred large baskets of rubbish that we picked up. There was so much rubbish that we had to clear it before we could walk down some of the roads, and when the large waggons had run over a lot of it, we had to use large shovels to get it off the roads.

Something similar happened with the other thing that all of those people left behind. When several thousand people need to relieve themselves, there is a lot of waste that is left behind – and we could not separate that out from the food left behind, small baskets, flower petals, packages, bits of clothing, a few toys, water bottles or jars, some plates and a lot of things that could not be identified. To some extent, mixing the flower petals with the human waste reduced the smell, but we were still not going to bury any of it in our village – or indeed anywhere near it. In the end, we sent down waggons that could be loaded up with rubbish, and we took it all up to a disused part of an old quarry and turned the waggon over so that the rubbish went into one of the holes – then we filled it over with gravel, sand and the like and forgot about it. We worked for a week clearing and tidying the village. That took us back to reality, and mundane tasks. Whenever I thought about our pageant afterwards, two images came immediately to mind. One was the crowds on the day, and the other the piles of waste. I still think of it as the rubbish of the 5,000.

The event was talked about for months. The committee also talked about it and analysed it for a long time, and during those discussions, the most frightening question that most people had ever heard was asked: "When can we do it again?" The realistic answer was that we thought we could do it again in another five years. By then, the war would be nearly over, but not quite. Lots more people would have died, including the Reverend White, and there was the start of an anticipation that the war was to be over soon. More people wanted to mourn their dead, and more wanted to wait until the war was actually over before we mounted another largely 'celebratory' event. We waited until after Worcester; some of us waited longer until some stories of our loved ones were resolved, and then some of our lives continued to change even after that. In the end, we never mounted another event of this sort – although others did in other villages and around the country, and perhaps we influenced them in their ideas. Like the 'Battle of Helmdon', the 'Pageant of Helmdon' became perhaps a rumour, perhaps just a story, and perhaps it would become a song that children sang.

TEN

NASEBY AND AFTER, 1645–47

The Battle of Naseby was on the 14th of June 1645. Once again, it was a summer battle (I noticed), and for the second time that I had heard, the Parliamentary army had won a decisive victory in a major battle. Perhaps the new military tactics that Edward had told me about were beginning to have an effect, and perhaps we were to see a turn in the way that the war was waged, and in the sort of results that we were to see. Edward had not given me any details of what he meant, so I could not judge what sort of impact his 'tactics' would have. Perhaps this sort of Parliamentarian victory had happened before in previous battles or skirmishes (other than Marston Moor), and I was just not up to date with the way the war and the battles were going. That was more likely. There were fewer battles in 1645 – Naseby being the second of seven battles.

We heard Naseby! It must be thirty miles from us, but we first heard a long low rumble which one of our older men said was cannons firing. I don't know how many they had there to make that sort of noise, but it happened again several times. When they told me, I didn't believe that we could hear it thirty miles away. We heard no rifles or muskets, no voices, just these rumbles. Some of the old men just sat on their bench and waited for the next one. Each rumble of cannon made them shake their heads and click disapprovingly with their tongues. We hadn't heard this sound before. We heard nothing for Cropredy Bridge, for example. I went and made myself busy. I couldn't sit around and think of the English dead! English killing English – it beggared belief! After a while, it stopped – and presumably that meant that either someone had won or the battle had moved around. Like any other battle, we would have to wait for the news, but the noise brought the war so much closer than other things had.

We had seen troop movements before the battle. With hindsight, we had seen more troop movements than we usually did, but we knew little about armies and battles. What we had seen were troops moving up to the area. I don't know whether they had planned a battle at exactly that place, but they must have known it would be that area – and so at odd moments for the previous week, someone would appear in the village announcing another troop. They didn't bother with small groups, just told us about the larger ones. People embellish stories – so they don't just tell of a troop of soldiers, they talk of banners fluttering in a breeze, muskets pointed bravely, bugles sounded, bright uniform colours. I have to say that whenever we saw soldiers in the village, the bright colours were some sort of brown or black – perhaps with a coloured sash. Whenever anyone said they had seen soldiers, it was reds and blues and all colours! I began to wonder if I couldn't see colours!

Some of the children went down to the road. They took one of the old men with them. We weren't going to let one of our girls go and sit by the roadside with the children with all of those soldiers going past! The children took a little food and apparently sat on one of the banks and played whilst they waited. They went down two days before the battle and waved at anyone who went past. I think they thought it was some sort of parade. They went for the afternoon, but being children came back with completely different stories of what they had seen. I think I didn't appear interested when they told me – because the image in my mind was of those bright young things happily waving at all those men going to die. Did the men think happily of victory and marching back down that road later – or did they think (like some I talked to later) that they had no idea what it was all about?

Robert Grey came home, for the first time in the war. He was wounded, and the news that he brought to us stunned us. What he said was to have a far-reaching effect on our lives, and he would shatter any threads of loyalty that remained between certain members of our group, myself included. "My father is dead," he said, without any preamble, when we saw him. I was with Stephanie (home for the day), and Harriet and Olivia were gathered together in the reception room of the Grey house. I had known something was wrong when we arrived, because Olivia had the red around her eyes from weeping, and didn't really look at us with the steady gaze that we were used to seeing from those blue eyes. Robert had arrived the day before, and it was Olivia's note to me asking to see us all which had sent me scurrying around to fetch them. It was coincidence that Stephanie was back on that day, and we had happily walked the distance to the estate, anticipating a warm and friendly reunion.

Instead, we were greeted by a clearly upset Olivia and shown into the room where Robert, bandaged and uncomfortable, was perched on a chair, a stick that he had been using leaning nearby against a table. "I have had to make the arrangements to have my father's body returned. He will be in our family vault in Towcester, and as you can see, I am having to take a little time myself away from my duties until this leg…" he gestured "…has healed, and I can return to take charge of my father's regiment. In the meantime, I find myself as the new Lord Grey, and I would very much rather that this were not the case. I am afraid, though, that this is not the only bad news I have, and what else I have to say will affect you all." I put my hand to my mouth. He would only say this, in this manner, if he was intending to announce other deaths, and for a minute I was terrified for myself and my family that he was going to say that Edward was dead. Only for a moment, though.

"Mark Green killed my father!" said Robert. Stephanie gasped, and slowly sank into a chair that was next to her. "I was wounded near the end of the battle, and Father came to see that I was alive and how badly I was wounded. The battle was nearly done, and we were both alive. We expected to be taken as prisoners, and to have to pay a ransom. It was possible, too, that we would be released after some sort of barter, but at least we were both alive, and we were both together. Father knelt beside me. We talked for a minute about how we were, and of people we had known and how they had fared. Then we saw Mark Green and his troop coming towards us. 'I will talk to him about our surrender,' said my father, and stood up. 'Mark Green,' he said, 'please—' and then Mark shot him through the head. Father was going to negotiate our surrender with him, and Mark shot him down like a dog, before he had a chance to say it. Father wasn't even armed! Mark just left him lying there beside me and walked away from us with his men. It was all over so quickly that I was stunned into silence."

Harriet sat down, ashen-faced, and Olivia knelt beside her. "Harriet – you will still be my friend?" she asked.

Harriet nodded but then said, "How can you still want me as a friend, after what you have heard?"

"You are not your brother," said Olivia. "You have constantly been at my side for the last three years, and you have never expressed any hatred or resentment to us."

"Olivia is right," said Robert. "In all of her letters, she has mentioned how supportive you have been, and how well you have demonstrated your love and your friendship for her and our family. You will always be welcome in our house!"

Harriet smiled at her. I knelt beside Stephanie – who looked horrified. I would not ask her in front of the others about her feelings for Mark – because I didn't know if they knew. I didn't know any longer – as far as I knew, Mark had not contacted her since he had left for the war, and now he had broken our friendships in half by his actions. I could see that Mark would not even give Lord Grey the chance to speak to him because of his jealousy and hatred, but to shoot him down like that was unforgivable.

Stephanie would know that none of us could forgive Mark after this, and that if she were to retain feelings for him, it might separate her from us all. She held my hand tightly, though, as Robert spoke again. "I was treated by a Roundhead doctor, and I had to deal with their leaders about what to do with my father's body. That was the only semblance of respect and decency I received. They accepted that we would want to bury Father at home – because of his rank – and not just to leave him lying there on the battlefield with the rest of the army. They treated my wounds and arranged transport for me and Father. It was an awful trip. Every mile jolted my leg badly, and we had to make frequent stops. It was very lucky that Naseby is so close. If it had happened in Yorkshire, Father would have had to be buried in a church there. We are lucky in another way. They were heading south-west when I left. Otherwise, they might have been billeted here or nearby, and I would be their prisoner. As it is, I hope to rest here for a bit and then rejoin my troops."

"Mark has become a mad, reckless fool," said Olivia, and I felt Stephanie's hand tense on mine.

"I cannot hate my brother," said Harriet, "but I cannot bear to see him either at this moment."

"Mark is failing due to his recklessness," said Robert. "Even within our ranks we have heard that his judgement is flawed, and that he is mistrusted by many on both sides. There will be a reckoning at some point – whoever wins the war – and Mark will not come out of it well."

We got up and took our leave at this point. Robert was clearly tired and in pain, and nothing was to be gained by staying at the estate and talking to him further. Stephanie separated from the two of us when we got back to the village, saying that she needed to return to Blakesley, but also, possibly, to stop me questioning her about how she felt. After the battles of Naseby and Langport, King Charles' army was effectively spent. Although he kept trying to build up a power base, his resources were exhausted and destroyed this intent. In May of 1646, he surrendered to the Scots, and later they handed him to Parliament.

Some soldiers, like Robert, returned to their home in these two years. Some were whole, some wounded, some without limbs, many lay dead. Whilst the war was not completely over, nothing was done in any organised way about clearing up the corpses on the battlefields. The dead were not buried in churchyards, and often their bodies were just moved into vast pits, or sometimes just ploughed into the ground to rot. Harriet went to visit friends near Northampton. They had a small estate, not far from the town, and although not too far away, it had been difficult for Harriet to make the trip to see them and stay for a while. She went there in the late summer of 1646, and whilst she was visiting her friends, known to be Royalists, the Parliamentary army arrived in the area, and Harriet – along with her friends – was placed under house arrest, and they were all told that they would not be allowed to leave until further notice. Harriet's friends were accused of treacherous activities, which included arranging passage for Royalist soldiers and the illegal detention of Parliamentarian officers. No one appeared to believe that this was true – perhaps even including those making the accusations – and it would seem that this was an excuse for the estate to be seized and confiscated.

Harriet and her friends were prevented from writing letters which might be intercepted, but servants on the estate were allowed to continue to buy food from the local village, and in this way, Harriet managed to smuggle out two letters – one to me at the village, which I then shared with her mother and Olivia, and the other letter was to Luke White, who she was in the habit of writing to. She told Luke where she was, why, and that her friend's family were threatened with treason, possible detention and even execution, and that no one believed that she had arrived only recently, and only by chance, for a social visit. We were unable to write back to her as she indicated that letters might be accepted, so we could only wait and see if she would be allowed free to travel home. We waited a month, and one evening Harriet reappeared in the village as a passenger in a cart with her belongings, escorted by two soldiers. The soldiers appeared to consider the escort duty as a bit of a chore, and although they accepted food and a place to sleep, they left early the following day. Harriet then told us her story.

She had written letters merely as a method of communication, not expecting them to produce any results, and she had been very surprised when one of her letters had had exactly the effect that she wanted. Two weeks after her letter to Luke, he had appeared at the front door of the big house with a troop of twenty men. Although Luke had now changed sides to the Royalist army before this, he and his men were wearing the sashes of the Parliamentarians. They were also all armed with muskets. Luke had entered the house and demanded to see the commanding officer of the troop. The somewhat startled guards took Luke at his apparent appearance as one of their officers, and had led him to the commander. "You have landed yourself in a lot of trouble!" said Luke to the commander. "And I am here for one reason only, which is to see if we can extricate you from this trouble without you losing your honour, reputation and perhaps your life!" This sentence was quite effective in stunning the commander, who was aware of nothing that he had done that would warrant such a statement from a strange officer. Luke unslung his musket and commenced to pour powder down the barrel. Whilst the musket was not actually pointed at the local commander, the act of priming it for fire was extremely intimidating.

"What have I done, why are you here, what is the matter?" burbled the commander, who, despite his troops, was starting to feel extremely alarmed.

"Have you heard of Sir Mark Green?" asked Luke.

"Yes, I know of him," said the commander. "A very dangerous man! Not to be trifled with!"

Luke was glad to hear this. He was using Mark's name as a weapon, and to find out that Mark's reputation was widely known was useful. "You will know then of what happens to people that upset Sir Mark?" Luke asked.

"Er, yes!" replied the commander. Luke then rammed a musket ball down the barrel of the musket, picked up the weapon, and levelled it at the commander. "Tell me why, then, you have kept Sir Mark's sister prisoner in this house," said Luke, with the feeling he supposed others had when they delivered a death sentence. "Furthermore, the owners of the house are, although Royalists, acquaintances of Sir Mark, and he is kindly disposed to them! Would you like me, then, to tell you what Sir Mark said, when he heard of your treatment of his sister and of your apparent attempt to steal the estate of his friends?" With that, he pulled back the catch on the firing mechanism of the gun.

According to Harriet, there was immediate panic throughout the house. When the commander had recovered from the shock of Luke's statement, he and his troops were given one hour to leave the estate by Luke, or after that (Luke said), they could not be guaranteed to leave alive.

The family whose house this was came out into the main courtyard to see their captors in a complete state of fear, loading up a waggon with belongings and saddling horses as they prepared for their long trip to Portsmouth – which was where Luke told them they were now required to go to. Once they had all left, Luke suggested the family went on a short holiday for a month or so to friends', so that if there were any repercussions for his actions, the other troop would not come back and find them there. Luke said that for the moment their lives were more important than their possessions. He also told a jubilant Harriet that she should go home the following day, with two of his soldiers as escort. Luke's men (those of his troop) had agreed to masquerade as Roundheads for the dangerous task of helping Luke to rescue 'the girl he loved, and his childhood sweetheart'. Harriet was delighted to see him, and completely overwhelmed to see this evidence of his affection.

Luke explained that he and the troop had to return before anyone complained of their absence – and possibly accused them of desertion. He made it clear to Harriet that Mark had no knowledge of this action and although he might find it mildly amusing, he might also be angry that Luke – a turncoat – had scored over his men in this subterfuge. Luke and his men left, too, the following morning – in the opposite direction to Harriet. In the climate of that time, Luke and his men were being kept as a holding force whilst they waited for further directions. Some soldiers, like Mark, were not welcome at home, and positively relished the chance of still further action. They waited to see what England would do next. My brother, Edward, now a captain, was also retained at his post, and he and his soldiers also still waited for the enemy's tread. Many found no rest, even at home. They put their pikes onto piles and tried to resume some sort of normal life, but too many things had changed for too many people. The country remained divided into areas that supported the King or supported Parliament, and an uneven, uneasy sort of waiting game was played across the country.

Near Helmdon, Robert Grey remained at the family estate. We continued to make sure that the village operated as it had done for the last three years – as many of our menfolk had not returned. Some were dead, some remained at post – like Edward – and some had simply disappeared. Soldiers who had been captured were often retained to rebuild fortifications or repair houses as a sort of unpaid workforce. Even if the war was regarded as officially over, we were not to be informed as to where the men had gone. Stephanie continued to nurse men who were unable to return home, Olivia and Harriet continued to run the Grey estates until Robert could be seen as fit, and the Reverend White still pottered about his duties. Every so often, I would receive a letter from Edward, and my father would ask me about it. Still we heard nothing from Luke White.

King Charles escaped. He came to an arrangement with the Scots. If they invaded, he could fight Parliament on two fronts. Charles found new support and new resources. It felt as if it was time for us all to resume a war that had just been paused for most of two years. Some of the men who had returned home had to decide whether their loyalty commanded them to return to the army. Many did not. My brother, Edward, had risen in rank, whilst others had returned home, and he was now a commander. Edward had come to the notice of Cromwell, and as he had done under Mark Green's tutelage, Edward learnt quickly. Under Mark, he had learnt about handling a troop and the art of command. Now, under Cromwell, he learnt the art of winning battles and campaigns. Once again, he showed aptitude. Mark languished. Still in charge of a troop, he showed no signs of rising in importance. He came nowhere near us, and we received no letters from him.

Robert Grey had returned to the army. He had taken over his father's soldiers as the new Lord Grey, and once again pledged them to the service of the King. Ironically, he was only able to do this as the Parliamentary army had let him come home to recover after his father's death. Olivia and Harriet had continued to run the Grey estates even with Robert at home – as they did not know what would happen to him. With Harriet's shock at her brother's murder of Lord Grey, she was even more of a staunch monarchist. The rest of us continued the duties and responsibilities that we had assumed in the first half of the war, and life in the village seemed to take the same path as it had before. Once again, our village refrained from obviously taking sides, and prepared again to assist those seeking assistance of refuge from us. Stephanie returned to nursing. We did not ask her what she felt about Mark; we just welcomed her on the occasions that she was able to visit us.

Then in January of 1648, Stephanie's story took a new turn. Returning late from a visit to the Grey estate, where I had been for a full day, I found a body lying on the ground, in a lane near the centre of the village. Snow had fallen during the day, temperatures were lowering, and it was clearly going to freeze overnight. I saw that there were marks in the snow to show that the body had been moved, but I was not sure if that was down to the body having moved there itself or if it had been dragged or deposited there by someone else – the marks were not clear enough. I was not even sure at first whether the body was alive or dead – but when I touched it, there was a small shudder and I realised that this was a live person lying there. I quickly called for help, and had the prone figure that I had found carried to our house and taken upstairs to my room.

I wiped the bloody face, and two things became obvious – firstly, that this was a woman, and as the features of her face became clearer, I realised that this was my friend Stephanie. Her body was bruised and bloody, and she had sustained several injuries – I was unclear at first what the nature of these injuries were, but there were marks of ropes, some cuts, and blood from several places on her body. I washed her, bandaged her, and over the next few days attended to her until she returned to consciousness. I fed her when I could and when she wanted to eat, and waited for the moment when she was able to tell me what had happened to her, and also when she actually wanted to do this. As she recovered, she showed no recognition at first, but later smiled at me, and then she tried to speak. Her voice was hoarse and rasping – and I didn't recognise Stephanie's usual voice.

This is Stephanie's story. She had returned to the village early on the morning of the day I found her. She had visited my house but had not found me – so instead she had headed for the Green house in the hope of finding Harriet. She saw a light and assumed that Harriet or her mother was in, so she had knocked on the door. As it happened, Harriet and her mother were both at the Grey estate, and as Harriet's mother was not very well, I had gone there too, to try and help. When Stephanie knocked on the door, therefore, it was answered and opened by Mark – who seemed to have made a surprise visit to the village. It seemed to take a few seconds for Mark to recognise Stephanie, and when he did, he asked her to come in. In the hall, there were two of his troop on guard, and Mark had clearly arranged food for himself in the dining room. She couldn't tell if Mark was staying there or if he was intending to leave shortly.

"Stephanie, yes," said Mark. "You have been working as a nurse, at Blakesley, I believe?" he continued, in what seemed to be a pleasant enough manner.

"That is right," said Stephanie.

"Blakesley is a Royalist stronghold, is it not?" asked Mark.

"No, not really," said Stephanie, "but, anyway, I have only been working there as a nurse."

"And living there, too?" asked Mark again.

"Yes, I have been living in the nurses' quarters," she said.

"So, it might be presumed that you might have overheard discussions about what the Royalist army could be expected to do next?" continued Mark, in something of a more challenging manner.

"No, I don't think so," said Stephanie.

"You see," said Mark, "I am in a bit of a backwater at the moment, Stephanie. I have not managed to attract the attention of important men like Cromwell, and what would be REALLY useful to me now would be to find out something about the moves of the Royalists forces as they regroup, and be able to show my leaders how useful I am.

"In fact…" continued Mark further, in what appeared to be a bit of a rambling chain of thought, "if I was able to find out what the King and his officers were going to do next, I would be seen in a really good light, and this would help me to rise higher up the command or possibly interfere with their plans."

Stephanie said that at this point she had started to be really afraid of the man that she had once thought herself in love with. Mark was unkempt in his appearance, his gaze was intense, and he was moving closer to her each time he spoke. She said that she tried to tell him that she had no knowledge of any of the Royalists' intentions, but he told her that she was lying to him. She tried to back out of the room and managed to reach the hall, but Mark instructed his two soldiers to hold her. They took her into the dining room and, on Mark's instructions, tied her to a chair, very tightly, so that she could not move. He instructed the guards to wait outside the door, and he sat down. Stephanie faced Mark across the dining table, and whilst she was tied there, he finished his supper.

Then he stood up, came over to where she was tied up, and started to ask her questions about the movements of the Royalists. Stephanie swore to him (and again to me later) that she had no knowledge about Royalist troop movements or their leadership, and he hit her around the face. He was wearing heavy gloves which had metal buckles on, and the metal cut her as well as the gloves bruising her. He choked her, too, which was why her voice was now so hoarse. This was all repeated, over and over. Stephanie knew that the guards could hear, but they remained outside the room. She started to realise that the interrogation was not just about Mark obtaining information, but it was also about him assuming control, and that he obtained a brutal satisfaction in causing her pain. He hit her wherever he was minded to, and, as a result, she received wounds all over her upper body. This procedure went on for what seemed to Stephanie a very long time. At length, she fainted. Mark threw a glass of water in her face to revive her, and then started to question her over again. This happened three or four times, and when she was eventually unable to raise her head to look at or speak to him, he stopped.

She assumed that the ordeal was over, especially when Mark cut the ropes with a knife – but then he carried her to the table, laid her on it and raped her. In Stephanie's injured state, and as someone who had never had a man before, he hurt her considerably, and seemed to take a tremendous amount of pleasure from her pain. Eventually, he stopped, buttoned up his clothing, opened the door, and called his men in. He told them to take her away from the house and to dump her somewhere in the village, "like a piece of dead meat," said Stephanie to me. She supposed she should be grateful that they could not be bothered to take her outside the village – where she might not have been found and might have frozen to death.

She was also grateful on reflection that Mark's men had not followed his example and raped her as well. She knew from her nursing that this had happened to some others. As it was, they took her a hundred yards or so and dumped her in a dark corner. Later, she had crawled to where I had found her – unable to move further.

I was appalled by Stephanie's story. I could not at first believe that someone who had once been a friend would resort to this sort of behaviour, but then I remembered Mark's murder of Lord Grey – and although it was in the heat of war, it was still a murder. I went to see if there was any sign of Mark at the Green house. I didn't intend to go in, just peer at the front, and if he had been there, perhaps I would have run and told others in the village. The house, though, was in darkness, and I was sure that Mark and his men had already gone. He had obviously moved on with his insane quest to try and obtain recognition or impress his leaders, taking with him men who would let him do as he wished to innocents or victims. Mark had descended into some new sort of violent madness. Perhaps he had always been destined for this sort of behaviour, and the war had just given him the excuse for the sort of behaviour that he had wanted to do.

"I used to love a man called Mark," said Stephanie, a few days later. "I hoped that he loved me at least a little, although he did not show this. He went away without leaving me news or writing me letters, and I tried to find out where he was." She summed up. "The war went badly for this man, and his actions became scorned by his superiors, due to his own disregard for human life. He came back angry, ignored my help for those who were wounded or injured, and focused on me as an agent of his enemies. He damaged my body, and destroyed my love for him. He had no answers that he liked and his men slung me out, like meat, to freeze and die in the snow. I hate him now, and I will find some way to avenge his actions and hurt him as he hurt me. Until I do this, I cannot move on."

She did not return to Blakesley. For a while, she was unable to move, and when she had recovered enough to move further than the house, she would sit around. She knitted, she whittled wood with a knife (the first time I had seen a woman do this), and unusually she questioned some of the injured menfolk in the village about their soldiering.

She was pleasant enough to me, but all of her delight and pleasure in life had left her. She observed and conversed but showed no emotions, and it was obvious that she was waiting for some chance, some opportunity. I assumed that Mark would not return to the village, and secretly welcomed this. If Stephanie had an opportunity to do what she had threatened to him, no one would see it as an act of war, because she was a woman, and she would be tried as a criminal.

I came back early evening about a month later. The house was very dimly lit by candle, and the shadows flickered on the ceilings. I called her name – and there was no answer. Then I saw a movement in the corner, and what stepped forward from the shadows appeared to be the thin figure of a man. "Who are you, and where is my friend?" I challenged the figure – picking up a saucepan from the kitchen range against the possibility of having to defend myself. Was it Mark, perhaps?

"Lucy, it is me," said a low voice that I did not clearly recognise – although in some way it was familiar.

"Who are you?" I asked, betraying my nervousness in the tremble of my voice. "Stephanie," the voice replied.

She had dressed herself in men's clothing, and bandaged her chest so that she looked less like a woman – and in a way, too, it made her chest look more muscular and more masculine. Her voice still rasped – partly due to the treatment she had received. She had cut her hair short – deliberately cut it badly, I thought. She had a knife in her belt, and from somewhere she had obtained a pistol. "What is this all for? You frightened me," I said, sitting down at the table.

"I had news of Mark today," she replied. "I am going after him. Now I know where he is going, I intend to get my revenge on him! It may not happen soon, but I will follow him until I do this." I told her that this was madness, that she should stay a few more days, and that the intent would leave her, but instead, she took a man's coat from beside her, a flask of water and a few basic food rations, and moved towards the door. She kissed me on the cheek, and my friend Stephanie was gone.

I watched her figure walk off down the lane in the dusk from my window. Stephanie no longer walked obviously like a woman, and if I had not recognised her as my friend across the room, then I thought there was a good chance she could pass as a man in public, as the soldier she intended to be seen as. I knew, though, deep within me, that one of the two of them – Mark or Stephanie – would not return to the village, possibly neither of them. Perhaps I was seeing Stephanie for the last time, and perhaps I had seen Mark for the last time several years ago. If physical appearance was determined in a person by the feelings within them, then I had seen them both as normal people for the last time a while ago. Perhaps none of my friends was still the same. Perhaps I was not still the same.

ELEVEN

DESERTION

Three of us had gone to Towcester market with old John Arkle in his cart. There were some things that we could not forge ourselves very well, and they were easier to buy at the market than to try and make (buckles on harnesses, for example), and a few supplies where we had not grown quite as many vegetables as we wanted, and we would see if we could pick up a few, and perhaps a bit more plain cotton sheet for bedding. We didn't like to go to the market too often, so we tended to save things up if we could until there were several things to go and get. There were a lot of folk around that particular market day, and we had to leave John and the cart some distance away from the market and then rely on being able to carry the goods back to him when we had got them. John was happy where we left him. He had spotted a couple of old mates he knew from before the war and was happy to have the excuse to spend time catching up with them.

When we got to the market, the whole area was jammed with people. A lot of them had come in for the market – but the market had been squeezed into a smaller space to make way for a frame at the other end. The frame was mounted on a low platform – about a foot off the ground. The frame rose 8 feet or so above that and had a crossbeam about 10 foot long and eight metal hooks on the underside of the beam secured by metal clamps. There were various braces which made the whole thing sturdy, and unlikely to topple over. Two gaolers guarded the frame and kept folk from getting too close. I knew immediately what the frame was, and it accounted for the market being so busy. Whilst a lot of people had proper business in Towcester buying and selling goods at the market, some had come there just to watch the hangings of convicted criminals on the frame that I have described. It had been designed and adapted to make executions easy, and visible.

I couldn't understand why people did this. The hanging of folk was meant to send a message to others not to do the same thing – but it seemed to me that just coming into town to watch a hanging or execution showed off the bad side of the watchers – and not the criminals. Some people even brought their children and made a day out of it, sitting near the stalls with food and drink. Imagine being hung, and the last thing you see before the bag goes on your head is a group of children eating their lunch! Children who were too young to understand and should not have seen that sort of thing were told that if they behaved badly, or did not do what they were told, "You will end up the same way." Punishments like this depended on which court heard them, or which magistrate made the decision, or how much pressure was exerted, or even just how rich and powerful the person making the complaint, or the victim, was. That means that the children should be told, "If you are poor and upset a rich person, you could end up like that."

Justice in the area was not really 'just', and human life was not valued as much as property – so the punishments meted out for those who offended the rich and powerful were always heavier. Often, punishment depended on who could buy the most witnesses, or even, sometimes, on whether it was easier to have the guilty person hung or get them to join the army or send them off to work for the complainant. Some were even sent abroad to the colonies. Punishments were often very heavy, and often for what seemed to me very small crimes. I realised that we had made an unfortunate choice in our day to visit, and wished that we had come on a week where the court was not sitting – but it was too late now. It would take us an hour or two to get home; we would have to come back again another time, and anyway, it was just for my sensibilities.

Accordingly, I went about my business in the stalls. We split up. Our temporary blacksmith went to look for the buckles, I looked for the vegetables, and our third member – Martha – went to look for the fabric. We split our few coins three ways, made arrangements where and when to meet, and went in the directions that we needed for our purchases. Vegetable sellers tended to group together, so I went to look at the range each had on offer and made discreet comparisons. Martha knew some of the cotton sellers – what is that word – haberdashers, is that right? – so she was best doing this. It took longer than I thought – I couldn't really find what I wanted from one seller, so either had to split my buying – which usually means you pay more – or settle for not quite what I wanted. I did what I thought was best – but by the time I got back to the others, I became aware that the condemned men were being brought out. The crowd had thickened and we couldn't really move. I found my way by the groups of the crowd. I remembered that there was a large group of people on a large waggon with an old grey mare – and once I found them, it was easy to find Martha and the blacksmith.

There were eight figures in a line roped together between the gaolers, and I was determined not to watch them all being hung. I knew what would happen as I had seen a hanging before – when I had not realised how bad it was. Unlike on the prison scaffolds with trapdoors, the victims in the town would stand on the platform, have the noose placed around their neck and literally be hauled off the ground to dangle kicking and struggling until they died. They could not do much with their hands tied together, and sometimes a whole set of men were hung at the same time, all roped together. It took longer than the trapdoor for them to die, because the trapdoor just snapped their neck when they fell. Sometimes, it seemed that the low platforms were deliberately designed to make the spectacle last longer, but it was probably the cost in designing a trapdoor that worked properly. I turned my back on the framework and concentrated on looking at the spectators.

There were (as I said) eight men to die, and their crimes and names were read out to the audience at the start. One had murdered a woman – and I suppose that if there has to be hanging as a punishment, hanging for murder is probably the most justifiable. One man had killed his lord's steward in a dispute about money he owed. Three were thieves – and I wasn't sure, but I guessed that they had probably committed several thefts for them to be hung rather than jailed or some other punishment. The final three were deserters from the army. I knew very little about deserters. The popular image was that they had run away from the battlefield, leaving their comrades in danger, and the deserters had taken the money that they were paid as soldiers – it was implied in the statement read out that their crime was therefore theft, too.

Most of the men said nothing as they mounted the frame. Two shouted that they were innocent – one of the thieves and the man who had killed his lord's steward – but most of the group seemed to accept their fate and went to their deaths with no word – just those awful sounds that are involuntary. As each man was hauled off the ground, there would be an awful cheer from the crowd that rose in volume until the man stopped struggling, and then the cheer would die away. It was awful to listen to, but it helped me to judge the progress of the event so that I didn't have to look. The last of the eight was different. The crowd seemed unhappier – and there were even a few noises of disapproval. Wondering why this was, I turned to see what was going on. Seven hooded bodies swayed slightly on the frame, and the eighth victim was being led to the frame.

The eighth person was smaller and slighter than the others in build, and a voice near me said, "Why, he's just a lad!" and indeed he was. There was some distance between me and the frame so I couldn't really distinguish his features, but I could see that he was much smaller than the gaolers, and I could swear that he was only about fourteen or fifteen years old. I heard the conversation near me continue. "What's he up for?"

"Desertion!"

"Desertion? Him? He don't look old enough to be a soldier!"

"Well, that's what I heard them say it was! He ran away from a battle, and that makes him a deserter!"

The crowd then quietened down a bit, and from the front I heard the

147

lad's voice. "No, sir! Please, sir! I won't do it again! I'll be good! Please! Give me another chance, sir?" I didn't think that his voice had even dropped properly as he cracked some of the words he spoke.

The lad continued to plead as he was led to the frame. I couldn't believe this. Surely a mere child could not be hung for desertion from the army in this way? Even if he had taken the soldier's shilling? The gaolers did not look happy, but they were going to do their job. The lad's voice grew higher in pitch as they put the bag over his head, and he let out a despairing wail as the noose was tightened around his neck. The wail was cut off sharply as he was hauled off his feet, and then there were gasping noises as he tried to take in air. His feet kicked and he moved in small circles with his arms jerking feverishly. It went on for ages. He was half the weight of the others, and the noose – although it was gradually strangling him – was doing it much slower than the other men. The noises continued from him, and then a tall fellow stepped forward from the crowd and hauled on the boy's feet. We heard the crack as his neck snapped, and all movement and sound stopped.

"See what happens to bad boys!" said a man's voice to his children in a nearby family.

"Shut the fuck up, you stupid bastard!" said his neighbour, and put his hand on the other man's necktie – shaking him. "You ain't fit to be a father!" he said, and then walked off, leaving the first man to slump to the ground, where his children surrounded him trying to help him up. The crowd melted away. Most of them realised that their happy spectacle had been ruined, and now they just wanted to get away and do something else so that they could wipe the hangings from their memories. As an example of justice, this had been a complete failure, and as a public execution, it showed more failure on the part of the law than the criminals. I swore to myself that if I was ever responsible enough to have to deal with a lad who had committed a crime, I would rather he escaped punishment altogether than go to that fate. I found that I could not walk steadily as we returned to the cart, and Martha had to hold me with her arm. I cried as we went – and she gently hushed me.

Of course, we had deserters during the war. We had them sometimes in the village, although often they would not say who they were, where they had been and what they had done. Male travellers on their own were not common. Usually, folk arrived as a pair or in a small group, so a man alone of the right age for the army could be heading to 'join up' or perhaps had leave of absence. Those that arrived alone, continually looking around to see if they were followed, and suspicious of authority, were clearly on the run from something or someone. The best thing we could do was to feed them, leave them alone, not ask them questions, and send them on their way when they were able. We didn't really think that it was our job to turn them in. If they had left one of our lads to die in a battle, that would be awful, but we didn't want to turn them in just on suspicion of something we weren't sure about. Most would disappear quite quickly – before we could send them on their way. There was something about sleeping in a village that made them think that the soldiers or authorities were just around the corner waiting for them – and when we saw them scurrying off down the lane, we wondered if they would ever find peace in themselves.

We had our own lad, though. Out of the twenty or so – perhaps one hundred people that we had our suspicions about in the war, there was one of ours who came back to us, and from whom we found out his true story. Most of the village did not know he was back, and those that did weren't really sure what had happened to him. Everyone who did hear his tale changed their views in some way, and although we had to be careful at first, support for this lad gradually grew to the extent that no one in our village would give him up for a hanging. Jack Joiner belonged to a family that had been in the village for hundreds of years. We knew that from the records. In most people's eyes, the Joiners were a good family – who tried to work hard and to do the best for their family or others, and although they were not always lucky, and were sometimes down at heel or destitute, they often found folk would try to help them with work and food as payment – because they were usually decent folk. They moved around a bit, because they couldn't always pay rent – but they stayed in the village.

Jack had signed up for the Royalist army shortly after the start of the war. He was not old enough, or old enough-looking, though, to be taken into the ranks of Lord Grey or Sir Henry. Even if he had tried to go with them, they would not have taken him as his family probably needed him for a few more years, and they knew that. Neither Lord Grey nor Sir Henry was cruel or ignorant enough to take all of the young men in one family. They took his father, though, and Jack accepted that he was needed at home for a bit longer. Ironically, it was our success as a village in organising resources and people that in the end enabled Jack, and two of his pals, to go, and they disappeared one night with a few stores from our hoards. They took enough food to get them to Northampton to sign up, and for at least a year after that they were frightened that we would charge them for the few veg, bit of bread and hunk of cheese that they took – and remove them from the army as criminals – so they didn't tell us where they were and what they were doing. If they had done, it might have been better for them.

They signed up into a regiment of foot that had several months of training before they were due to take part in any fighting. These few months were long enough for the older men in the regiment to teach our three lads how to steal properly from town or village people, or even soldiers from other regiments. It was drilled into our lads that they must not thieve from their own regiment – and although they gradually lost the few belongings they had, it was explained that this must have been raids from other troops for which they should take revenge the same way. The lads were unofficially adopted by the older men, although Billy – one of the other two, and the most handsome of the three – didn't seem so keen on this adoption, which required him to sleep in the same bed as two of the men. Billy didn't talk much about the sleeping arrangements, or whatever it was that kept bruising his face. It was explained to the officer that Billy fought a lot with the other lads – so that was why he had the bruising. Jack and Pete fought more, and had fought more as children anyway, so bruising was normal to them, and the fighting as children had made them less handsome than Billy.

Billy didn't stay very long. He just upped and left one night whilst the regiment was still training, and both Jack and Peter, the other two boys who stayed, accepted the story that he had run off one night without saying goodbye. It was considered thoughtful, too, that he had kindly left behind for them a few things to help them carry on as soldiers. Jack thought it was a bit strange that Billy had left his boots for them as well as other things, like his knife and his bag. The older soldiers said that Billy must have switched to some shoes so that he looked less like a soldier, and he had apparently left his belt, too, because he didn't really need it. Jack started to feel that this story might not have been completely true when he got a bit older, but by then some of the people who had told him that story were dead or had bits of limbs missing, so it didn't really matter any more. Also, how do you go about finding another lad in a war when you haven't heard from him for several months? In any case, things really started to change after the regiment moved. All of the skills of thieving and bartering they had learnt really became useful when depriving villagers of the things 'their' soldiers needed.

Wasn't it wonderful, too, when they were able to creep into another camp and steal lots of really useful things! They were treated as heroes by their 'friends', especially when they returned with that whole piglet, and the whole platoon ate pork for the first time in weeks. Strangely, it didn't seem to matter whether the other camp was on their side or the enemy's – except when Lord Maltraver's silver watch went missing, but it was found in a village shop, so that was all right! By the time that Jack and Peter – or Pete as he started to want to be called – fought in their first battle, a lot of the skills they needed had been honed into them. Crawling, not being seen, appearing from a different direction, keeping low (well, they were small anyway), keeping important things dry, dressing warmly (possible by stealing clothes), buying food with stolen money or stealing food made them excellent soldiers and impressed those 'friends' of theirs. Both boys celebrated their fifteenth birthdays within days of each other on battlefields. Their closeness in age had always been of interest to them.

Interestingly, though, it actually turned out that the other fatter, bigger, slower, older soldiers that had 'adopted' them were not quite as good at dodging the musket balls, or the sword slashes, and those 'friends' started to get fewer in number – as did the number of them that had all their limbs. Jack and Pete became able to decide for themselves at first sight if a wound was fatal, enough for discharge from the army or just a light wound. They also found out that a soldier who lost an arm might not be worried about the rings or bracelet left on it. There was always a market for boots, and there was always a bit of time after a battle to look for a few souvenirs. Always go for the officers first! No one told them where they were going, no one told them – until the actual day when they were fighting – and no one said who they were fighting. They simply got down to the business of not being fired on by keeping down, until they could get to the main business of looting. Jack even saw a few soldiers who were very badly injured and near death – who were 'helped on their way' by older men. Jack couldn't really do that – he felt it wasn't quite right.

No one, unfortunately (young or old), could avoid cannon fire. Although you could often hear cannonballs coming, if you took any time to work out where from, it was too late. Because they never knew where they were fighting, Jack was unable to say which battle it was that almost wiped out their troop, just that the cannon fire had been much more accurate than before, or they had just been unlucky. Dazed, Jack sat up after the barrage, left the ditch he had lain down in, and went to find Pete. Pete was dazed too. Jack could tell that as Pete looked at him. Pete was still alive, and Jack was really glad about that. He grasped Pete's hand to pull him up, and it was only then that he realised there was only half of Pete left. Everything beneath Pete's waist had disappeared, and although Jack looked around, he could not see anything that looked like the bottom half of Pete. Much later, he thought that even if there had been, he could not have put Pete back together. Pete kept gasping for a bit, but he wasn't going anywhere, and eventually he stopped gasping. Jack went through his bag – found a few bits and pieces – and then left to find the rest of the lads.

Jack kept on fighting for a few more months after that. He had got to the stage where he had suppressed his feelings almost completely. Death and mutilation had little or no effect on him. Money and property – especially other people's property – was, though, very important. It was the difference between cold or warm, hungry or full, dry or wet, popular or unpopular, and Jack carried on a one-person campaign of battlefield theft.

It was logical that with such a complete suppression of feelings, when something did penetrate this wall, it was possibly going to destroy Jack completely. When this did happen, it was, unsurprisingly, on a battlefield, and the cause of Jack's complete destruction turned out to be the body of a soldier. He could see the rings on the hand of the soldier, but they wouldn't come off, so he cut the fingers off with his knife. He pulled the boots off, but then he caught sight of what looked like a bracelet chain under the body of the soldier. He pulled, and the body turned over. The first thing Jack saw was a bracelet, the second thing he saw was the wreck of the chest that was split open by a cannonball, and the third thing he saw was that the soldier had his father's face. The bracelet that he held was attached to a locket, and when he opened it with a catch on the side, the locket had a picture of his mother inside it.

For several months after that – perhaps longer – anything that had the identity or personality of Jack ceased to exist. The shock of all of the things that he had done and seen, and the witness of his father's death, had caused some part of him to shut itself off – possibly for protection. At some point, he must have pocketed the locket, checked around for other soldiers, found none, crawled into the centre of a tangle of brambles, and waited there until dark. He must have then crawled out and stolen away from the battlefield. He had his knife and a stolen pistol, and although he could not remember this (or anything really for that period), he may have used the knife and pistol to threaten others as he crossed the country. He must have robbed for food and drink, possibly slept in barns or haylofts, or in hedgerows, and gradually he retraced the routes that he and his troop had taken earlier in the war. He went near no towns, no barracks, no battlefields, talked to no one, spent as little time in one place as possible, left no trail, and survived unscathed by using all of those skills he had developed as a soldier. If this had been a school and he had been marked on these things, he would have been marked top of the class, and would have sat at the front desk. It wasn't, though, and he didn't.

One day, he was hidden in a hedgerow near a house on the edge of a village. He had been in the hedgerow for a whole day. This was a long time in one place, and it was longer than he had stayed anywhere else. Jack had no real idea of time, but he was aware that he did not feel the urgent need to move on, and he spent the first part of the day watching the comings and goings of the occupants of the house and the local villagers as they moved around the area. He ate a little of the food that he had, stayed still so that no one would see, hear or smell (in the case of dogs) his presence, and eventually the light started to fail. A candle was lit in the house. He left his hedgerow, walked towards the house, silently opened the door, and then walked in, and handed the locket to his startled mother. Then he went into the room which he had slept in as a child, and went to bed. He slept there for two days, and when he woke up, I was sitting by his bedside. He was curious rather than frightened, and he recognised me. "Hello, miss," he said. "I bin away!"

"I know, Jack," I said. Jack was then still only sixteen when I saw him.

Jack's mother had come to me the evening he had arrived. She knew (as did quite a few of the village) how inhuman I had found the hangings in Towcester, and I had, on several occasions, debated the case with others in the village. Others had the popular opinion of most, that the soldiers who took the money and left their comrades to face death on the battlefield were criminals, and should be punished as such. I had never believed that the boy I saw at his execution had deserved his dreadful fate, and I had made it my business to try and find out stories from those others who had had some dreadful experience as a soldier. I had found no one that had had a positive or enjoyable experience, but I found lots of those who had had negative experiences, and they had all developed different ways of coping with it. Some, like the boy at Towcester, had not been able to cope, and some just preferred death by hanging to the fright of the battlefield, and just wanted peace. They didn't actually say that, but they owned up to crimes that they might have concealed – or sometimes just marched into a barracks and handed themselves in when life became unbearable.

When Jack's mother came to me, she knew that she would not send her boy away. She knew that her man was now dead, and she knew that if Jack's presence became common knowledge, it would spread too far, and the authorities would find out. She had sworn Jack's sister to silence, and frightened the girl enough so that she would not talk, but she needed a place for Jack to hide, either until he could be reintroduced to the village or placed somewhere where they would not question him. She thought that if we could place him with a farm with the story that he was soon to be called up – but was a bit young and needed another year – he might be useful to them and accepted. I knew of such a place. It was far enough away so that the people would not know Jack (or of Jack) and would accept the story. We also introduced another aspect: that Jack would not speak. It meant that he could not be questioned over his story and trip himself up with contradictions, and the farm would accept this as another reason to avoid being called up.

Jack stayed at his house for another two days, just because it was easier to move him then. We agreed that one day each week, I would come and get him and take him to meet his family somewhere other than his home, and he would spend the day with them – until the time came for him to go back to the farm, which he could probably find again without my escort. This worked very well. After a while, I introduced one or two others into the secret – the vicar and my father, the two people I trusted the most. I introduced them to Jack so that he knew they were trustworthy, and for the next two to three years we took turns to deliver Jack to his family each week. There were still a few others in the village who knew – but we didn't expect them to do anything, just keep their mouths shut if they saw him. Eventually, we got to the stage where the Parliamentarians were so much in control of the country that they didn't care about the deserters any longer – especially those who had originally been Royalists. Further, the Parliamentary army eventually stopped needing new soldiers, so recruitment parties stopped being seen in our area.

Jack eventually became such a necessary part of the farm he lived in that he started to take more responsibilities. We also made a plan that he would 'learn' to start speaking – perhaps a word at a time – and so he started to 'learn' how to instruct others or take control of them. Eventually, too, Jack became so physically different to the fourteen-year-old who had left that he didn't need to worry about his appearance any longer. The farm knew him by another name anyway, and he stayed there for many years. It took him several years before he could tell me all of the things that he had done as a soldier, and even when he did, I refused to condemn or judge him, and nothing he told me changed my mind about the iniquity of hanging people and the absolute abhorrence I felt at the idea of public executions. I also felt that the army had taken our boy and shown him how to be really bad, and in the end, Jack had decided for himself that he didn't want to be bad anymore, and he had come home to us. To me, that meant he had chosen the right course in the end.

TWELVE

1648: PRESTON

The Battle of Preston was fought in August of 1648. Once again, this was a summer battle, and it was set to be the last major battle of what became known as 'The Second Civil War'. After it was over, Parliament and the King had to resort to negotiations – that neither of them wanted. What took place in them, what followed those negotiations, and the refusal of the King to negotiate according to what Parliament called proper procedure or rules of negotiation became known the world over. Whilst this was all happening, we in Helmdon began to find out what had happened to those of our former friends from the village who had been at the Battle of Preston. Preston was not quite the end of the war and our story. The end of the war (and our story) would not come for another couple of years, but Preston left its mark on some of us. Some reorganisation of the administration of England took place as a result. The Parliamentarians took over running more of the country, and one autumn evening, their troops arrived at the Grey estate in Stuchbury.

Olivia arrived back at the estate one evening from a visit to a neighbouring hall, to see that there were troops at the door of her house. The evening was closing in a bit and shadows were pointing towards the building. Olivia was aware from the soldiers' banners that they were a

Parliamentary troop, and they stopped her from entering when she tried to walk up the front steps. "Who are you, miss?" they asked her.

"I am Olivia Grey, daughter of Lord Grey. This is my family's house and how dare you stop me from entering."

The soldiers looked at each other, unsure how to deal with someone of this importance but needing to obey their instructions. "Go and tell the commander," said one soldier, who appeared senior to the others. One of the other soldiers entered the house, and there was a brief pause after he disappeared inside. Olivia was left waiting at the door with her bag, although another soldier took her horse and led it round to the stables for her.

The first soldier reappeared at the door, a little more hurriedly this time. He bowed politely. "Miss Grey, will you please follow me. Our commander will see you now. He apologises that you were stopped at the door of your own house and kept waiting by us!"

A little mollified by this apology, Olivia followed the soldier into the house. There were more guards standing inside in the hall, but they were not ransacking or looting the house, merely guarding it. The soldier led the way for Olivia down the corridor to the study. This was intended to be politeness, but it irritated Olivia that she had to follow a soldier in her own home. The study was formerly Lord Grey's study, but for the last few years it had been the centre of organisation for the estate whilst he was away, and Olivia had used it. The soldier knocked on the door of the study, and a voice called "Enter!" The soldier stepped to one side and gestured for Olivia to enter. He then politely shut the door behind her.

The room was candlelit, and at first the light did not quite reach the face of the tall figure who stood behind the desk. "Miss Grey... Olivia," said a voice that was faintly familiar to Olivia.

"Who are you?" she asked the figure.

"Do you not recognise me?" said the man, who was obviously the commander.

"Your voice is familiar, sir, but I cannot see your face," she replied.

"Forgive me," said the man, and advanced so that his face was more clearly in the light.

"Edward!" she exclaimed. "Edward Brown, but older now and with more important a manner, and clearly dressed much better than I remember. Are you now the commander here?"

"Yes," Edward replied. "I am commander of the Parliamentary troops in this area and, in fact, of the residents, too. My military rank is that of colonel, and I am responsible for garrisoning this area, so I am the commander, too. I arrived earlier today intending to ask your permission to come in, but you were not here…"

"….and your soldiers could not see you stand patiently waiting for me outside the door of a Royalist family house that you were visiting!" finished off Olivia for him.

"That is right," said Edward, a bit ashamedly, "but that is not all I needed to say. I am expected as commander to live in the most important house in the area, so that I may be seen to be in charge, and because the local people expect instructions to come from this house – so they will see it as a continuity of the normal way of things. That means that I need to ask you if I can use this house as my base."

"Does your father know that you are here?" asked Olivia.

"No," said Edward. "Not yet. They tell me that he is away for two days, so I have not seen him yet."

"That is right," remembered Olivia. "He took some corn…"

"…took some corn… to a Royalist house near Towcester," finished Edward for her. "Yes, we know, and we will not hold that against him. We know that this estate has been supplying the Royalists, and that was understandable in a Royalist house in a Royalist area, but I am afraid that supply will have to stop now that we are in charge of this area. You cannot reasonably expect us to supply troops from the other side!"

"I suppose not," said Olivia. "I suppose that I also have no choice at all in this matter?"

"No, not really," said Edward. "I am afraid you will have to have me as an 'honoured' guest in this house, but I would rather that I did not have to have you guarded and escorted everywhere. If you give me your word that you will not try to smuggle further messages to the Royalist troops or continue to supply goods to them, then I will accept your word for you and your staff."

"Then I will give that word for as long as you are here," said Olivia, "but, please, if there is to be fighting again, don't let this house or this village be the site of a battle!"

"That will not happen," said Edward. "We do not have a large force here, and if a large force were sighted, we would have to withdraw. This house is not really defendable, and I have no intention of sacrificing my men unnecessarily. Now to more pleasant matters. Would you perhaps permit me to dine with you tonight?"

"That would be a pleasure," said Olivia. She was aware that this more mature version of a girlhood friend was someone that she did want to talk to more and ask about the war.

I, too, received a note the following day from the new commander. 'Please report to the new area commander at Stuchbury Hall – former residence of Lord Grey – tomorrow, 13th of this month at eleven of the clock.' I was terrified by the note and its terseness. I had heard of new troops arriving at the hall and that they were Parliamentary troops, but I had had no more information than that. I had heard nothing from Olivia, either, so as far as I knew, this was no friendly request for a visit, and in any case, what would an area commander want with me? I was an unimportant person except for what I did for the village – in terms of messages and recording notes for the committee. Perhaps there had been a complaint. Perhaps someone had told the Roundheads that I was working for the Royalists. It couldn't just be that I had not done all of my tasks well enough – that would not concern them. Perhaps it was something about my father working for the Royalists. I had to admit that after Mark's treatment of Stephanie, I had more sympathy for the Royalists, but there was Edward, too.

I spent a sleepless night thinking about all of the things that I had done, and whether I had done them right or wrongly, or if I had said or done something that might be misconstrued. I allowed myself plenty of time to walk to the hall the following day so as not to annoy the new commander by being late to arrive. It was a pleasant day for a walk, so it was not really a chore having to go to Stuchbury, but I was still nervous as I walked through the big double gates and up the drive to the front door.

There were two soldiers there guarding the doors. They had coloured sashes that indicated they were in the Parliamentary army, and they both had big swords in belts – which frightened me more. "Yes?" said one, shortly, to me. I said that I was expected by the commander and showed him my note – which he didn't look at but just took from me. He opened the door, went inside, and I heard a murmur as he spoke to a more senior person. I got the impression that the first soldier was unable to read – so the note I had brought had meant nothing to him.

He came out and gestured me into the hall. There, inside the front door, was my brother, Edward, facing me. I didn't think about it at all, but ran to him and hugged him. This seemed to amuse the soldiers around him very much. Edward looked a lot older than I remembered. His face was thinner, and it had more lines – but he looked wonderful. He was very well dressed – better than those around him – and he looked, well, important. "Lucy," he said, "I am the new area commander here!" I put my hand up to my mouth in surprise. "I asked for someone to write to you, asking you to come here, but this note…." and he held it up to me "…has been badly written by someone who didn't realise that you are my sister, and wanted to convey importance and instruct you rather than request you to come here. I shall have words with them later!" I was very relieved at what Edward said, and relieved that I was not in trouble. He took my hand, and as we walked to what was now his study, I bombarded him with questions about how he came to be here, and about the war.

Olivia was sitting in the study on the window seat that I remembered from a previous visit. She rose as we entered, smiled at me, and explained to me that Edward and his men had 'politely' occupied the hall (smiling at him as she said this), and he was required to live here as befitted his status as the new area commander. He in turn told me that he had been picked for this area as he already knew the people and could make deductions quicker about what was needed and where things were. He had been told about the village and its committee, and he wanted to see if they could expand the way that we operated out to neighbouring villages as a better way of producing resources (food and the like) for a country that was very short of organised agriculture and industry after six years of war.

He was interested in the quarries, too. He had sent for me as a way of making initial contact with the village committee, to explain to them what he wanted, and to ask them for suggestions on how this might be done. I was very happy to accede to this request (or was it an instruction?).

I was also very impressed by this new authoritative Edward. He looked completely at home in the hall, was respected by his troops and was very much at home giving instructions to them. I saw something else, too. He and Olivia were very much at ease with each other. Edward did not act as her captor, but neither did he act as the gawky village boy in her presence. When she spoke, she often looked at him, and just as often, she smiled. They were comfortable with each other, and unless I was very much mistaken, there was a friendship there, and maybe more than that? I was happy for the moment that the situation was not awkward, and excited, too, about the possibilities that Edward had discussed with me. At length, he (and not Olivia) called for tea to be brought, and we settled down to talk about the people that we knew or had known. I also told Edward that he had a half-brother on the estate. Olivia had felt unable to mention it to him and was relieved that this had come out.

Father was still not back from his trip, and Edward found it amusing that he would return to the hall to find his son in control of the place where he worked. He also found it amusing that his father was still supplying corn to the opposing forces. When Father did come back, a few days later, Edward played a trick on him. His soldiers greeted Father in the courtyard and asked him about supplying food to the Royalist troops from a house that was the area command base of the Parliamentary army. Poor Father did not know what to say. He thought he was being accused of stealing food from the estate. He was then brought into the house for an 'interview with the new area commander', and found himself facing his son! I think that it took Father the rest of the day to stop shaking, and a while longer to forgive Edward for the trick, and Edward perhaps should have behaved better. Father had to accept that he could no longer supply the Royalists, but he felt that this meant he could not do his duty as he saw it, and as he felt Lord Grey would have wanted him to.

There would be quite a few more requests for help from groups that did not know about the change of control in the next few months. Edward found it quite amusing to send them a reply letter which said 'Edward Brown, Area Commander of Stuchbury, and Colonel in Lord Cromwell's army regrets to inform you that he is unable to agree to your request for further supplies. If you wish to appeal against this decision, please appeal in person at Stuchbury Hall.' Not surprisingly, no one arrived at the hall in person to appeal against the letter! Edward may also have talked to Father about his half-brother, but no hint of such a conversation was mentioned to me. Edward knew, of course, about Lord Grey and Sir Henry. He had also seen Mark Green more recently than most of us, and knew about Mark's murder of Lord Grey, but he did not know (and I could not bring myself to tell him or Olivia at that time – although I told him privately, later on) about Stephanie, and her treatment at Mark's hands. Harriet was in the village and I did not know if she had been told that Edward was back. I was also unable to find out at that moment what she felt about him, or his rise in position, or even to ask her about my supposition of the friendship or a possible relationship between Edward and Olivia, but I must admit, I was extremely keen to ask her.

I had imagined that Harriet's relationship with Luke would let her feel favourably towards Edward. I was keen, too, to return to the village and tell the villagers about Edward's ideas to extend our 'co-operative working' out beyond the village, to the area, as a pioneer for other areas of the country. Harriet, though, was completely occupied with another matter. Edward was not the only one who came back after Preston. Luke White had come back to Helmdon, too. Whilst Edward rode back at the head of his troops on his horse, Luke came back in the back of a cart, severely wounded, and likely to die. He was delivered to Harriet at the manor and promptly installed in a spare bedroom by the men that Harriet directed to carry him upstairs. Luke was another example of the injured men from a battle who are not properly treated afterwards by a doctor, or just bandaged up on the basis that they would get better or die. In Luke's case, the irony was that he and his group had set off to rescue some other soldiers and had been fired upon by the Roundheads – who had either mistaken them for reinforcements or who had not really cared who they were. By the time that Luke reached Helmdon, death was a certainty, and it was not far off.

Harriet sent a message for the Reverend White to come at once to the manor, and when he arrived, he was immediately faced with the need to reconcile himself with the son he had thought spiritually lost, whom he had then avoided trying to converse with or understand, and who now needed him as he neared death. Harriet told him most of this, and as he arrived at the bedside of his son, who was conscious and in some pain but recognised him, all he could bring himself to do was to sit with Luke and to grasp his hand. Harriet looked on as they tried to speak properly to each other for the first time in years. "Father, I was partly wrong," uttered Luke in a weak voice. "I thought that a simpler religion was a better one, but those fighting this war are only really interested in what they can get for themselves. They only want to believe in God if He supports their desires, and it doesn't matter to them what His Church does! Half of them just want to steal silver from the Church. I was wrong about some of the things that I thought, and some of the things that I said to you!"

"Hush, my son, it is not your fault!" said the Reverend. "I think I knew all that you have said had a point, but I was also too obstinate to see that there might be other ways. I wanted you to be more perfect than the others, and I could not face it when I thought that you had betrayed me. In my heart, I knew that you had not betrayed God, but I thought you had betrayed me! Save your voice and your strength, my son. I love you, and I know that you love me!"

"There is also another that I love," said Luke, looking at Harriet. "I love Harriet, and I want to marry her! I know that I am dying, and I cannot be a proper husband to her, but I want the world to know that I did here what I should have done years ago, and that Harriet was in my final thoughts. We must marry tomorrow, in your church! Don't tell me about waiting for banns and things – because we cannot wait for three readings, maybe not even for three days. It doesn't matter to me if the world doesn't really accept this marriage – as I have nothing to leave Harriet and we will have no children to label as illegitimate."

The Reverend looked at Harriet and she nodded to him. I think it was at that moment that the Reverend White's religious beliefs again crystalised into what was important in his soul and his church, and what was just ornamentation or custom. Luke would be married. He would be married in Thomas White's church because that was what Luke wanted to do. If Luke had wanted to marry at that moment, Thomas White would have conducted the ceremony there and then in the bedroom, but Luke wanted the wedding to be seen properly in public, and he wanted to be married in his father's church as a sign of reconciliation between him and his father. Flowers and vestments and banns became suddenly superfluous. What was important was that the church had to be made ready, people had to be informed and attend the ceremony, and Luke had to live long enough to get to the church. Thomas White would face any consequences from his actions afterwards!

Thomas White tried to get round to every house in the village that day, and it was in his visit to me that I found out what was going on upon my return from seeing Edward. I did not waste his time by telling the Reverend about the events at the estate but instead wrote a note to Edward telling him of the events in the village and Luke and Harriet, asking him and Olivia to attend the village church at midday on the following day – partly to set an official seal on the events and possibly to deter any protests or fuss that might arise from others in the village. Then I set off around the village to spread the load of delivering the news for Thomas White, and between us we not only told everyone in the village what was to happen but also those who lived in the farms and buildings around the village, too. Privately, I also told a very few religious hardliners that this was a dying man's wish, and it might be better for them not to attend the wedding at all rather than bring themselves to the notice of the new military commander who would be there to ensure order. I don't think there were any real objections, but I didn't really listen properly to what others said to me (not for the first time).

Those who were told and approved wholeheartedly offered immediate help. They arranged garlands of flowers for each pew, and cleaned and polished the church more thoroughly than it had been done in the previous six months. The villagers all knew Luke and Harriet, and most of them were determined to make sure that everything was done as properly as possible for the couple. An uneasy hush settled that night over the village. Those of us who knew Luke knew that he needed to stay alive through the night – and that would not be easy for him. Luke himself, too, was torn between his need for rest and the need to talk as much as possible to the woman he loved, and whom he was soon going to lose. Harriet told me later that the night passed in stages. They talked for a while and then Luke slept whilst she watched him, and then he would wake, talk some more and then sleep some more. He continually repeated his feelings for her, his memories of her in earlier days, and what he would have wanted them to do if he was to have been spared. This pattern continued all through the night, and Harriet was one of the few who actually slept not at all – frightened as she was of losing Luke whilst she was asleep, or before the wedding that he wanted.

Luke had to be carried to the church in a chair by four men whom he knew. All that he needed to be able to physically do was to stand up in front of the altar if possible, and to make his formal declarations to his father in front of the congregation of people whom he knew. He was cleaned and dressed as nicely and respectably as it was possible to do in the circumstances, and then he was literally carried straight to the front pew of the church in time for the appointed hour. An armed guard manned the approach to the church, appointed as a mark of respect to a wounded and dying soldier (even an adversary) by Edward – who was there in his best uniform with Olivia at his side. Their appearance together marked official approval for the event, and some sort of reconciliation within those of the village. It also suggested to the villagers that they were very good friends. Harriet looked lovely. She had dressed simply and carried one of the garlands that the villagers had made, and I swear that when Luke looked at her, I saw strength for the forthcoming ceremony flow into him.

They both declared their love for each other clearly, with some strength and in firm voices, although Harriet gave an audible sob at the line 'As long as you both shall live', and Luke took her hand at that point to give her his strength. We all 'robustly' sang the hymns that Harriet had chosen, and threw flower petals over the both of them as they left the church. Luke had to be carried from the church, though, and although a meal had been laid out for the two of them and their guests, he was unable to sit there for more than half of an hour before being carried back to the manor. Luke died later that night. Harriet stayed awake with him until his last ragged breath, and then, too tired to tell anyone or say any more at that moment, she slept beside the body of her husband. The two of them were found together by a maid the next morning. Both of them were immobile, but one was alive and one was dead, and the word was quickly spread around the village. I could not find anyone afterwards who regretted what we had done, or regretted attending the event. We wept for Luke and for Harriet.

Luke's death had been foretold, although the village had only known this for a day or so. When the news was spread of his death, therefore, the village had had some small chance to prepare themselves for it even if they found it hard to bear. Luke's father could say nothing when he was told. He put his head in his arms, and they left him to cry. Mentally, he had not really prepared himself for the event, and physically, doing what he could for his son after their reconciliation had taken him to the limits of his own strength. That evening, the Reverend Thomas was found immobile in his study, having succumbed to some sort of seizure. He could not move or communicate to anyone in any way. He was taken to his bedroom and laid in bed there. He was cared for at every moment, but within a day, he, too, was dead. Our knowledge of science was not enough to tell us what had caused him to die – but we thought his heart was broken. He did not live long enough to oversee the funeral of his son. His daughter was missing; possibly she was dead, too, and as far as Helmdon could tell, the White family was no more.

THIRTEEN

DESECRATION OF THE CHURCH

Our village church of St Mary Magdalene was perhaps a third of a mile to the south side of our village, on one of the lanes that ran down to join together to approach the main road. It was probably sited at that distance so that the graveyard was clear of the village and had room for expansion over the years. It also meant that we had a little bit of a stroll to go there to church, and a little bit of time on the way back to reflect on God's message if the children were not too loud, and work up perhaps a bit of an appetite for lunch on Sundays. It was pleasantly proportioned, and had a small tower at one end to watch over the rest of the church and to summon us with one or more of its four bells. Despite its physical site, it was the centre of a lot of the village's thoughts, and it was important to us. It dominated the lane and road to the main road, and sometimes we felt as if it – and God – were guarding us. The church became more important to a lot of us in the war, and we found ourselves visiting it more to take a moment of peace, and to whisper a prayer to Our Lord for someone we knew – either a soldier or a relative, or someone else in the village.

The absence of loved ones made it harder still for those of us at home to cope with small disasters. I always liked the church, and having it as a haven affirmed that love for it. I mentioned before that the fabric of the church was important to me – in terms of the decoration and content making it feel as if I was welcome, but it was more than that. I have little experience of large churches, but some that I have seen seem stern and forbidding – as if you are being told off by God before you enter the church. Our church felt like the right size, though – and I know that is silly. In my mind, I pictured the church on a sunny, windy day when the trees nearby were blowing around and there was a rush of sound in the air. On wet or cold, dark winter evenings, the lights of the church would draw me towards it, and I would anticipate the feeling of warmth and light when I got inside, but in my mind and my memory, when I thought of our church, it was the church and the tower against that blue sky and the clouds, and the pleasant greenery around it. The church was often warm. I think there is something about the type of stone used that protected us in the congregation from the cold outside. In the summer, the building was still warm, but not hot. I think God protected us from the elements.

I carried on my work, I did my duty, I valued my independence – and was grateful that I was not too tied down by family. I continually worried about religion, though, when I had time to think about it. The war was being fought by men on both sides who professed themselves to be doing God's work. Many of these men were more highly educated than I was, and I didn't see how I could have the arrogance to assume that they were wrong in their beliefs. The war was also being fought by men on both sides who didn't care at all about conscience or God, and as Luke had once written, some of them were putting their immortal souls at risk. Although I was sure that God would see into them, it was possible that some of these men would be in a winning army and might dictate the lives of the rest of us after the war. Would that risk our souls as well as theirs? Was it possible that God looked at the world He had created, and saw one country where men killed each other, whether or not they valued their God? Was it possible that our whole country was damned because of this? What about the men of conscience who fought because they firmly believed what their wiser rulers told them to do? Were they also damned? Did it matter what you thought about when you fought?

I tried to talk to our new vicar about this. He said that each man would be judged by God on his own merits (I am sure that he meant women, too) – and that God could see everything – but I still worried. I worried when I saw flashes in the sky one night. The doctor told me that these were shooting stars (he used those words) and that they were a 'scientific' discovery. He didn't want to say whether God had created them, and when I said that people in the village saw them as a 'portent' of disaster, he just poo-pooed them. Privately, I thought that if something bad happened in the near future, I would believe what the villagers said rather than the doctor. I don't always think that men of science know everything, and I am certain that they don't admit to not knowing things. They think they have to provide an explanation for those of us who seem to know less than they do. The Civil War had made all of us think about the village in a new way, and one of the things we had to consider was whether we were all in danger – and whether God would warn us, or damn us. I admit that I didn't think of this every day, but when I had time to think, it all seemed very important to me. We had already had one example where men who tried to show that they cared about God had tried to damage our work. By that, I meant the Puritans who had tried to sabotage our pageant in 1645.

Was it possible that men of God had been sent to warn us and we had laughed at them? Worse, we had stripped them of their clothes and painted them in garish colours. We didn't believe that they were right, but THEY had believed that they were right. We had done the opposite of Joseph's brothers in the Bible (where they removed his coat of many colours – because it meant favouritism). We had compared them to the gunpowder plot – where a group of men dressed in a similar manner had been found attempting to destroy Parliament one night, and they had suffered horrible punishments. Logic told me that the gunpowder plot men had been punished because they had also tried to kill the King – who had divine right – but surely that was what my brother, Edward, was trying to do, by fighting for the Parliamentary army? I had spent several years trying to treat people from both sides equally, but I still felt on balance that my sympathies were more with those who didn't want change. The church continued to be a haven for me, but my worries also continued. They were eased a bit by an event that took place in 1648.

This event didn't solve anything for us, but it did send a message to me as an ignorant country girl that even if God disapproved of what we were doing, at least we were trying to do his work – and maybe we could use that as evidence on the Day of Judgement. It made me happier about my opinions of others – at least for a while. The church (our haven) could be seen from the main road, whilst the rest of our village buildings could not. When the main road was in use during the war, we did not always want the folk using that road (soldiers, renegades and the like) to see us, but the church appeared to be designed to be seen from a distance, and seeing the tower from the road sometimes directed visitors to us. The rest of the buildings were lower and hidden mainly by bushes and trees. This was why we had felt the need to post children on guard earlier in the war to let us know that visitors were coming up one of the lanes or the drovers' road. It was not, though, until later in the war that we realised that the distance from the village to the church put it at risk.

The new priest was sent as a replacement priest soon after the Whites died. He was a nice jolly fellow. Young, single, and with a bright positive view on life. He seemed to want to take care not to have a 'side', and in a country divided by a war, not dividing his congregation was important – but it also left us village folk with the impression that he did not have too strong an opinion on anything, and I suppose we looked for more evidence that he devoutly believed in God. We were used to a priest who told us what God wanted us to do – so that we knew what was important to God. The new priest seemed to be suggesting that God would not mind very much if we preferred rituals and paintings, or wanted an altar or a table, and where it was placed in the church. It was important to folk to feel that they had not alienated God – but some of the village thought that 'God would not mind very much' if they missed church or how often they prayed. The new priest also did not know the names and houses of the village folk to 'chase' them down in their homes on Sundays.

I am not putting this very well, but I suppose that there are two things here. Do we want our priests to be all 'fire and brimstone' and 'you will burn in Hell if you put a foot wrong', or do we want them to be (as Jesus suggests) forgiving and more kindly? Do we want to be told what to do, or do we want a commentary on what we decide to do? Do we take responsibility for ourselves? I think that England needed forgiving for all of the crimes that had been committed in the war, and I liked the idea of personal forgiveness, but kindness did mean that some people thought they could do anything they liked as long as they repented at the end. Also – when you grow up with a priest and think that you know their expectations, it is a bit difficult to respect a change of ministry. It feels like the Church has changed. What is worse is that it is difficult to feel that you can actually trust someone that you do not know. The Church seemed to expect us all to trust our vicar just because he was a vicar – not because he had shown to us that the trust was warranted.

Father Andrew's first job as our new vicar was to conduct the funerals of Thomas and Luke White. Thomas' name went onto the little wooden board which recorded the village's previous vicars, and where one supposed that Andrew Thompson would be recorded, too, in some twenty or thirty years. Thomas and Luke were interred into adjacent graves, with a headstone for each of them. They were buried, too, next to Luke's mother and Thomas' wife. The church paid for Father Thomas White's headstone, whilst Harriet Green – or perhaps I should now say Harriet White – paid for Luke's stone. The new priest did the services very nicely, but he had known neither Luke nor his father. Perhaps he did them better because of that. We felt as the coffins were carried out that we were saying goodbye to an older way of life, to older patterns of behaviour and to an earlier church, rather than just the familiar faces of two of the people that we loved. Perhaps we were saying goodbye to the haven that I had always felt the church to be. I still felt that Luke and his father belonged to us, and not to God!

On one evening in October 1648, though, our new vicar – who was still to earn our trust – became aware of unfamiliar sounds within the church as he approached it for an evening visit. He hadn't been in the village very long, but he knew what he should hear (very little at that time of the night). Instead, he heard the sound of things breaking or cracking, stone and glass (he thought) – and he thought that he heard muffled voices inside the church. Rather than go into the church on his own, he turned round and came to our house for my father, and Father and I both went with him, picking up another strong-looking man on the way. I sent a message with one of my neighbour's boys to Edward at Stuchbury Hall, asking Edward to come to the church, too, at his earliest convenience. When the three of us approached the church with the vicar, we could indeed also hear the sounds that the vicar had heard earlier. We saw, too, the flicker of candles, shadows moving, and it was obvious that there were people in the church.

We pushed open the door, pushed aside the heavy curtain that hung on the inside, and stepped into the church. We saw several figures clothed in plain dark garments, and with hoods over their heads. They had pinched the hoods together at the front so that we could not clearly see their faces, and they were engaged in several different (and destructive) tasks. One figure with a large hammer was raining blows down on a small statue of St Mary, which was lying on the ground and which showed some evidence of having received several blows already. It had chips to the paint, one arm had been broken off, and at the moment we entered, the attention was on the face and head. It had been hammered off its plinth. A second figure had some sort of brush and was scrubbing whitewash over one of our two murals that were painted on one wall. The murals were something our children liked to look at – although we knew that some worshippers were not in favour of them in Protestant churches. They were of biblical scenes that were easy for the children to understand, and I often wondered if they had been painted deliberately to explain stories to the village children.

A third figure was just mounting a small ladder in front of one of our few coloured windows, clutching another hammer in one hand. We loved our windows, and although not all were coloured, we believed that some were very ancient – perhaps several hundred years old. We regularly cleaned them so that they didn't get dirty, and so that the light came through them in lovely colours. The ladder was being held at the side by a fourth figure, and the window was in imminent danger of being smashed.

"Stop, I tell you, stop!" shouted our vicar in a loud voice that I didn't think him capable of producing. At the sound of his voice, two things happened. The figure on the ladder overbalanced and fell backwards to the ground – landing on his bottom. Another figure appeared round a pillar from the direction of the altar, clutching another hammer – and past him, I could see another statue on the flagstones. The altar had been turned over, its coverings pinned underneath it, and it looked like it was about to be attended to with a hammer, too. It was brave of the vicar to shout, because I had heard of other clergymen being attacked when they had tried to stop their churches being vandalised.

The figure from the ladder got up and walked towards us purposely, and his associates lined up behind him. They presented a menacing line of men – with their hammers held in their hands, although it has to be said that the one on the end with the large brush was not as menacing as his friends. They were made more menacing by the candles behind them and the hoods they wore. It didn't feel real for a minute. I had never seen a play in a theatre, just the ones that the children did – or we had done as children. Occasionally, too, the church in the town would have a tableau – and I remembered as a girl being taken to see one with other children from the village. It had been really exciting going there for a day out, but watching the gospel in the darker church with different people's voices had been a bit frightening for me. Now, and just for a minute, it was like that, here. The figures in their cloaks lined up in front of us, the flickering of the candle flame emphasised by the darkness outside, and occasionally excited by movement in the air. In a play, I was told that you had to believe the story in front of you, and for a minute I believed in the menace of those in front of us. I shivered and drew closer to the vicar, perhaps as my spiritual protector. Then I was snatched back to reality.

"This church is an abomination!" said the central figure – who it would appear was the leader of the gang. "It is covered in images and decorated as the Catholic heretics have their churches. This is not a church for English folk. It has an altar to hide the priest's heretical doings and a screen so that normal people cannot take part in the worship properly. As for all these painted statues, they are obscene in the eyes of the Lord, and we are doing his work in removing them." He gestured at the objects of his content as he described them. He was the image of a strict Puritan – or he had rehearsed well! I had heard this man's voice before, I knew. I had heard it in anger, too, and raised in a higher complaining tone. It had not been for a while, though, and I would have to think back over some time. If I could only remember where and when that had been…

"This church is beloved by all of its parishioners," shouted the vicar back at the figures. "If my flock wanted it any different, they would have discussed it with me, and if there were things here that were unacceptable to them, we would have considered taking them away! This is not your church. You do not have the voice of one of my parishioners. You have no business here, and by desecrating this church, you are breaking God's law and that of the authorities."

"You are wrong there, priest!" said the lead figure. "It is everyone's duty to cleanse the church of papal practices and painted idols, and we are doing God's will in removing the idols and imagery! This country will be improved and returned to God by our actions!"

"Actually, that is not true!" said the voice of my brother, Edward, from behind me as he pushed aside the curtain that hung in front of the door. I had never been so glad to hear his voice. "My Lord Cromwell indeed wants simplicity in the churches of this country, that much is true, but it is the folk who worship in each church who should take part in cleansing it. What you are doing is simply vandalism and desecration, and my lord has also said that we need to protect innocent God-fearing folk from looters and thieves, like you."

"Oh, and what are you going to do about it?" said the lead figure.

One of his friends tugged at his cloak to get his attention. "Eli…" he whispered, and then I knew who the lead figure was.

"You are Elias Wright," I said. "Elias Wright from Wappenham. I saw you there in the stocks once. You were put in the stocks for doing no work. Your squire had you put there. I knew that I had heard your voice before when I heard it just now. You are no genuine religious zealot. You are a thief, a wastrel and a vandal!"

"We are leaving!" said Elias, clearly quite upset that he had been recognised. "You lot aren't going to stop us!" and he raised his hammer in the air.

"No, you are quite right there," said Edward, much to my surprise. He motioned us to one side, restraining with his arm the vicar, who appeared to want to tackle the cloaked figures. They sidled past us, heading for the door but making sure that they still faced us. When the last one was past, they started to move much faster. "Get them!" shouted Edward, and from outside we heard the glorious sound of five church desecrators and vandals being apprehended by twenty Parliamentary soldiers. They had no chance to run; the soldiers had grabbed hold of each of them as they left the church. When we left the church a minute or so later, the five were being held fast by the soldiers. Edward had chosen his largest men, and their sense of menace was much greater than that of the vandals, who they visibly terrified. All except the leader. Without his hood, his face displayed the betrayal and lack of fairness that he felt. He had obviously seen his mission as one that he should emerge from triumphant, and that he should escape any following counteraction.

"I am Lord Cromwell's commander of this area, and you are charged with desecration of this church!" said Edward, and again I was very impressed by his commanding statement and his posture. I wanted to hold on to his arm – but I had the feeling that would not improve his standing in the eyes of his soldiers or the villains they had apprehended.

"They had these as well, sir," said one of Edward's men, holding up a cloth bag and producing from it two silver candlesticks, and our chalice and plate – all of the valuables that our church held.

"...and theft," added Edward to what he had said before. "Take their masks off," said Edward, and the hoods were pulled backwards so that the faces could be seen. As I thought, the leader was Elias Wright from Wappenham. I could not swear to it, but I thought I had seen the others around that village, too. The figures were led away by the soldiers towards Stuchbury, where they would be held overnight.

"What will happen to them?" I asked Edward.

"We will probably get the weakest one to list everything else that the group did, and then let that one go. All sorts of things might happen to the rest; forceable enlistment in the army, gaol, possibly even death!"

"Death?" I exclaimed.

"What do you expect?" said Edward. "They had in their possession several pounds worth of silver that they had stolen from your church. Forget for a moment about what they claim to be their religious beliefs. Stealing from a church is a serious crime. We will investigate them and see if they have committed any other crimes."

We went into the church. As we walked around, the vicar listed what damage had been done. Fortunately, the coloured glass of the windows had not been touched. The vandals had obviously left them until last, because they thought they would be more likely to be heard from outside whilst they were damaging them, or perhaps it had just been a question of finding a ladder – or doing the harder work first. As it was, we had only become aware of the vandals because they had been heard by the vicar, who was close to the church. If he hadn't been walking that way, the closest houses would not have heard anything. "I don't think that we can save two of these statues," he said mournfully. "I can't bring myself to throw them away, but they will have to be stored out of sight for the moment. Perhaps in the future, we can do something to them. I think they are nearly a hundred years old, and the story is that they were given to the church as a present." We helped him to right the altar. The cloth fabrics had been damaged – but when they were replaced or repaired, they would hide the chips that had been made in the stonework.

The mural, though, that had been defaced was irreparable. We decided that it would all have to be whitewashed over, because we could not face looking at half of a mural. This was a shame, because it was one I liked. It represented the Feeding of the Five Thousand, and I liked the boat on the lake from where Jesus talked to the crowd. The children would miss it, but perhaps it might be replaced in the future. "I have seen damage from the Reformation where all the statues in a church lost their faces," continued the vicar. "It doesn't solve any problems within the churches' worship, though."

"Those men were not really reformers," said Edward. They came here for theft and were going to sell the silverware on. Perhaps we can get them to tell us who would buy it. There has been a lot of theft and pilfering in this war!"

"That Elias did nothing before!" I said scornfully. "I don't understand how that lot avoided the army. They must have been hiding under someone's bed to avoid it."

"Well, they won't be doing that from now on!" said Edward. "Unless it is the bed in a cell!" We left the vicar finishing his list so that the magistrates would have the evidence of the damage, and we walked out through the door. Two of Edward's men were now on guard there.

"I think we will keep a couple of men there for a few nights," said Edward. "There are often cases where thieves hear about a robbery and others go back the next night assuming that no one will still be there. I'd rather catch a few more thieves than have the village upset by more theft from the church – or elsewhere in the village." He took my arm and walked me back to my home. I was glad that I had not seized his arm before and had not embarrassed him in front of his men, but I was as glad to have his arm now and I clung on tightly. I was very grateful, too, for his presence in the village, and very proud that my brother was such an important figure here, now. I was conscious, too, though, that at the centre of my beliefs were the law of God and the rule of the King. Edward had fought for change and I didn't think rebellion against the King was his main aim, but I didn't want to ask him. My family had always felt unimportant. Now I felt as if we were at the centre of things, more and more. We were greeted by several folk as we walked home, and I invited Edward in, but he wouldn't stay as it was late. We became aware that the story circulated in the village in the next few days – being exaggerated each time the story was told. Lots of people asked me for the details whilst the story was still fresh. Some asked me several times. I think they liked to hear the story.

Father Andrew got the respect from his villagers that he had never had before (and had maybe secretly desired). His reputation (as I think I have said) was that of a peaceable man who preferred his flock to come to services because they wanted to, and so he didn't shout or rail at them. This story gave a completely different impression of him and his actions on this day. The story was told that he had found the desecrating thieves in the church and, entirely on his own with nobody else around, had ordered the thieves to stop 'in a voice of thunder that rattled the windows'. It was said that his voice alone had stopped them in their thievery, and they had cowered timorously in front of his commanding figure. He had been supported by us, but (in the story) the soldiers had arrived just in time 'to stop the reverend striking down the thieves with their own hammers'. The implication was that the thieves had needed the soldiers to protect them from the vicar's wrath, and however much Father Andrew protested this version of events, the story was maintained and embellished. His congregations swelled with a mixture of those who were afraid of being punished for not attending church and those who wanted to see evidence of his voice of thunder. In time, of course, things returned to normal.

Elias Wright was sentenced to be hung by the neck until dead. This was only partly for the theft of the silver from the church – although possibly this theft was enough to have warranted such a punishment on its own, but there was also a small matter of desertion and theft from the army. Elias Wright had joined the army with other men of his village in 1642 in the first excitement of the war starting. He had joined the Parliamentary army, protesting about change, and had deserted after the first battle he had seen. Clearly, the bodies he had seen from the safety of the store's waggon had frightened him witless, but unfortunately they had not frightened him so much that he forgot to take a small pay chest from the waggon with him – and consequently, he had been looked for by the authorities ever since. The authorities took the line that deserters needed to be punished in a way that sent a message to others, but, obviously, taking the money could be construed as planning the action before the event, and that is what the magistrate said at his trial. According to the magistrate, Elias had been lucky to live an extra year or two after his original crime – and that was only due to the difficulty of finding such as him in a country torn by war!

Elias was hung in Towcester the following spring, having spent the winter in prison in Northampton until the full scope of any other crimes was known. I thought that just the very idea of the punishment of spending the winter in that cold jail with little food, always in darkness, the rats, disease, lack of drainage would have been enough to stop me committing a crime – but it hadn't stopped Elias. In the spring, he had been returned to his local town (as was the custom) to be hung by the neck in front of those who had known him – to deter them from the same activities. His 'friends' in the robbery were luckier. They were told of Elias' activities and former crimes, and then were told that they could either join the Parliamentary army or face accusations of being accessories to theft, possibly desertion, hiding a fugitive, conspiracy (anything that could be levelled against them, in other words) and take the chance that they, too, might face the noose. Unsurprisingly, Elias' friends had chosen the army as the easier option. They had signed their marks and had to serve the first six months with no pay – because it would be put against the value of what they had conspired to steal.

It was felt, also, that they were likely to be unreliable regular soldiers in a regiment and that they were the type of men whom others wouldn't fight with, and so they were detailed with others of their kind to be gaolers in local prisons. They were separated from each other so that they could not conspire, but placed (again) with others of a similar nature. All of them were warned that if prisoners escaped from their gaol, they would be punished in their place. They were brought back together for one particular duty, and it was no coincidence that they were lined up to watch Elias Wright's hanging. The last thing that Elias Wright saw on this earth before the noose was placed around his neck was his erstwhile colleagues stood in front of him, holding gaolers' pikes, shuffling their feet and looking shamefacedly at the ground whilst a large crowd jeered at Elias on the scaffold. Once again, I felt how bad it was that families gathered for the ultimate punishment, and threatened their children with it.

I wondered if the hanging felt for a minute like a stage play, too, to Elias when he saw the crowd in front of him. Did it feel real for him? Were the crowd all laughing and jeering? Was there any sympathy for him? Did he have any relatives who had come to weep for him and regret his passing? Did Elias feel just for a minute as if he were the sole actor on stage in a play, as I had briefly felt when he and his men had lined up in front of us in the church? Did he see his ex-comrades in front of him as the bit players nervously waiting for a speech so that they could be given directions – or were they the comedy? Did he genuinely think it was unfair (as I had surmised when I saw him outside the church), or did he feel in any way that he had deserved his fate? What did Elias actually feel in the moment when the 'curtain came down on him' at the end of his play, as the hood descended and his show was over – forever? Would God be the next thing he saw? I shivered again – as I had done in the church – and drew my shawl closer around me. What or who would I see at my ending? Who would be waiting to guide me into the next life?

To me, with hindsight, Elias had died for being evil. He had stated that he had religious principles, and those principles had commanded him to desecrate our church. To me, that made it easier to believe that others who wanted to change the Church and the way we worshipped were also bad. My brain followed the pathway that if the way we worshipped was bad – or not what others wanted – then they should found their own churches, and have the services that they wanted in them. They should not try to change the churches of those who were already happy in them. Further, my brain told me that if people were unhappy with the way that the country was being run, shouldn't they leave it, and perhaps go to one of the new countries that we were discovering? America, perhaps or Van Diemen's land? Perhaps it was a sin of avarice to want to stay in this country, but for it to be changed? My heart, though, worried that we were not all good – and that if God was dissatisfied with what we did, or our behaviour or our morals, then perhaps he wanted the change and simplicity of the 'rebels'.

I couldn't bring myself to debate – even in my own head – the concept of the divine right of the King. This was the way it had always been in England, and if it was not acceptable, then either England should be split – which would be impossible, because of the number of viewpoints – or instead, those who didn't like this England as it was should leave it. I didn't number Edward amongst those people. Edward hadn't said he wanted change for change's sake, he had said he wanted a more equitable society, which would give him the chance he wanted to make something of himself. The trouble was, though, that he had attained his goals by fighting with those others who did want to change England – and, ironically, he was accepted in his new status by those like Olivia, who were part of the old world! Once again, I couldn't deal with this in my head. I could only feel that I didn't believe God hated us for the way that we worshipped, and that we weren't completely bad in his eyes, even if all of us occasionally committed minor sins. I hoped that I would be greeted by St Peter when I died – or (as I was unimportant) perhaps one of his more junior officials.

FOURTEEN

CRIME...

They executed the King! They put him on a block at Whitehall and chopped off his head! They did it in front of hundreds of people! Surely, if there actually is a divine right of kings, there must be some reaction from God for the 30th of January 1649, when his trusty servant King Charles, the first of that name, was executed by his subjects? His son was crowned Charles the Second, in Jersey. He vowed to fight on – and I think he was only nineteen years old at the time! I think that the Parliamentarians thought that executing the King would end the war and sort everything out, although others say that because he wouldn't recognise their truth, he had to die. They say also, though, that it was because King Charles would just not accept their cause, or share rulership. I was not sure if the King's army had faith in Charles' son, and that he would win, or if they had just lost faith. Perhaps it was their last chance to prevent change in England. There don't seem to be as many Royalists as there were, and there seem to be a lot more Parliamentarians. I suppose it is easy to say that you are part of a winning team?

The gap left by our friends and relatives was to grow larger. Often, when we walked round the village, we were reminded of them in the things we saw. We heard nothing properly from our absent village members for the next two years. There was a very small trickle of returners to the village, but they showed some things in common. They did not want to talk very much about the war, and we did not force them to when they were silent. The horrors of what they had seen, or possibly done, or let others do on the battlefield seemed to stay with them. They seemed less enthusiastic about life. We were told about nightmares, or witnessed sudden flares of anger, or lassitude, or a refusal to take part in social events. It was as if there were two levels of humanity. Those who had stayed behind in our village valued our lives, and those who returned here seemed to feel guilty about living, or resent those of us who had not gone to war and knew nothing of it. Of Mark Green, Robert Grey and Stephanie White, we heard nothing. Harriet tried to fight back to her normal busy life. It seemed, though, to us that the return of more men of military age increased the amount of crime.

There had always been some level of crime in the village, just as there has always been crime everywhere. Most of it was what they call 'low-level' or petty crime. Someone would steal a chicken – or a chicken would go missing and someone would allege theft. There were constant allegations of theft of items that could not be proved – like corn or firewood or stone. I think a large number of alleged 'thefts' were made simply because someone thought they had more goods than they actually did. If they had promised a quantity of goods, perhaps corn to the miller, and that quantity was not realised, it was easier for them to claim theft than to admit they had made a mistake in weighing or calculating it. Of course, the miller was allowed by law to claim a proportion of the corn for his 'wage', and it was up to the farmer to check if the miller did that honestly – or whether he 'took a bit extra'. There had been two occasions when the amount of small crime had diminished, one being when the Royalist soldiers had been billeted on us, and the second was now that the Roundheads were stationed at Stuchbury Hall, and still regularly patrolled the village.

To sum up, most crimes of this nature had no lasting effect and did not change the quality – or course – of someone's life. Injury could be a different thing – in affecting quality of life – but was not always considered an actual crime. There were lots of cases of workers in the quarries being injured, for example. When large quantities of stone were being moved, it was only by regular careful supervision that accidents were avoided. They were not always supervised carefully, though. Technically, of course, this was not regarded as a crime. It was always put down to carelessness of the workers, and it was only if the quarry owner cared that the injured worker was able to maintain some quality of life after the event. Some quarry owners did not care and were not careful, and I think should have been considered criminals. If a farm worker carelessly injured another labourer, he was blamed – but quarry and farm owners were not. Is that fair? Is life as important as property?

We knew, too, that certain families and people in our village were poorer than others. We knew that if some could make their existence better by 'acquiring' extra goods, then they would. We made efforts as a village to help people like that before they needed to commit a 'crime' that we would have to take note of. If that meant we found extra work for them or told them that we had 'extra' food that we could spare, then we would do that. We were left pretty much on our own to deal with criminals in our village. Often, that meant that the vicar would preach a sermon about theft, if there had been thefts. If that failed, the vicar would arrange to call on people to ask if they were all right – or even to see if they had things around that perhaps they shouldn't have. The next move was sometimes a deputation. Leading figures such as the vicar, employers, perhaps even Sir Henry, would visit. There were the magistrates, but they were almost never involved by us for very small crimes.

Those who continually thieved could also be asked to leave the village. Most folk did not own their houses, and those who did own a house usually did not need to steal. A lot of us (my family included) lived in a house owned by their employer – and if they were short, they would often talk to the employer or ask the vicar's advice. My family's house belonged to Lord Grey and his estate. I thought that we would be allowed to live in the house until my father died, and after that, Edward and I would have to ask the Lord if he wanted the house back, and potentially find another. It was also possible, of course, that Lord Grey could ask us to leave after Father died – although technically Lord Grey was now Robert Grey, who I didn't think would ask us to leave. The point was, though, that if we committed enough crimes, Lord Grey could tell us to leave the house – and if we could not find another, we would have to leave the village. The point, too, was that some of the people who thieved were dependent on others – sometimes on those whom they stole from.

Then there were 'crimes' that people did not like to discuss. There are crimes that people often ignore or look the other way from. We had had at least one case where a man was forced out of the village for beating his wife and children. I think that he was unhappy in his life and was taking it out on them, but he had been talked to by the vicar, and he had still not stopped. When his children still appeared with bruises, and then his wife's arm was broken, he was thrown out of his house. His wife and children were told that they were welcome to stay, and that we could find a job for his wife in the village – but in the end, the wife and younger child chose to leave with him, and his older son – then eleven years old – was taken on by a local farmer who gave him work and a place to live, and trained him to become a farmer. I don't know if he ever saw his family again – although I believe they settled later in Brackley, which was not too far away. I think there are a lot of these sorts of cases.

In the category of crimes that people did not like to discuss, we also had to consider sexual crimes. I don't like the word that I use but can't think how else to mention them. There had been a case in our area where a man had forced himself on his daughter – incest, I mean – and another case where an uncle had done the same with a boy. There are unpleasant things like this all over the country, I understand, but I can't really understand how people can hurt someone that they say they love. Perhaps they misunderstand what is meant by love and confuse it with 'debt'. Perhaps they just don't care what other people feel or want. In both of these cases, we went to Sir Henry about them, and after questioning the men he sent to Towcester for an officer. I think they use the title constable, but the men we get seem to just be the men who are gaolers, who get sent out sometimes to collect suspects. In both cases, the men were tried, and I think they were sent off somewhere – but I didn't spend any time trying to find out. I just know that they didn't come back to the village, and that Sir Henry looked really grim when it was mentioned.

We had no killers or murderers before the war. We had plenty of killers and murderers during the war – but they seemed now to be traitors or patriots or renegades or 'duly designated officers' or whatever. We didn't have them in the village much – unless you count those of our village who were away killing other people in the army, or you count those men from the village who had taken part in the Battle of Helmdon, and had perhaps killed twenty or so of the renegades just outside the village. I think that is why the army was so popular a choice in 1642 and 1643. Men suddenly realised that they could shoot or kill other folk, although they never thought that the same thing could happen to them! For a couple of years, the idea of leaving and fighting (I believe) started to take violent folk away from the villages – and gave them a chance to be violent somewhere else. Someone once told me it was a 'power' thing, and I have been told that people in other areas of the world believe you become more powerful by killing someone – and in some cases by eating them!

In 1648, particularly following Preston, things began to change. More soldiers came home. There was the period when King Charles I was captured and then tried, and suddenly there seemed to be less of a Royalist army, or it was further away. Even following 1648 and before those thoughts about the Royalist army, people seemed to start believing that Parliament had already won the war, and that fewer soldiers were needed. Some folk were sent home in 1648 and 1649, and some drifted away from the army. Gradually, areas of the country started to receive home men – who for six years had lived by killing and looting and stealing and plundering or even raping. These men were no longer satisfied with just going back to their old jobs, and it seemed as if many of them needed some sort of break from normal behaviour to satisfy those old needs. They had been 'educated' into bad behaviour by what they had been expected to do. As I have said – we seemed to get more crime.

Men engaged in drinking sessions with their old army friends, they started fighting with those who used to be on the other side of the war, and they showed violent behaviour towards anyone who would not agree with them or didn't appreciate them, and that sometimes included wives, children, friends and relatives. There were groups of offenders in the towns, whilst in the villages it seemed to be more individuals – although I suppose that was because there were fewer ex-soldiers in the villages. We had a couple of them in Helmdon. They seemed to meet up at the end of the week and drink rather a lot of beer, but, as far as we know, they didn't break windows or attack members of their family – and as far as we could tell, during the week, they were quiet and sober – although they seemed more serious and less good-natured than they had before they left. They had left a fair number of friends behind on battlefields – so their nature was understandable.

In late 1648 – November, I think – we started to get some odd incidents in Helmdon that were out of the usual pattern of village life – or crime. We had a case where a young woman of seventeen was on her way home from working late as a servant in one of the houses. She lived in the village, so she went home at night rather than (as was common) living in the house where she worked. According to what she later told the vicar, as she walked past the entrance to an alley in the dark, she saw a figure come out of the alley. The figure was wearing a cloak, and she couldn't see clearly who it was in the darkness, but she assumed it was a man – and it advanced towards her. After a few steps, it raised its hands and rushed at her. She backed away, turned and ran, and as luck would have it saw the torch of someone else a little way down the road. She shouted to attract their attention, and when they turned around she ran up to them. It was a local couple whom she knew. She pointed back down the road, but, of course, there was no one to be seen in the road by then.

The girl told the couple what she had seen and done, and they walked back a little way but could still see no one else. They then escorted her home, and all three of them told their story to the vicar the following day. The girl was asked to repeat her story in front of our committee, too, and she told exactly the same story as she had done before. She was not known for lying or exaggerating or daft behaviour, so she was believed, and as a committee we decided not for the minute to report to the local town – as we had no evidence and only one event. Instead, we advised folk in the village to take care, walk after dark in pairs if possible, and, in the case of the first girl, to perhaps ask for an escort home or sleep more nights where she worked. We also reported the story to other villages, and in return got several replies that there had been instances in other villages where someone had been seen prowling the area, and had either run away when challenged or had not been there when others went to look for them. These could not be accounted for.

Unlike us, one of the villages – Slapton – had reported an incident back to the authorities in Towcester. It would appear that they were not the only village, either – although other reports came from outside our area, and we did not know what they consisted of. No one knew what Towcester had done about it, but it would seem that very little had happened. Two weeks later, in December, we had another case – and this time it was a bit more serious. After a two-week gap, there was a bit of a return to "This is a small village, it is safe for me. I know everyone, and maybe it was just one silly girl." One night, one of our women had been to assist at a birth at the top end of the village the other side of the river. As she walked home, carrying her torch, a figure leapt out at her from behind a hedge. The 'assailant' let her pass before moving, so the first she knew was when a hand went over her mouth, another hand grabbed her cloak, and she dropped the torch. Light blinded as she was, she could not see her attacker very clearly, but she was of strong character and fought, lashing out with hands and feet. She was dealt a few heavy blows, and it was obvious that her attacker was someone of strength.

Luckily, one of her kicks managed to disable her attacker – landing somewhere near (if not on) his groin. I say his, because she was sure that her attacker was a man – perhaps a man felt different when you kick them! He let go, she ran off and rained blows on the door of the first house where she saw a light, but when the area was searched, again, there was no one. We reported this to Towcester – this not being the first incident that had been reported to them. The authorities in Towcester decided to take action to affect the area and deal with some crime. They decided to recruit some twenty ex-soldiers, men with good characters and references from local landlords or employers or men of the church. They would have two duties, the first being to wander the town at nights on a Friday or Saturday, and to break up fights by persuasion, or separating men, or even in the old way of 'knocking a couple of heads together' so that violence was confined and damage to property was limited. The other duties of these enforcement men were to circulate the villages either alone or in pairs, to promote good behaviour and keep an eye on the bad.

Slightly more than half of the twenty men (twelve, I believe) would circulate the villages to check the behaviour of the inhabitants, and to make sure that ale houses were properly behaved and that drunkards went home, and again to limit violent and damaging behaviour. Authorities never take action quickly, and it wasn't until the new year that this forming of a troop was to take effect. There was a parade, where this new citizen militia was paraded. They were duly sworn in, by the magistrates and in front of the townspeople. They did look quite a 'solid' body of men when they lined up. They had a helmet and breastplate, and a cloak that went down to their thighs – presumably for protection from the weather. On the breastplate was stamped the county coat of arms so that they could work in any of the towns and cities in Northamptonshire – although they were to be based in Towcester. They had a solid wooden cudgel, which was about 18 inches long. This was intended to restrain attackers but not to cause them permanent damage as a sword would have done. I think that if a sword had been swung at the cudgel, it would have stopped it, too. They raised their cudgel when taking their oath. I think that the cudgel could have done some real damage if raised in anger – but that it would depend on the man wielding it.

We were told that some officers would patrol our area (south-west of Towcester – towards Brackley), whilst others would do the other three quadrants (south-east, north-east, north-west). It seemed to me that twelve officers might not be enough, but then I suppose this was down to money – and I did not know where this was being funded from. The other way of looking at it was that this was to be a regularly funded force to ensure good behaviour, and that the law was followed. If this idea caught on, I thought that it might be something very good around the country. After the parade, we and the other village leaders were introduced to the three officers who would be working our area – so that we could recognise them when we saw them. Their names were Peacock, Carroll and Jenks. They were large men – and although they were civil enough to us, I thought that they were not particularly impressed by us as the representatives of the villages. After all, we were volunteers, and I think paid men never value those who do things for no money!

When we spoke to the officers, I was aware that whilst they smiled politely at us, the smile did not reach their eyes, and they did not make an effort to talk, just acknowledging our greetings. I could see how big they would have appeared in the ranks of the army, and I didn't think that they would make much effort to converse with us. They knew that we were there, what we did, and that potentially information from us would be passed to them through their officer. I didn't really see them making many friends with our villagers, either, but perhaps I was judging them unfairly. They were there, after all, to protect us and the village. The idea with patrolling the villages was to not tell the villages when they were being patrolled. This partly worked – as some officers followed this and varied their routine. Others, though, seemed to have a regular route depending on what night of the week they worked – and possibly where they lodged – so their movements were predictable.

Despite the formation of these groups and the patrols of officers, we had more incidents. These took place over a few months, always in the dark, and however much we tried to restrict movement alone around our village in darkness, people who assisted at births, or those who worked in the ale houses, or those who looked after or cared for other people, often found themselves having to scurry home. Given the nature of the war, these might be young lads. They were often women, and rarely older men. So far, we had had four attacks, and they were all on women – and all appeared to be by the same man. We paid more attention to those old soldiers. Without actually following them, we tried to find out who had seen them on the occasion when someone had been attacked. We could not be completely certain – but it seemed that each of them had been at home during at least one (maybe more) of the attacks, so unless we were looking for a group of attackers, it seemed unlikely to be them.

We looked at people who came into the village. We had some regular visitors – tradesmen, mainly. Our tradesmen took their goods out to other villages (and we watched them, too), and some came in. Candlemakers and leatherworkers spring to mind – but they didn't usually come at night or stay late. We had one or two tradespeople (not all men) who had formed relationships in the village, and they would stay over at a house – but again, they usually had a 'witness' to their activities! Again, we talked to other village leaders, and they said that they were experiencing the same problem. Possibly, they had not identified it as consistent behaviour or as a consistent problem. One village definitely said that two girls had complained of being molested, but they regarded those girls as 'silly young things' whom they considered immature, and had disregarded their story. If their complaints were taken as genuine, though, the area might have had as many as twelve to fifteen assaults in a three- to four-month period.

It was about to get worse. One of our girls, Ann by name, was raped one night. She was eighteen years old, and she was popular in the village without being flirty or silly. She had helped a lot of folk, and again that was the reason for her being out late at night. She had helped out at a birth, and left when she was no longer needed. She was unable to say what happened to her after that, and indeed unable to speak for two days. She was examined by our doctor, who confirmed that she had been sexually assaulted – seemingly with force – and there were several bruises on her head and upper body. Under her fingernails were small traces of blood, and her hands and arms were bruised, too. It would seem that she had fought her attacker but had been hit savagely on her head, and this had stopped her making any further resistance. The bruises around her head had removed any memory of the attack but had also changed her as a person.

As Ann recovered, it was clear that the chatty, happy girl we had known before was replaced by a slower and less confident person. Every so often, we caught a look in her eye as if she knew that she had forgotten something, or perhaps had had a fleeting memory of the girl that she had once been, but then that would go, and she resumed her life as it was now. She did less work, and the work that she did now needed to be supervised. She did not go out in the evenings any longer, as she now couldn't do the jobs that she had done before, and now spent more of her time helping her mother in the house, although we suspected, too, that the standard of any work she would do at home would be of lower quality, too. It was awful for those of us who had known her to see the changes in her, and the lack of potential and happiness in her future. It now looked as if she would stay at her home for the rest of her life. It sounds callous to say, but it was possibly a relief for her and her family that she had not also been made pregnant by the rape.

As spring drew on and turned to summer, there seemed to be fewer attacks in our area. Just possibly this was because it was light until later on, and by the time it was full darkness, it was very late. If an attacker wanted to approach our village but not to be seen, then they would not want to come until it was full darkness, after nine and then ten o'clock, when there would be less folk around. We still had our 'officers of the law', too. We did not see them very often, and I think that was part of the plan. I saw them twice, I think, but both times were in daylight, and unless you knew that they were officers, you would not realise this. They carried their cudgel under a cloak – which also concealed their breastplate. We did hear that they had caught criminals and had had some success in stopping pilfering in the towns and villages. A few suggested that these were small crimes that hadn't been worth reporting in the past, and that they had made no difference, although there were incidents where late-night revellers had been brought to the cells by these officers. The constables did not catch our attacker, though, and the problem continued with other assaults.

We checked with the other village leaders. We sat down and checked locations of attacks. There seemed to have been around twenty-five to thirty assaults by this point, all within the last six months. The attacks had started shortly before the constables had been employed, and had carried on with no let-up after they had started. We had nothing that we could identify as a pattern before that. All attacks took place in the hours of darkness, all with no witnesses, and the pattern across five or six villages suggested an increase in violence as the assaults went on. Recently, the number of attacks had slowed slightly over the whole area, not just in our village – perhaps due to the lightness of the evenings that I mention. We agreed to send all of our information to Towcester, but we did not think that they would do much else. They had provided constables, and the only thing we could hope for might be more of them – but usually finances were set for a period, and we did not think that there would be an increase in the numbers of men until the next year. All we could do was to sit and wait, and hope that a constable would catch somebody in the act or be told who it was.

We tried various other things. We tried to have a group of people around at night, but we didn't have enough people to do this properly, and when they went round as a group they used torches – and perhaps that made them more obvious – and they didn't see anyone. Of course, it meant there would not be attacks on those nights – so perhaps they had an effect. We tried to make sure that more people had someone with them – but practically that was not going to work, either. If someone arrives at your door saying, "Mrs Simpkins is giving birth – can you come at once," it is not reasonable to reply that you will just send for someone else to walk with you, and that she will just have to hold on until you get there. What happens is you go, and you take your chances. We did have more girls, though, that would stay overnight in the places where they worked, or in the houses that they had helped out in, and I think with hindsight that might have reduced the number of incidents, but it didn't stop them.

There will always be crime. Crime happens because someone wants what someone else has – either because it is 'unfair' that they don't have it, too, or because it will take too long for them to get it. When a person identifies that they want something, the need for it increases with time, and a realistic expectation of how long it will take means nothing. If life is taken, or injury inflicted, it cannot be returned or undone. In 'justice', we take the life in return for the one that was taken, or we remove freedom. If property or wealth is taken, repayment is expected – and perhaps the law protects property more than life (as it does when a worker has an accident). Perhaps the repayment is an excuse, too, for war. Perhaps it is important that someone's lands or property are returned, and the death of soldiers is necessary in this context. After all, the war started because King Charles thought that his rights and privileges were being 'stolen' by Parliament. There is also one further type of crime, and that is crime that is committed for the benefit of someone else. Is crime permissible if, like Robin Hood, theft is done to give to the poor? Is killing a soldier permissible if it is the only way to stop your friend or a member of your family dying? Is killing permissible to stop any other crime?

FIFTEEN

...AND PUNISHMENT

kept up my usual village committee activities. I continued to deliver messages, news and packages. I did this in the daytime, and I had to do this at night sometimes. I tried to make sure that I (as we were suggesting to other people) was not wandering around, alone, in the middle of the night. I tried to finish my duties earlier, and I undertook to wear trousers in the middle of the night, so that if I had to move at speed, I could do so faster than if I was wearing a dress. This caused some raised eyebrows the first time I delivered a message late at night, but I did not wear trousers in the daytime, because I did not want to become the subject of a village-wide scandal. I wore a cloak with a hood at night, too, as even in the spring and summer it was sometimes cold at night. I carried a basket, too. I was immediately identifiable as me to anyone who saw me.

Most of the people that I delivered messages to regarded me as slightly strange anyway, and as they saw me as the village message system, they put up with me so that they could get information on time and correctly. There were, though, still occasions when I would be walking through our village, deserted, in the middle of the night, seeing the occasional parlour light and passing like a ghost did – unseen and unheard. I also had a secret weapon. I took to carrying our kitchen poker with me, so that I could defend myself if need be. It was about 18 inches long, and the top was looped – so I could put a string through it and hang it round my neck or over one arm. I did not tell folk this, though, as I (myself) thought that this was a bit too much preparation, and that others would not understand. ("Trousers and a poker? I tell you, there's something wrong with that girl.")

Thus, one night, in the summer of 1649, I found myself walking from the vicarage to deliver a message to the top end of the village about some supplies due early the following day. It was a warm evening with a moon. I kept looking up at the moon as it showed me the branches of the trees above my head. I had quite a way to go, and as I walked up the Wappenham road, I realised that there was someone ahead of me with a torch, who was walking slower than I was. It was a girl, and I was gradually catching her up. I had that moment when I worried about approaching someone else from behind in the darkness but decided to let things take their course. As I got closer, I realised that the girl was Florence Kirby – I could tell by the colour of her hair in the torchlight, because she had long auburn curly hair. I had known Florence Kirby since I was a young girl – she was two years younger, and she regularly ran errands and was helpful to me and for others. I had no torch, and I knew that the night would feel warmer and safer if I walked with a friend and a torch.

I did not get to her, though. Whilst I was still 200 yards off, I saw a big black shadowy figure rise up from the side of the road, rush across to Florence, and literally pick her up and carry her off to the other side behind a bush. She dropped her torch in the road as they moved. I heard muffled cries and realised that one hand was over her mouth. I dropped my basket and ran towards the bush, and then hesitated for a moment. Florence was lying on her back behind the bush with the shadowy figure crouched over her, and as I looked, the figure delivered a powerful blow to the side of her head. I could see all this from the flickering of the torch that was still burning. Florence ceased her cries but gave out a little moan. "No," I said to myself, "this monster is not going to have Florence!" The figure rose up slightly, and I realised with distaste that it was removing its trousers, obviously with the intention of raping Florence whilst she was not completely conscious. I struggled with my clothing to free the poker

I was carrying, and then with all my strength raised it high in the air and brought it down on the attacker's head. The attacker shook violently but remained partly upright, and for a second I thought that he was going to get up and come for me.

I brought the poker down a second time, and the figure let out a horrible gasp and collapsed, unmoving, across Florence, who gave another gasp, showing that she was still alive and, as far as I could tell, just immobilised by the powerful fist that had hit her. I stood for a moment, uncertain what to do, with the poker still in my hand – and realised that I needed to get help. I was also very conscious that I was standing next to two immobile people, with a poker in my hand. My imagination told me that the poker was very slightly bent, too. I backed away from the pair on the ground and started to look around in the dark silence for a light somewhere, anywhere, but there was nothing. I moved a bit further – but still I could see no light or sign of movement. I had gone about 100 yards when Florence (and it must have been her) screamed. There was a moment's silence and then a shutter was flung back – the other side of Florence from me – and I heard a voice shout, "Who's there?"

Florence screamed again, and suddenly it felt as if the whole street had woken up. Windows and shutters were flung open, doors opened, heads appeared, feet clattered down steps, lights appeared in windows and folk started to appear with torches and head to where Florence was now calling for help in a broken voice. I ran. God help me, but I ran! I could not cope with the sudden appearance of what felt like half of the village, and I felt immediately that I would be taken as a guilty party – for something. I would be held and taken off to a cell somewhere and executed like those other poor souls I had seen. I ran back towards the green and towards Church Street. With the commotion around Florence, no one saw me go, a figure in black in the dark – with just possibly a little glint of light reflected off the poker I still held in my hand.

I ran to the only place I thought I would be safe, which was the church, although as I ran, my mind changed, and instead I headed for the vicarage. I was not sure what I thought the vicar could or would do, but I could think of no one else that I might run to. Edward became a figure of the law in my mind, commanding but apologetic as he explained in my mind that he could not help a fugitive; or even my father, getting old and unable to understand what I told him – so I headed for the vicar. New, but a man of the cloth, and was it still possible that the seal of the confessional still applied, even though we disapproved of Catholics? I hesitated as I reached the vicarage. The building in front of me had always seemed a friendly, welcoming place, but now, in the middle of the night, there was a hint of menace in the shutters, in the moonlight glinting off the windows, and perhaps for a minute this friendly building had become the home of conscience or justice – and perhaps it was my downfall. Waiting behind the door might be disgrace, punishment, judgement and shame. Perhaps I should run, home, or through the fields to another village or a town. Perhaps I would just start a completely different life somewhere else.

I pulled myself together, banished these thoughts, and then hammered on the front door with the handle of my poker. There was a pause, and then a shutter opened, and I heard the vicar's voice say, "Yes? Who is there?" I had frightened myself by this point that I would be apprehended by the villagers before he could open the door, and hammered on it again. There was movement within, the bolts were drawn back, and there (thank goodness) in front of me with a lit candle was the vicar. The vicar opened the door slightly tremulously as he was not sure what being was on the other side of the door. It had an extremely loud knock, and for all he knew, it might have been Satan himself come to drag him to Hell for envy of his neighbour's vegetables. He was wearing trousers, and a smock, and I don't think I'd woken him. Perhaps he had been studying something – the Bible perhaps. Outside his door he found a small figure clad in dark clothing with a hood up, its face in shadow, and it was clutching a poker, which appeared to have blood and hair on the end. Understandably, he took a step backwards. He made the sign of the cross and asked hoarsely, "Who are you? Fiend or human?" I pulled my hood down and he looked at my face. "Lucy?" he said, moving forward again. "What on earth? What are you doing here at this hour?" I had started to feel strangely unwell by this point – but I knew I had to reply to his question.

"Father, forgive me, I think I have killed a man!" I said to him. He took me by the hand, led me into the house, and shut the front door behind us. I think that he knew me well enough to know that I was not a murderer by habit or by inclination, that something awful must have happened, and that I was not there to harm him. He led me into his parlour and sat me down in a chair by the fire, which was still smouldering gently. He held out his hand for the poker, and I let him take it. He fetched me a small glass of sherry and made me drink it, and then he asked me what had happened. Before I was able to answer, there was another thunderous knocking at the door. He sighed, rose, left the room, edging the parlour door shut behind him, and walked to the front door. I couldn't hear what was said, but I could tell by the tone of voices that someone else had come to tell him what had happened. After a few moments, he shut the front door on them and came back to the parlour where I sat.

"I have to go with them," he said. "You stay here! Don't answer the door to anyone, and if you get tired, curl up in the chair and get some sleep. I might be some time, if what they have told me is true!" I nodded and then leant my head on my hand. He fetched a cloak from a hook, put it on over his clothes, and lit a lantern from the fire. Then he looked at me again for a moment, made the sign of the cross again, and left the room. I stared at the window. I felt unable to move my gaze away from it. I couldn't lose the feeling that someone was going to come after me. If I looked at the window, I would see it come, or I would see the reflection of it. The villagers, the man I had hit, perhaps, his spirit, or even Satan himself. I sat for a long time looking at that window, and eventually I slept. I shouldn't have slept, but from the time I arrived at the vicarage I had started to feel strangely removed from the events of the night, and it all became confused in my head.

I don't remember anything else at all for a while. There is a complete gap in my memory between going to sleep in the chair in the vicar's house and when I woke up one morning in a bed in a bright, airy room that I had never seen before. I felt refreshed, and walking to the window, I looked out onto quite a nice garden, and beyond a hedge, a field of corn, and then a wood. The whole place smelt fresh, and wholesome, and although I had trouble putting my thoughts together, I was fairly sure that I had never seen it before. I heard the door open behind me, and a pleasant-looking woman with dark curly hair came in with a glass of milk. "Ah, I see you are up, Lucy!" she said brightly.

"Who are you, mistress, and where is this?" I asked her.

"This is the village of Akeley, near Buckingham. I am Mistress Thompson. I am the sister of your vicar, Father Andrew Thompson, and you have been here for two weeks," she said. "And I have answered you the very same question every day that you have asked me. You have asked it whenever you have woken up since you came here!"

I had a moment when I could not quite take all of this in. Two weeks? I had been here two weeks? What? Why? Then as a dream, fragments of a previous life started to return. There was something I could not quite put my finger on, but I needed to try and make sense of it. "Helmdon?" I asked her.

"Ah, now that IS different!" she said. "You haven't mentioned your home village before. Perhaps this is what brother Andrew meant when he said that things would start to come back to you! He will be here, tomorrow. He has visited once a week to see how you are. It is quite a long way from Helmdon to Akeley, but he wanted to see how you were. He has to stay one night each time to do this journey. Do you remember your name, too?"

"Lucy, I am Lucy," I said. It was an easy question, and I couldn't think why she was asking.

"That is the first time that you have remembered that, too!" said Mistress Thompson. "You definitely are better!"

I could not remember everything, though. My memory returned to me piece by piece. At first (that first day), I remembered the young days before the war, and then like a water tank filling up, I started to remember our lives as young adults, the start of the war, and almost everything else. By the time another two weeks had passed, and I saw the vicar for the second time, I could remember everything except the days before I had come to Akeley. I told the vicar this, and he said that he didn't know when my final memories would return, or even if they would. He told me that

I needed to stay at Akeley for another week, and then he would come for two nights. He would tell me everything that I needed to know, and it was important that I did not return to Helmdon before I was ready, and knew the story that he would tell me. I suppose that I should have spent the next seven days in a flutter of anticipation, but I am afraid I didn't. I enjoyed the things that I did with Mistress Thompson and found them relaxing and enjoyable. I was not conscious of needing a rest – but I think that is what my body and my mind needed.

The vicar returned. Mistress Thompson let us use her parlour and sat with me in case I needed support from her. I was grateful for that. I did not know how I was going to react to what the vicar said. When we were all sitting comfortably, the vicar lit his pipe – and just the familiar smell of the tobacco was reassuring to me, although his sister got up and opened the window with a disapproving frown. He started to tell me the story that he knew, in stages. He paused after each stage, because I think he wanted to be sure that I would not react badly before he moved on in his story. He told me what he knew for a fact, what he knew that was specialisation, and he did not question me on what I knew – because he believed me when I told him that I had no memory at all of that last day or so in Helmdon – but he felt that I needed to know what they thought had happened. Indeed, I had no memory of some period before that, either. There was a blank of a few months.

The vicar had left me in his chair, when men from the village said to him that there had been another assault on a girl, and that the attacker was dead! It was not known who had killed the assailant, but his body had been found on top of a young woman who swore that he had knocked her unconscious first. She said this when she recovered a bit more. Her story was borne out by several things. She was still under the assailant when her screams had brought help. She could not have mustered enough force to hit and kill the assailant from where she was. The assailant had clearly been hit from behind with some sort of metal object which they had not found, and they had been unable to find whoever attacked the assailant. An empty basket had been found about 100 yards from the incident – but it was not known whose basket it was or if it was connected to the incident. No one had seen any other person in the area before, during or after the incident.

I had arrived at the vicarage with a bloodstained poker. The vicar had thrown it in the river the day after the assault. The vicar saw that a dangerous man who had targeted young women and girls (in at least one case), and who had ruined at least one life, had died. He felt that in running to him, I had intended to confess confidentially or needed God's help – but the stress I had felt had prevented me doing so and taken my memory. He presumed that I had killed the assailant with the poker. He felt that I should not be taken to the cells in Towcester and tried for this. If I had not been sentenced to hang, I might have been sent to a prison or a mental institution or to a colony. He felt that ruining my life in some sort of legal retribution was not a good thing and it was not really justice. He thought that he would have to account for himself to God at some point, and he would do that.

"Will I go to Hell?" I asked him. I still had no memory of this, but I was convinced by the vicar that I must have done this.

"I don't think so, Lucy!" he said. "I don't know if there is some sort of purgatory where you might have to repent, but you have done a good thing for others in doing a bad thing. You have saved many other girls from a lot of pain and harm!" The vicar then told me that when they turned over the body of the assailant, it was one of the Towcester constables. The vicar was the only one there who had been at the 'swearing-in' ceremony – and therefore the only one who recognised him as Constable Peacock. I recalled meeting the officers and my feeling that they did not think very highly of us. A shudder ran through me. They had covered the face and head of the body before anyone else arrived, so the vicar was the only one who knew that one of the constables had died, and he was the only one who knew that the constable had to have been the attacker.

The vicar couldn't be sure, but it looked as if the constable had been attacking women since he came back from the war – even before he had been made a constable, and he had taken that opportunity to carry on his activities. When they found him dead that night, he had none of his uniform on – but he had an excuse as a constable to prowl round the villages at night if he was challenged as to why he was there. The vicar made 'discreet' enquiries. Towcester had no idea that their constable had died in our village, and one month later, they had still not asked us if we had seen him. We had been one of three villages that he patrolled, and there had been attacks in all of those villages. There was no record of which nights constables had been patrolling, and if they had discussed it amongst themselves, they had not written it down. There were no checks made on when attacks were made, and if they coincided with patrols. The authorities in Towcester made no real attempt to find who was doing the attacks, and it was clear that the patrols were only in place to guard the property of the rich. This all went over my head a bit. I still had the vicar's image of what I had done and said, might have done, and might have said – but some of it still didn't feel real.

As far as the village went, an unnamed attacker who had assaulted several of their girls had died whilst attacking another. They cared not, and if they had been asked to search for the responsible person, they would have put no effort in. What they did not want was a body conveyed to Towcester, and other patrol officers coming in, looking for an offender and possibly finding a quick fix with someone who could not answer for themselves properly. "Who else knows about me?" I asked tentatively.

"Your brother, Edward," said the vicar, "although I decided with the villagers that we would give a proper funeral to the 'unnamed' attacker' and he is buried in the bottom corner of the churchyard, I decided that I needed some unofficial response from a member of the civil authority, and who better than Edward?"

"What did he say?" I worried.

"He said that he was very proud of you, and, given the chance, he would tell you that himself! I think that he may have told Olivia Grey, too, but no one else – not even your father." I relaxed a bit. I was glad that my father did not know. He was a bit of a stickler for rules and laws, and he still treated me as his little girl. I didn't want him to look at me with a question in his eyes, or think the worse of me for my crime.

"And you, Father, what do YOU think of me?" I asked, and Mistress Thompson reached for my hand – not for the first time in this ordeal.

"You have saved perhaps a lot more women a lot of pain and suffering," he started. "You have made it a bit difficult, as what should have happened was to see if you were actually guilty of any crime, but that would have been a trial, and that might not have been fair. You have been very lucky that no one saw you, and perhaps I should not have done exactly what I did." He drew breath and I wondered what was coming next. "But I have been told so many good things that you have done over the last seven or eight years, so many people you have helped, even directing a battle? I think you are basically a good person, and it is just that you should not be punished anymore. I think that at some point, you are going to punish yourself further for what you have done. I don't want you to do that, and I want you to be happy. I don't want you to languish in the cells at Towcester for months whilst they work out what to do with you!"

I was crying by that point. I had really underestimated Father Andrew in the past, and he had done so much to help me to put things right that I did not really know how to make it up to him and what to say to him to thank him properly. "There now, Andrew, see what you have done?" scolded Mistress Thompson, and she gathered me into her arms and gave me a big embrace. The father was right. I was sure that when I had truly grasped what I had done, I would be sure to feel some real guilt, and I was not sure how to deal with it. We had a pleasant evening after that, and Father Andrew left for Helmdon. We agreed that he would return in a week and take me home in his cart. I had meant to ask him how I had arrived at Akeley, but I forgot. He had told other villagers that I had overreached myself in my duties, and that I had needed some time for a rest. Everyone who he told this to reacted by agreeing that I had worked far too much for far too long, and the story was accepted without question. No one seemed to tie it in with the death of the rapist.

And so, I went home. Father Andrew turned up the next day, with a little surprise of his own. He brought Florence Kirby with him. He said to her that a nice day out would be good for her, and Florence thought that missing the laundry for one day would be just what she needed. I gave her a hug, and looked at the vicar with a question in my eyes. He shook his head, and when we had a moment he said that Florence knew nothing – and was quite confused about the whole incident anyway. We had another pleasant evening, and then we set out quite early the following morning. I made Mistress Thompson promise to write to me, and to come and see me if she visited the vicar, and she said that she would do that. It took us several hours to get back, and I must admit that I started to feel more nervous as we left the main road on the final stage of the trip. I needn't have worried – as we had several friendly nods or waves as we passed people in the cart.

Father was at home, and the house was very tidy – so I suspected that others had been in to clean and polish for him. He was glad that I was well, and tried to make sure that I had behaved properly "when the vicar has taken so much trouble to make sure that you were well, Lucy," and hoped that I had shown my gratitude. Edward and Olivia appeared very soon after we arrived – so I guessed that a message had been sent quite quickly. My brother gave me a big embrace. This was quite a rare thing, but I guessed that he wanted to show me how much he cared and had worried, and that he was glad that I was apparently unharmed. Olivia hugged me, too, and I was sure that Edward had told her, and I was grateful for her care. Father behaved as I expected – in that he didn't want me to cause too many problems – and he was so keen for normality to be re-established that he would have had me put the kettle on and make his supper, if others hadn't already taken care of that.

My crime was to have killed a man. My punishment was to live with that on my conscience. I potentially might live another fifty to seventy years, and I might have to expect punishment in the next world for my actions in this one. My problem was that I had no memory of what I had done, and I am afraid that, as a result, I didn't feel able to dwell on my actions and force myself to feel guilt that I didn't have. If the vicar and the Church are right, we can expect salvation if we truly repent for our sins. What happens to us if we don't repent for something we can't remember? Perhaps I would have to face that realisation in the future, and then I could properly evaluate what I thought about the events of that night. Would I feel like an avenging angel as it happened, or did I feel some sense of rectitude as I hit the man? This was above my level. I was not able to decide about forgiveness for someone who couldn't remember their crime. I wasn't sure if anyone could do that.

Was I just concerned about saving the girl? I had spent years in the war feeling sick of the thought of violence. I had not even put my name on the list of those prepared to load and shoot a musket at another man, and then *in extremis* (as I believe the word is), I was told that I had picked up a poker and hit a man over the head with it to save a girl. In the end, of course, my memory came back a year or so later. I was not conscious of exactly when, and I felt no awareness of the arrival of the memory. I saw Florence one day, and one of the memories that came into my head was of her spread-eagled on the ground in the darkness, under a dark shadowy figure of a man as he prepared to rape her. I felt again the sense of rage that I had felt on that evening, and I remembered the strikes of the poker as it descended twice on his head. I was aware, too, that I had not remembered this before. I was not initially aware of any horror at myself for what I had done. I saw it as a necessary action.

I spoke to the vicar about the return of my memory. I told him what I have said above – about what had triggered this – and he listened to me. At length, he told me that now I had the memories, I was truly free to repent to God for what I had done, and that repentance was the first step on a ladder towards forgiveness – being a true Christian – and God's forgiveness. He didn't ask me exactly how I felt about the memory, and I was unable at that point to tell him – but I have thought about it since. I have to say now that I do not feel sorry about what I did, and I think that if I was in the same situation again, I would do the same. It is not on the same level – and the only way I can explain it is this. If someone was able to prevent the death of their child, would they kill? If it was the rape of their wife or child, would they kill? If the answer is 'yes' to that, then they potentially could be in the same situation as I was. At what point would they decide not to kill? Would that make it more forgivable?

I did not plan this event or my actions. Even armed with a poker, I had not set out to kill anyone. I had merely set out to protect myself, and at a particular moment, I felt such anger that I killed a man who was about to harm someone that I knew and valued. When I remember this now, I feel no guilt or sadness at his death. I think that if he had got away, he would have done the same again – perhaps even to me. I can anticipate being in the same situation again, and I can see that my reaction would be the same. I am unable to repent properly, and if the vicar is right, then I cannot expect God to forgive me. I cannot expect to be received in Heaven when I die. I still believe in God, and in the teachings of Jesus, and I feel sad about the lack of God's forgiveness, and that I cannot expect to be received in Heaven. In the end, I expect to have to answer to God for my crime, and I will have to tell God that I am not truly sorry for it. God will then have to decide what to do with me.

SIXTEEN

A TALE OF HELMDON

'Once upon a time,' this tale begins. I know that people who were not around for the times and events that I describe will not accept it as fact, and might even dismiss it all as a 'fairy tale'. Stories that people don't accept are often reduced to 'tales' or 'songs' to make them acceptable. The children here sing a song called *Ring-a-Ring O'Roses*. The vicar tells me it is actually about a great plague of old. The ring of roses is the marks that appeared on the arms, the 'pocket full of posies' is about flower petals wrapped in linen, which stopped the smell of death. 'Atishoo' was the sneezing, and 'all fall down' was dead! The children here have started to sing another song, and I am told it is about our war. It is called *Humpty dumpty* and it is about something big and heavy from the army – which was either pushed onto a wall or up against a wall. Either the mud or the wall wouldn't take the weight, and 'Humpty' had a great fall. Something to do with the city of Bristol, and 'All the King's horses and all the King's men' – well, it is obvious where that all comes from. This is a tale of Helmdon, and it can be turned into a rhyme or song if anyone wants it to, but it goes something like this:

A great battle was fought at a place called Worcester in the Year of Our Lord 1651, and it ended a great war that had lasted for nearly ten years. The defeated army and soldiers were killed, taken prisoner or fled from the battle. Some fled in groups, some fled as troops, and a few fled as individuals. Unimportant men simply went home. Nearly a week after the battle, a young maid of my acquaintance was up one bright autumn morning – running an errand or milking a cow or some such. The sun was shining and had not brought any heat to the day. The colours were bright, as they often are first thing in the morning, and the long shadows from the low sun contrasted with the bright colours of the new day. As our maid neared the river that flows through the village, swinging her small basket as she walked down the road, she saw a small group of men sitting on or near the riverbank. They had a small fire going and a small cooking pot on it, and were boiling some water, or perhaps soup. They had horses tethered to a bush nearby, and the horses looked tired. All of the men wore large dark cloaks, but the maid could see evidence of some brighter clothes underneath the cloaks. The men all looked dusty and tired, too, as if they had done too much riding on a dusty road. Some were standing, others resting.

The maid approached the men, and one of them asked her, "What village is this?"

Being a good-mannered young maid (as they all are in tales), she replied, "This is Helmdon, good sir!"

He looked at his friends – perhaps they had heard of Helmdon? It would appear so, because at least one of the others nodded. "And are the villagers here the King's subjects?" he said, putting a slight emphasis on the word King.

Knowing that this meant that these 'gentlemen' were likely to be Royalists, and possibly fugitives from the Parliamentarians, our young maid replied, "Well, most of the men who left in 1642 left to fight for the King, although one or two fought for Parliament, but also at the moment there is a small detachment of Roundhead soldiers at Stuchbury Hall, three miles up the road." At this, one of the men rose to his feet, the first gentleman looked at the others with a touch of alarm, and our young maid mentioned that there would be a regular patrol of those troops along this road at around mid-morning. This did not seem to ease the minds of the men very much – but at least they left the cooking pot on for the moment.

Our young maid further added that the village of Helmdon had always provided hospitality for anyone who wanted it in the war, and that they had done this several times for soldiers of both sides, and that was still the general policy of the village. Helmdon tried not to mind at all what people had done or what side they fought upon, but tried to provide them with a refuge from the fighting.

"That is very good!" said the gentleman nearest to her, who had spoken to her before. He appeared to be the main spokesman for the party, and the others seemed less keen to speak. "That is a very noble policy for a village, and perhaps unusual at this time. As it happens, one of our party, erm... John..." he seemed a bit uncertain of the man's name "...is not very well, and we need to find somewhere for him to rest for a few days, perhaps a week, to recover! It would be best, though, if the gentlemen from Stuchbury Hall were not aware of this!" It was clear to the maid that she had been right, and these were Royalist fugitives from Worcester. The other men nodded their agreement at their leader's statement – as if the first man had said something very wise. He moved aside, and one of the other men – who had been lying nearby – raised himself up from where he had been resting.

Our maid noticed several things. This other man was young – she guessed he was in his twenties – almost certainly a few years younger than she was. He had a noble countenance that was strangely pleasing to her, and an engaging smile. He looked, though, tired and haggard, and as his friend had said, it looked as if perhaps he had a small fever. He was a little sweaty, and was intense in the gaze he fastened onto our maid with bright eyes – which may also have indicated a small fever. "He is not really ill," continued the other gentleman, "but he really needs a few days' rest, and a few days out of the saddle! We have a long way to go, and I don't think our friend can do the whole trip in the state he is in at the moment."

The young maid thought quickly. She knew several houses where this noble man could rest up, but there was only one place where discretion could be guaranteed – without gossip around the village – and that was in her own house. That was also one of the closer houses to the path from the river. She thought that it would be possible for the young man to use one of the bedrooms for a few days without it being spoken of all around the village.

She said all of this to the gentlemen but added that they would have to move quite quickly, or other folk would be up and about, would see them, where they went, and might be asking questions of them. She said that they would have to trust her not to speak of this, and they seemed to accept this – perhaps they felt that they had no choice in the matter. Perhaps they also felt that a young maid looking after their friend would be a bit unusual in 'normal days', but then this was not normal. Perhaps, too, they felt (but did not say) that a village house with one young maid in would be beneath their friend's station! She walked with two of the men assisting the tired young man on a smaller path up to the village – whilst two of them waited with the horses by the river. The man was walking slightly unsteadily, but that was usual for someone who had done too much riding. When they got to the top of the path, she carefully looked around but could see no one, and so they assisted the man across the road to the other side, into the backyard and then through the back door of her house.

The house seemed a bit small with four of them in the downstairs room, but they all helped him upstairs to one of the two bedrooms, and then his friends went downstairs again with her. "Someone will look in, in two to three days, to see how he is doing, when there is no one else around, but we will return in one week today, at this same time, to take him away with us. Please take very good care of him for us – as he is important to us – but, please, would you tell no one else?" they asked, and she agreed. The maid had a father who was away on a trip, and she was not expecting him back for a week. This was convenient, because although she trusted her father, it would make things more complicated and the house would seem smaller. She did, though, have a young friend from nearby who came in most days, cleaned and helped her around the house. Our maid rubbed a little butter into her forehead so that it looked sweaty, and rubbed some ash into her cheeks to make them look a little grey. When her friend arrived at the door, she hunched over a little and told the friend that she had a little fever and wanted to rest in bed for a few days and not do too much.

She told the friend that cleaning the house would raise dust and she had a sore throat, too – which the dust would irritate. It would be best, she said, if the friend didn't come for a few days, although perhaps she could knock on the door of the house each morning to ensure that the maid was alive! Her friend readily agreed to this unexpected holiday from work – because although she enjoyed doing the cleaning and helping out as a rule, a break was always welcome, and she left. Our maid went upstairs to find her new guest asleep on the bed, and so left him to sleep. She found herself doing quite a lot of errands for this man over the next few days. He recovered quite quickly from his fever, although for two nights he was quite restless but was obviously used to having people run around and fetch and carry for him, and didn't perhaps quite understand why he couldn't have everything that he wanted to have. As it was, our maid had to send her friend several times to the shops to buy things for her. Perhaps her friend thought she was eating a little more than normal – but, if so, she said nothing. After all, 'feed a cold and starve a fever'.

Our maid's guest showed few signs of wanting to get up and move around for a day or two, and this as well was useful – as she didn't have to worry about keeping him away from the windows or the door so that anyone passing would not see him. It also made it quicker and easier to get things ready for him if he was not in her way. All she really had to do was prepare food, empty the chamber pot and check that the bedding was still suitable for him. After two or three days, he started to get bored with being upstairs most of the time. He could come down in the evenings, when she could lock the door and pull the shutters across – when it didn't seem unusual. She brought him a copy of the Bible to read – as it was the only book that she was able to get hold of, and that occupied him a bit. She sat upstairs sometimes and taught him the games she had learnt as a girl – guessing games, a card game or two. He watched her sew and knit, but neither of them had the least interest in him learning to do those things properly. Sometimes, it rained, or was dull. He found those days easier to be indoors with her. On the bright days, he seemed more anxious to be out and moving. He had more purpose.

Our maid also found her guest very attractive, and on perhaps the third night, whilst she was giving him water, he reached over and stroked her cheek. She was never quite clear exactly what happened after that, but she joined him in his bed and stayed the rest of the night with this man. As we have said, she was a maid – with all that the term means – but this man was surprisingly gentle with her – perhaps because of his illness – and she was happy to sleep with him not only for that night but for the few other nights he was there, until the early morning that his friends came for him. She was surprised in herself that she had done this with a man that she did not know, and without a period of getting to know him properly, but she had become aware over the last two years (or so) of her loneliness, and she wanted some of the companionship that she saw others have. To sleep with a stranger, too, possibly avoided the complication of a longer-term relationship that she did not want to have or to try and sustain.

They talked a bit, too, but he did not want to tell her what he had done in the war, or who he really was, or where he had been. Occasionally, he would let slip a chance remark, and from that she gathered that he expected to head south after he left her, stopping off with trusted friends – and she thought that he might end up catching a boat across the Channel. He certainly seemed to think or suggest that there was little for him left in England for the foreseeable future. Perhaps he had lost family or friends. Perhaps there was no one left for him here. Perhaps he would be sought out by Cromwell and his officers and punished, or worse. Her guest started to regain interest in his appearance, so she repaired and washed his clothes so that he appeared more presentable. She washed his hair for him – this was difficult for him to do with a basin. She had shaved her father's face in the past, so she was able to provide this service for her guest without failing or cutting his skin. There were also a few occasions during the daytime when he 'reached for her' again – but she didn't feel easy being in bed with him during the day as anyone might knock on the door, and this only happened once or twice as a result. He didn't seem to take offence, though, when she laughed and left.

Our maid's guest was not content to stay in her house for the whole week. He wanted to see what the village was like, and he wanted to see the soldiers of 'the other side' as they patrolled the village. She wasn't happy about this. She did not want anyone to see a strange man leave or enter her house during daylight, and there was a great danger that the soldiers would apprehend her guest as a stranger. There was only one way to do this, and John, the noble man, had to agree to give his word to make only one visit outside the house. The way of getting him outside the house and into the village was to dress him literally in a dress. To say he would be a washerwoman is perhaps too much of a cliché, but he would dress as an older woman. If he carried a basket of pegs, he could pass as a trader from outside the village, and with a low bonnet, clean shaven and with a neck scarf shielding his face, his maid could see that it would work for a short period of time. The soldiers were likely to patrol between eleven in the morning and twelve midday, so the two of them knew what time he would have to leave the house to get to the centre of the village.

Before eleven, they picked a moment when there was no one in the back lane, and he left the house. She had told him which way to go, and she had arranged to follow him to the green. Indeed, she left the house shortly after him, also covering her face. She was supposed to be ill, but it would not matter that much if she was recognised – because she could say that she was getting a little air and was 'feeling a bit better'. Accordingly, she followed him to the green, and there they sat in the low branches of an oak tree – as she had seen other folk do during the day. Around twelve, the soldiers arrived. There were only twenty of them, but they were quite impressive to the villagers. Edward was riding at the head of the troop. She saw her guest stiffen slightly at the sight of the troop and reached to hold his hand. "Who is their commander?" he whispered.

"Edward Brown!" she said. Edward saw her as they passed, and lifted his hand to his helmet as the troop went past.

"He knows you, then?" whispered her guest.

"Yes, he is my brother!" she said, and he pulled his hand away from her. "Don't worry, I am not going to tell him about you! I promised!" she said, and took his hand again. "Anyway, my father is on your side!"

"And you are in the middle of it all?" she heard him whisper. He shook briefly, and she realised that he was shaking with laughter at her situation.

They watched the soldiers walk on, and then they returned to her house as discreetly as they had left. He didn't ask to go out again. He had realised that seeing twenty soldiers quite closely was quite different to seeing the massed rank of the opposing army on a battlefield, and perhaps the soldiers had appeared too similar to those he had seen killed on those fields. It was also possible that he had realised the possible risk to her being seen with him in front of her brother, his soldiers and the villagers. In any case, he only had one more night in the village to spend with her in her house – and her bed. She was relieved in a way that he was going, but she felt something for him that she had not felt for another man before his visit – and she felt it had changed her in some way. She was sure that the war was shortly going to end, and that this might be her last chance to do something out of the ordinary in the course of the war. Presumably, when the war ended, there would be a return to normal customs and behaviour, and expectations of a woman's conduct, too. Hiding men in a bedroom might be suitable for a war, but she would be judged badly if she did the same after the war was over.

There were, too, to be more soldiers in the village over the next month or so. The last battle had been won, and, to all intents and purposes, Parliament had one. They had no intention of rounding up those of the Royalists who could still cause mischief. Individual soldiers were not a problem, and indeed a few had started to return to the village – but there were more patrols of more soldiers passing through Helmdon. Sometimes, they would ask returning Royalists what their intentions were – and on most occasions the answer was "To go back to my farm" or plough or shop or family. They were looking for troops of men, to disband them, or to find out if they intended to fight more, and of course they were still looking for leaders of the Royalist army, such as the man that our maid was concealing in her house. If estate owners were to accept the new regime and return to their estates, or be persuaded to serve the new regime, then they were of use and could be permitted or even helped to do this. If, though, there was any chance that the former leaders saw a return to battle or war as possible, they needed to be captured and restrained. With no large Royalist armies still in existence, Parliament could spare more men to look for their leaders.

The maid's guest's friends came for him on the following day as they had said they would, and quite early in the morning. He was quite ready for them by then, healthier in appearance and manner (obviously because of her good care of him), and they hurried across the road and there mounted the horses that they had brought with them. She saw from the doorway that he looked back once and blew her a kiss, but then they all rode off – slowly at first so as not to disturb the neighbours. She saw them change to a canter, further down the road, and then they all disappeared around the bend. She was sorry to see the man go, but she had her own life to live, and if he had stayed any longer, there might have been questions about him staying in her house. As it was, she cleaned the linen, washed the pots and tidied up the house, and when her friend came round the next day to knock on the door, she told her that they could go back to normal on the following day and that 'she was all well'. After two weeks, it started to feel like a bit of a dream, and she valued her solitude – and the tasks that she did around the village, which had had to wait whilst she was 'ill' for a few days.

After another month or so, she realised that her noble guest had left her an unexpected present, and that the description 'maid' could no longer be applied to her. Her little 'present' was going to become more obvious in her belly in another two or three months, and then she would have to start thinking of excuses and explanations, and to make plans for her future. She went to talk to the vicar, and then together with him talked to her father when he returned from his trip. Neither man was overjoyed at the turn of events, but after nine years of war, it was something that had happened lots of times in the village – and it was no longer really a surprise when a woman without a husband became pregnant and had a baby. Further, although the vicar was a good man, her father was not perfect, and understood that a single maid was going to make some mistakes. Perhaps he was surprised that she had not made mistakes earlier. In any case, he didn't feel quite as able to shout at her or insult her, and in the end he would prove to be very supportive. Gradually, our 'maid's' friends and other folk grew to know about the baby, and whilst some were surprised and some were horrified, others were pleased about her news 'if she were also pleased' as they put it. It became an accepted fact.

The baby boy was born in June of 1652, and at her request he was baptised one month later. Baptisms were done early in those days due to the fear of child mortality, although her son seemed to be very strong and healthy. There was only her, the vicar and the two godparents at the baptism. Her 'guest' and his friends had said that the guest's name was John – but he had seemed surprised when she called him that, and she suspected that this was a made-up name for convenience. She had only heard him use one name – a name that he had called out twice in his sleep – and that was 'Stewart', so she christened the baby Stewart John, and gave it her surname. The father's name was given as John of Worcester on the birth certificate so that the baby had a father, and to give her story some credence. There were a number of children in the village with 'unknown' written on the certificate, or in some cases just a blank space, and she felt it would be better for the baby later in life if it appeared that she had known and cared for its father – even if that was not exactly the case.

The baby grew up happily with her in her house, and they had a nice life together for the next few years. Her friend helped her with the baby as well as cleaning the house, and there were other women in the village with babies of a similar age. They helped her as well, and they all shared in the care of their children. Many years later, though – more than ten years later – she saw a picture – a print – with a picture of the baby's father on it, and at last she knew the true identity of the baby's father. Once she saw that picture, she knew that she could never tell the truth to her son, or about her son, and if she did it would mean that her baby would be taken away from her – if she were believed, and possibly her life would never be the same again. It was more likely, though, that if she told the truth, she would be called a liar. The story about this young man that went with the picture mentioned something about this man hiding out in an oak tree somewhere, but it said nothing about Helmdon, so there was no suspicion that the oak tree was in that village, and that was the way that our young woman was determined it was going to stay!

If this was written as a song, it might go:

'A great man of England once stayed with us here.
He ate off our dishes, and drunk of our beer.
He loved a young maiden, who he found dear, but
He was long gone, when her time it drew near!
And then probably fa la la la, etc.

A moral tale, then, for you in this song.
Some things are right, and some things are wrong,
Do not judge folk if your morals aren't strong
But help if you're needed to help them belong.
With a Hey Nonny No and an Oopsi Down Daisy.'

SEVENTEEN

MICHAEL'S STORY, 1651–52

The final battle of the war was that of Worcester in 1651. I was nearly ten years older than I had been at the start of the war, and whilst I did not feel older, I was respected much more as a member of the village. People asked my advice instead of just telling me what to do. I was still a member of our committee and I still helped make decisions. What I missed very much, though, was the presence of a lot of the older generation. I realised that as we get older, we welcome the freedom that we want, but then realise that we valued the guiding hand of our parents or elders that we had when young, and sometimes freedom seems like a less solid footing – where we take responsibility for the consequences of our actions. The war felt as if it had been started by the elder generation, but with the deaths and destruction of a lot of the country, it was our generation that had to finish the war off, and the people that I spoke to, or knew, did not want it to go on.

At Worcester on the 3rd of September, Cromwell's New Model Army defeated the Royalist army – mainly consisting of Scots under the leadership of King Charles the Second. This was the last, I think, of thirty-nine or forty battles that had taken place over nine years. We got our news of the battle in the village late, as usual (I think it took at least two months to arrive), and I think that none of us (in the village) knew that this would be the last major battle of the war. None of us really knew that this was a last round-up of anyone left who would fight for the Royalist cause. Even when we did get the news of the battle, and then that it was the final defeat of the Royalists, it was fragmented and piecemeal, and it took some time for us to get news that we might want, or which we felt was relevant to us in Helmdon. News often came with individuals returning to the village, or walking through it to return home. It was often sporadic, inaccurate and contradicted others. We got no news of Robert Grey, Mark Green or Stephanie White for some months after that.

The first thing we heard was in late October, and that was that Robert Grey, like his father, was dead. We did not know how he had died, but we did not really expect to know what had happened to one captain in a large battle. The news hit us harder than it had done for Robert's father, or Sir Henry, as they were older, and one might expect that they would suffer more from a war. Robert was in his twenties and could have been expected to come home, take over the estate, and rise to some position of responsibility in the country. He was a friend of mine. All of his potential was wasted, and worse, it was wasted in a kind, honourable man – who had done what he felt he had to. The future of the estate now rested solely on the shoulders of Olivia. She could cope with that, but she had lost two of her family now, and that was not easy – even with Edward's support.

It seemed that the army would not arrange to bring Robert's body back for interment in the family tomb as they had done with his father. It seemed that there were so many dead that it was no longer felt desirable to bring all of the dead home, and although Robert had briefly inherited his father's title, he was not regarded as a major public figure. Instead, Robert would be buried in a churchyard in Worcester, and if he was to have a headstone or memorial, then Olivia would have to arrange and pay for that, and have them transported to Worcester or built there, and then arrange for them to be located correctly. I saw her briefly, after the news, ashen-faced and hollow-eyed. She was to leave the following day to make these arrangements, and the only thing that seemed to hold her together was Edward, who would go with her to help.

It was clear to everyone now that Olivia and Edward were in love with each other, and with Edward's elevation to senior military rank, that he would probably marry Olivia and live with her at the estate before very much longer. The title, now, would lapse as there were no close relatives, and the Grey estate would potentially change name to whoever ran it. My father and Harriet Green were to organise the estate whilst Olivia and Edward were gone, but my father had aged considerably during the war, and had felt the death of Lord Grey and Robert very keenly. I thought, looking at him, that this might be the last time he would take any real responsibility in running the estate, and that it was very likely he would retire to our cottage after this and sit in the sun or relax with those of his age group – those who had been left unscathed by the war. That would certainly save him any possible embarrassment in stewarding an estate which his son might take over!

We entered a 'commonwealth', where Cromwell took over the country. The title had first been used in 1649, but it didn't seem to mean much to us. Cromwell seemed to us to be a new king – although he refused to be called that. The country was (in name) run by Parliament – but they never seemed to meet. No decisions were made, and as far as we were concerned, there was no real change. Our only decent 'squire' had died. His son never came back. His daughter still owned the quarries, and she did her best to follow Sir Henry's way of supporting local folk and treating tenants properly. Village discussions involved her less than they had Sir Henry. They were more likely to come to the village committee. We changed it to a village council in 1649, and although there were grumblings from the richer families in the village, they took no part in making decisions – and truth be told, they did not want the responsibilities.

The country needed money to repair towns and their walls, to help villages restart their farming activities, and there didn't seem to be any money. Most of the major landowners who had joined the war still had their estates – or their sons did, or their close relatives did – and whilst there were some cases of property being handed over to the victors, it made very little difference to anyone else. Across the country, churches were plainer – a lot of them having been made that way in the war. Some villages (like ours) had survived the war with buildings, farms and housing all intact, and we carried on our farming and small businesses the way we had before. Goods were sold, rents (and some taxes) were paid, God was worshipped, and as we felt better off than most, so we thanked God for that, even if I thought that I was not his favourite person.

That was it for a while. We were told that the war dragged on for a year or two after that, but I have to say that we didn't see any sign of it. We were aware that there was a 'commonwealth', and we were aware that certain things, like Christmas, were disapproved of, but we found that if we kept to ourselves and did not boast about what we did, then no one bothered us. Because there was no real news, we would not know if we were still waiting for people to return from the war, or if they were still in the army, or if they were dead. What happened after Worcester was that we saw more folk on the road, some of them heading south, a few coming back to our village, and some who just said that they were not needed and were going home. Just once or twice, we had someone come to us in the village with news or information that we wanted to hear, and one of those (and the most important of all of our sources) was a man called Michael.

Michael appeared in Helmdon in the autumn of 1652. He was the sort of man we had seen on the roads, either looking for a meal or a bed for the night. Generally slightly untidy, often with the look of those regularly underfed for a few years, sometimes with a pike or another weapon, rarely really threatening, and often nothing like we imagined a soldier in the ranks of an army would look. An army (or at least the few bits we had seen) looked menacing, whereas these few remains of an army looked half-starved and pathetic. Michael was perhaps a few years older than me, not unattractive, and seemed both restless and nervous in demeanour. I was approached by a neighbour who told me that there was a strange man sitting against a tree on the village green, and what should they do with him. Apparently, I was expected to know!

I went down to the green with another neighbour – a more elderly man – and we approached the man, who was sitting (as I had been told) against a tree, and who appeared to be sewing up a tear in his shirt. He was looking around at the people who passed, and seemed in no hurry to move on. He wasn't known to us, but he didn't look like a danger to us.

We greeted him, welcomed him to Helmdon, and asked him if he was looking for a meal. He acknowledged that a meal would be very welcome, and that he hadn't eaten for the last day or two. We told him that we kept a barn where strangers could be fed. We did this because we had done this for a few years, and it was helpful to have somewhere regular where we knew we could put up a guest for a night, rather than have to arrange it each time someone arrived.

The man gathered up his belongings and followed us willingly enough down the lane from the green to the barn. We sat him down on a bench in the barn, heated him up some broth and gave it to him with some bread, cheese and a small glass of our beer. He ate (as you might expect) quite quickly, but not as messily as some folk we had seen, and he obviously enjoyed the food that we had given him. We sat down with him so that he would have someone to talk to if he wanted, but, like a lot of our visitors, he was either not used to talking at meals or it was something he preferred not to do. At length, he finished the food, took a last drink of the beer, and stood up to stretch himself. He refrained from belching, which to me was always a good sign, and then sat down again – perhaps wondering what we wanted him to do next.

"Now then, stranger," I said, "we ask for no payment for food, but we would ask you to tell us about yourself, and your story. We don't get much in the way of news around here, and we don't hear enough of the war and those people in it, so we ask for your information, in repayment. Does that sound reasonable to you?"

"Aye," he said, "it sounds very reasonable, and I will happily tell you my story, but first I have a question for you both. Two questions, I mean." We agreed to answer his two questions if we could. "Is this village called Helmdon?" he asked. We told him that this was indeed Helmdon. "Home of Sir Mark Green?" he asked. We hesitated. He could be asking as a friend of Mark's or an enemy. Mark was not here, and no one knew where he was, but we did not want to get drawn into any reprisals or debts of Mark's. Eventually, we nodded, and the stranger told us that he had been looking for this village, and that he wanted to tell us his story.

His name was Michael. He did not give us another name but said that he came from a village in Devon called Bow – in the middle of that county. He said that as he had given that answer so many times in the years since he had left Devon, he had come to be called Michael Bow by the people he had met and fought with. He said that like several young men he knew, he had joined the army rather than carry on the same boring life in the village he had left. We nodded at that, because we had heard the same story from many young men. It was not so much that they had a clear idea of what soldiering was like, or that they had a great desire to kill, or even that they had strong beliefs, but that the world of a soldier seemed so much more interesting, and the excitement of flags, guns and uniforms carried them away – often from their homes, and their common sense.

Michael Bow had walked the few miles down to the local town of Crediton with his three friends from Bow, and had then joined another twenty or thirty young men. The area was predominantly in favour of the Parliamentary cause – taking its lead in this from the county town of Exeter, and in fact some of the Royalists had taken against the country towns because of this, sacked them, and caused more resentment of the King because of the soldiers' behaviour. This, though, was all after Michael and his friends had already left the area – and were in a roundabout way headed for Lansdowne, which was to be the first major battle that they saw. The first soldier Michael saw killed, however, was one of their own lads who was killed whilst they were learning how to use muskets. "It hasn't gone off!" said Bert as he swung round with a loaded musket. Michael and two others hit the ground as the musket did 'go off', shattering the head of another poor lad who now happened to be in front of Bert and his musket.

The man in charge hit Bert very hard for disregarding the training he had been given, and took him out of the camp. If Bert hadn't been in training in the army, he told them, he would be hung for murder, and none of them would want an idiot like that besides them in battle. Michael looked at me apologetically at this point as he told us this story – he thought the detail would be upsetting for a woman, and maybe it would have been a few years ago. They buried the poor dead lad there and then, just outside the camp, and they carefully made a wooden cross to stand guard over him. There were more crosses in their future to be made by the troop, but by the time they had seen another twenty or thirty potential soldiers die from accident or carelessness (or even just because the banners were the wrong colour), they had stopped bothering to make crosses, and in battles they had even stopped burying the bodies, because there were so many of them.

Michael said that the usual practice in a battle was to kill all of the prisoners but to keep the noblemen for ransom – demanding money from their families. If the families wouldn't pay, or the money wasn't enough, they killed the noblemen as well. There were exceptions to this. Sometimes, when a battle or skirmish was lost, the victors would take the losers into their army. If the losers were known to be from a force that strongly supported their cause, they would be killed. If they were Irish, apparently, that meant they were dangerous and should all be killed, and Michael had been told about losers who had been killed in a church after claiming sanctuary. That didn't seem right. If the losers were like Michael and his friends, who had joined a local band, they could be taken into the winning army. They would be put on the front rank so that they weren't behind those who had captured them, but often after another battle, they would just become like the others.

Once they had complained with the other soldiers, slept beside them, eaten with them and occasionally raided with them, it seemed to matter very little which side they were actually on. There were even occasions where their officers were persuaded to change sides, and the soldiers were given no choice but to follow them. Michael swore that his group had changed sides at least twice in the ten years, and he also said that in one place they had lined up near the battle and had only joined in when their commander had been sure who was going to win. Joining the winning side of a battle was seen as 'an acceptable military strategy'. After all, for many of them, their lives were going to be much the same whichever side actually won the war, but if they joined the wrong side at the wrong time in a battle, they might well be dead.

Michael thought that he had fought in five or six of the major battles and a much larger number of what were called skirmishes – which were smaller battles between smaller forces. As time went on, the number of men whom he had known at the start of the war got fewer and fewer. To start with, they were 'The Crediton Lads', then they were part of 'The Devon Company', whatever that was, and then they were the 'West Country Brigade'. At one time, he was absolutely certain that he had been part of Fairfax's troops, and he was certain that at another point his captain had shouted out "Hurrah for Prince Rupert" as a garish figure in bright colours had cantered past on a thundering great big horse accompanied by two large dogs! He had even seen his captain praised by Cromwell, and Michael was only six feet from that man. Michael had realised that comparing Cromwell to Prince Rupert might not have been taken well by his officers.

For the last two years (since the Battle of Preston), Michael said that he had come under the command of Sir Mark Green – at which our ears pricked up, and we started to follow the details of his story more closely. Michael had come into contact with Mark because the troop he was in had been transferred to Mark's command. Mark did not seem to operate as part of the larger Parliamentary forces but operated as a smaller separate group. Often, they would go out raiding for food for the army, or they would scout out the surrounding area for other forces, or they would collect information, and increasingly they would be sent to round up small groups of Royalists as Parliament took over control of more of the country. Sometimes, they were just used as a force to show that the Parliamentary army was present.

Michael learnt quickly that Sir Mark was an angry man. Mark had demonstrated that he felt he had not been treated fairly or given the right chances, and whilst it was obvious that Mark liked the freedom to take charge of a troop away from the army, it was clear that he really saw himself as having the same ability as the colonels or the generals, and that he was being deprived of his chance to make a difference to the war. Michael learnt, too, that when Sir Mark was sent to 'round up a few Royalists', this invariably meant that Mark would just instruct his troops to shoot them all, whether or not they had surrendered. Michael knew that there was very little he could do about this without being killed himself, and he quickly learnt that if he fired a musket just over the head of a prisoner, he would not actually be killing unnecessarily, and sometimes even just a minor wound would give someone the chance to slip away later. This was preferable to murder.

Michael also learnt that Sir Mark assumed that all civilians were spies, and if the 'spies' were left alone, he was sure that they would give information to the enemy, and so Mark invariably slaughtered civilian men if he had ammunition left, often raped their women 'to get information', and even locked their children up – uncertain whether they would be released before they starved. Sir Mark had become a name associated with suspicion, violence and hatred, and had caused deep distrust of the Parliamentary army by civilians. In battle or skirmish, he took foolish risks, and regularly needed reinforcements of extra men because of the risk at which he put his soldiers. He was distrusted by his superiors and equals, and hated by his soldiers. He was sent off on separate missions with his troops because no one wanted him in their command.

Sir Mark was at Worcester with his troop, because Cromwell wanted the largest amount of men possible to defeat the Royalists one last time and send them a message that all hope was lost. Sir Mark wanted to be there, because Michael thought that they all knew this might be the last battle. The Royalists seemed to have been losing for four years – but no one had told the Royalists! Cromwell himself was not blameless in the war, and was known for killing prisoners. To that extent, Sir Mark Green would serve under Cromwell – especially if he had the chance to bring himself to Cromwell's notice, and he believed that he followed in Cromwell's footsteps. Cromwell, though, it was rumoured, had heard enough to distrust Mark. At any rate, Mark and his troop would find themselves in the middle of Cromwell's 28,000 troops and fairly near the front rank of them – away from Cromwell, and in quite a dangerous position.

The battle was wearisome, and seemed to last a long time. Michael had heard enough before the battle to know that the Royalists were seriously outnumbered, and like many others, he assumed that this would be a quick battle, easily won, and quite short. It wasn't, or it wasn't anything like as short and easy as Michael – who was growing tired of nine years of fighting – would have liked it to be. There seemed to be move and countermove, charge and counter-charge. Every time soldiers were pushed back, they seemed to move round and come the other way – but perhaps that was just Michael's tiredness making him think that. Towards the end of the battle, there were some more counter-charges from the Royalists. One group came past Sir Mark's troop, and as they drew level, Mark shot the leader of the group through the head. To Michael, this would have been just another Royalist casualty, if it hadn't been for the reaction of Mark.

"Mark made a great song and dance of this one," said Michael. "He swung round to his men saying, 'See, that was Robert Grey, Lord Robert Grey! I said I would have my revenge on him and his family. Dirty Royalist dogs that they were!'" Michael stopped his story at this point. My hands had gone to my mouth (this seems to be my immediate reaction to shock – I have noticed), and I must have gasped. "Does that mean something to you, miss?" he asked.

"Yes, it does," I said. "We knew that Robert Grey was dead. His estate is about three or four miles that way, and his sister went up to Worcester to arrange for his gravestone. She didn't know how he died, and I don't really want to tell her. Mark hated her family – and he didn't really have a good reason for the hatred. None of us knew that he had killed Robert Grey, just that Robert was dead."

"I am afraid that Sir Mark Green didn't have much reason for hatred towards a lot of the people that he killed," said Michael, "but that is not why I am here. I didn't know that Lord Robert Grey lived so close. I came here because of what happened to Sir Mark Green.

"We had won at Worcester – there was no doubt about it. All that remained was some mopping-up of the remainder of the King's troops, and sorting out the lords that we could ransom from the rest of the survivors. I was standing guard near our leaders with a couple of mates – and Sir Mark was discussing what to do next with some of the other generals. They had a bit of a chat and then Sir Mark moved apart from them to look over the last bits of the battle. This young lad appeared through a bit of a haze. He was wearing one of our banners – so we assumed he was one of us. He was holding his musket in front of him, and it took us a few seconds to realise that this wasn't just random, because he was facing partly away from us, but his musket was deliberately pointed at Sir Mark.

"The lad spoke to Sir Mark. I heard him call 'Mark,' and Mark turned and then the lad said something that I didn't hear. Sir Mark said, 'What about her?' The lad said something else and Sir Mark said, 'No, you can't be!' Then the lad shot him through the chest. We shot the lad dead immediately and we rushed over to them. Sir Mark was still alive, but only just. He opened his eyes, looked past us and said, 'Stephanie,' but blood bubbled up through his mouth and he died in front of us. We took a look at the lad, then – but he had been shot in the head and he was obviously dead, face down, lying in the mud. He had a small bracelet tied to a powder bag – which I took off him. It seemed a shame to leave it lying there in the mud. I have it here, still. It must have been a present from his sweetheart, or maybe from his mother. I have no idea why the lad killed Sir Mark, though."

He showed me a small bracelet which I recognised as belonging to Stephanie White. There was no point in looking at it closer, or asking questions, or getting involved in giving explanations to Michael. It was a shock that Stephanie was dead, but I think I knew that the last time I saw her, she would not come back to us – or if she did, she would not be the same person that we knew before the war. I also knew that Stephanie's body now lay amongst the thousands buried at Worcester – or even with those who were not buried and were just ploughed into the ground.

I turned to Michael and asked him what his plans were for the future. "I don't really have any," said Michael. "I just thought of heading back to Devon to see what was available. I don't have family there any longer. There may be someone there who remembers me and will give me work, or I will just move on."

"Stay here awhile," I said. "I am not sure how much I can let you tell the families, but both Mark Green and Robert Grey have sisters here. Harriet Green still lives in the family house, and even if she just knows that Mark is dead, at least she will know, and not spend more time wondering if he will come back. Perhaps the village will accept her as the mistress of the house instead of just a stand-in for her brother. I don't think we should tell Olivia Grey that Mark killed Robert, but I might tell Edward – my brother. We could find work for you here. We are short of menfolk, and I am sure that we can find you lodgings. If you stay and then want to leave, that will be up to you, but you could give us a chance and see how you find us!"

"Aye," said Michael, "I would like that. It has been so long since I have been invited to stay anywhere."

Harriet was never told the full story. After a little practice, Michael told her that he had served under Mark in the war, 'and he had been a really good commander', at which Harriet looked a bit sceptical as that didn't really fit correctly with other things that she had been told. Michael told her, too, that he had been present at Mark's death at Worcester, 'where he had been heavily outnumbered and had died heroically protecting his men'. Harriet looked more sceptical, and I wondered if we had overdone the story just a bit. No one else seemed able to tell her about Mark, and there was certainly no argument from any other source – so she had to accept it from Michael. She paid for a memorial plaque in the church, and she told me that he had done a lot of bad things – but perhaps deserved the plaque. I never hinted to her, by look or smile, that Michael had told anything other than the truth.

Michael never left the village. Two years later, I married him and became Lucy Bow. Privately, I consider that a slightly funny name, but it suits, and it is how I, and our children, Stewart, Robert and Stephanie, are named some five years later. We live in my family house, and my father did indeed retire there, although he is now dead, having been weakened more than we thought by his activities in the war. He approved very much of Michael, and was happy for us both. The house was quite full at one stage, with us, Father and our first baby, Stewart. Father died before we had our second or third child, or the house would have been very difficult to stay in. Michael now has part ownership of one of the local farms, and when the other owner, the widow Haskins, dies, he will be permitted by her family to buy her share, and it is possible that we will then all move to the farm to live.

We are tenants in our house, so it will be passed on by Edward and Olivia to another family when we move. I keep up to date with my half-brother, Robert, and his mother, Susan. She agrees that when he is older, we will tell him who his father was, and of our relationship. We won't tell him everything, though! I eventually told Michael the story of our group of friends – and what had happened to them. He was grateful that I was alive, and impressed by all of the things that I had seen and done. In the end, I also told him about my great crime. He said he was impressed by what I had done. He said that I had killed one person for the best of reasons, and that he might have killed more people for the wrong reasons. He said that if we faced the day of judgement, I was more likely to be the one who was accepted into Heaven than him. Again, I have not told him absolutely everything.

I married Michael, obviously, because I was very attracted to him, but also because he showed that his humanity and common sense had not been affected by the war. He had come to us with memories that he wanted to forget, but he was not permanently scarred by those memories. His faith in the general goodness of people and his faith in some sort of God were unharmed. He believed that we would not want God to interfere in everything we do, because it would affect our freedom to choose. He believed wars were the result of our inability to do things properly, or our selfishness, and he had the sense and judgement to link together what he knew, put it all together and talk sensibly about it. I think in another time, he could have been some sort of priest or advisor – but, of course, his views didn't really fit with those of the Church. Michael was happy, too, to take me on, a single woman with a young child. He believes that my son Stewart was the son of a man who died in the war, and it is best it remains that way. He doesn't ask if we were married.

I married Michael, also, because he knew nothing about me as a younger person or girl. He knew nothing about what had formed me, and that meant that I could accept his feelings as they were for me as an adult. I was older than a lot of brides, but I was unable to relate to any of the village men that I had known when I was young. I could never marry anyone that I didn't respect, and I didn't respect those who would judge me as an adult but perhaps confuse that with the child I was. It is also possible that they might speak to me or judge me on the things that I might be seen to have done wrong, and Michael doesn't do that. Finally, I wanted to forget that earlier time myself. I wanted to forget the responsibility, the bad news and the judgements that we had all made about people and other parts of society. I wanted not to make the decisions, and that meant that I wanted to be in a family where I could consult or ask about things. Michael and I became respected as a married couple, and that was important to me.

Olivia and Edward, too, are married, and live at Stuchbury Hall. They had a much bigger wedding than us, and even Cromwell was invited. It is still called the Grey estate by those of us who remember, and I don't see that changing. There is still a great amount of cooperation in what is farmed in and around the village, and what is farmed on the estate. I am constantly awed by the fact that Edward's prowess in the war made him a local figure of authority. He is fair, just, makes sensible and well-thought-out decisions, and he has taken on a lot of the responsibilities of Lord Grey, and there has been talk of giving him some sort of title – although I don't see how that works with no king to grant it. At the moment, he is referred to as Commander Brown, and if he ever regrets the fact that his sister is a village girl, he makes no sign of it. He treats me with respect, and often asks my opinion. He says that he has nothing but respect for (as he puts it) the way that I ran the village during the war, "Oh, with a little help from the vicar and a few others!"

They have two sons. Robert (who in appearance is like his dead uncle) and Luke (deliberately named for Luke White). Harriet is Luke's godmother and I am Robert's. Like all boys, they sometimes fight, and they sometimes play as soldiers. Edward doesn't stop them – but when he needs to talk to them about their rough play, and as part of their education, he teaches them two things: one is about how to soldier properly – spying out the land, considering plans of attack, what the other side might do, etc. The other thing he teaches them is about tolerance and understanding. He teaches them that the village survived partly due to the actions of Black soldiers, and how differences in religious and political opinions led us into a war that did serious harm to the country, and in the end did not really solve anything. He has debates with them where they have to understand what the other is saying, why they are saying it, and sometimes they are made to argue for the other person's side. He says that if one of them wants to be a soldier, he will not stop him, but he wants him to be a tolerant soldier.

I told Michael all the work that we had done in the war, and he, too, became part of that work after the war. Then he took over part of the farm, when the owner decided to sell part of it. We were lent the money for the share in the farm by Edward, and we will pay him back when we are able to do so – although he has constantly said that was not necessary. He said that he thought I was owed it (but that must be wrong). Harriet now works helping old soldiers to recover and find work around the village and the area. She ended up running all of the three quarries that we used in the war, but the monies from them also fund village projects, and some goes to helping the soldiers that Harriet also finds jobs for. I think we will never have quite enough men to replace those we lost, and each summer we have to call in seasonable workers from the towns. At other times, we cope with what we have. Each year, the memories grow fainter, and the country slides back towards what it was before the war. Harriet seems happy as she is, and has not looked for another man. Her mother died recently, but I don't think that left a gap in Harriet's life – it was one less person that she needed to help.

Father Andrew, much to everyone else's surprise, married Florence Kirby a year or two after the end of the war. I wasn't as surprised as many people were by that – because I thought that I had detected a glint in his eyes when we had returned in the cart from my 'stay' in Akeley, although he had behaved impeccably – and continued to do so after we returned, to the extent that Florence had to guide him or lead him a bit in their romance – as she told me later. It may even have been a surprise to her that he actually managed to propose. I think that married clergymen make the Church authorities happier – as married vicars look like more solid citizens, and it means they are happier in the church where they work and are less likely to want to move on and find other challenges. I know of one other church where three single

233

clergymen in a row all decided to become missionaries. Every time I visited, there was a new vicar.

Cromwell died in 1658 and his son Richard took over. That really said to us that whatever Cromwell had meant when he rejected the title of King, he had established a reign of sorts, where the son took over from the father. Surely, control should have gone to the next person of ability, and perhaps we could find our way out of the whole mess. Then they removed Richard and, with glorious ceremony, invited Charles the Second to take over the country again – which he did in 1661! I think the dead of the war must have been rolling in their graves! Inevitably, there were further reprisals against a few of the Parliamentarians, and a few estates were returned to their previous owners. They even dug up Cromwell and hanged him, but in practice nothing changed about the way the country was governed, and perhaps nothing ever will! Oh, and we all lived happily ever after!

AUTHOR'S WORD

The village of Helmdon is in Northamptonshire, between Oxford and Northampton. It lies about 5 kilometres (or 3 miles) from the A43, which is the main road between those two cities. It also lies between Brackley and Towcester, both of which are closer to Helmdon – Brackley being 6 kilometres or 4 miles away and Towcester being 11 kilometres or 7 miles away. Traffic drives up the A43 now a lot faster than it did in 1642, and fewer folk will take the time to drive off the main road to investigate or explore what villages there are around.

Helmdon is almost exactly in the geographical location where I wanted to place my book. I grew up in Oxford, and although I never lived nearer Helmdon than Oxford, I spent enough time in the area just to the north of Oxford to know some of the roads, towns and villages of which I speak. I wanted to write about a village that was close to a main road, in an area which saw combat and was sited similarly to other villages in the area. It was near Oxford so that I could visualise the area. I looked at the map, saw Helmdon, gave it a few days, and it settled into my mind.

The basic story for this book and the original eight main characters came from the idea for a musical opera that I wrote in 2015. I researched the dates, events and history, and I think that it provided about 10,000 of the original words. I had probably written another 5,000 words on top of that before I settled on Helmdon as the location, and then it was easy to 'flesh out' the detail for another 5,000, before I added more stories. It is a moral tale. Outcome relates to behaviour. Often, outcomes changed when a chapter was rewritten or the behaviour changed. The lives of all of my characters were affected in some way by change.

After I had decided on Helmdon, the village itself wrote some of the stories – for example, the one about the quarries being an obvious subject, but even the one about the Royalist troops was suggested by Helmdon's location – and subsequently the 'Battle of Helmdon'. The location and size of Helmdon made it more likely to be a centre for places like Stuchbury and Wappenham and Astwell. Historically, it seems to have had quite a range of facilities and businesses. Having decided all of this, I mainly ignored Silverstone – because of its location on the main road. Sorry, Silverstone!

There is a lot about Helmdon in the public domain. It is possible to find out names of villagers, even their wills. I have used two or three Helmdon names, whilst others are generic. I have avoided too much specific information about individual Helmdon houses – although I found a historical reference to three 'manors' and that it was linked, too, to how the village grew and spread. I have mentioned a vicarage, too, as it was needed for one of the stories, but I have 'named' no real other houses (although several are in the public domain). I have regularly used the maps on Google to define directions.

The quarries are documented – as is the information saying which major houses (Stowe and Blenheim, for example) they supplied stone to. On the other hand, the information about the railways in the nineteenth and twentieth centuries hinders research: I refuse to believe, for example, that Station road existed earlier than the 1800s, although the Drovers' road was obviously there – but Station road (and two stations) later dominated the village. The church features heavily. It always had to, because of the differing opinions of the time. Once it was in, there was no stopping it, and it wrote some of the stories, too.

Logistically, Brackley and Towcester would have acted in the seventeenth century as the local 'towns', which could be visited in a day, and Oxford or Northampton would have involved at least overnight trips. I have used the towns and cities as places to visit, or learn lessons from, or for judicial administration, or for their markets. They are not central to the story but act as background detail. Once I had decided on Helmdon, I deliberately tried to avoid writing a book that residents would find offensive to the village, but I am aware that there are inaccuracies and fictions.

I have deliberately blurred specific locations in the village – because I didn't want to deal with accusations of inaccuracy. In some cases, it is possible for the story to be either side of the river – but there is enough detail for each story or sequence to be plausibly in Helmdon. I have suggested (although not stated) that the spread of the village was bigger than it may have been. If there were 300 people there in 1642, then they would have been concentrated more on one side of the river, whilst I suggest that more of the houses are located further up the Wappenham road.

There will be no surviving intelligible gravestones for people of Lucy's rank or status in St Mary's churchyard. Any graves or memorials that survive will be for those of the Greys' or the Greens' social level – but don't look for them, or for the murals that once covered the walls. Look instead for the stained glass. Churches in England had decoration removed twice; once during the Restoration and once during the English Civil War. I am torn. I like clean stone walls, but I like painted walls. I have seen both (and the ubiquitous whitewash), and cannot make my mind up which I prefer.

I invented some sort of public transport, I invented a constabulary, and I invented the idea of cooperative farming and industry in seventeenth-century England. I invented recovery wards for soldiers and therapy for those who were disabled or injured. I invented the start of the Army Medical Corps, and I even invented the cart park. I invented a parish council and I invented several Helmdon families. Yes, I could have changed the surnames, but if they acknowledged the connection between the colours, I didn't think I needed to. I invented a historical pageant, too.

All of the battles I mention happened in the English Civil War, on the dates I say, and with the results I have given, but I missed out mentioning perhaps twenty-five or thirty of the other battles as not germane to my stories. The main battles I wanted to include in came from the original idea, and structured the whole time period in the sort of time sections that I wanted. I wrote about ten to fifteen chapters before I had to seriously consider if there were big enough had gaps to fit in any more stories. For money, I will tell you which stories came last!

As far as I know, Prince Charles II never visited or stayed at Helmdon. Where he did stay after Worcester is documented and accessible, but it is not impossible in that month or so that he could have been elsewhere. As far as I know, too, he fathered no children who lived in Helmdon, and if you didn't pick up the fact that it was him I referred to, then I am sorry for the spoiler. He was about four or five years younger than Lucy was at the time I write about him.

Lucy was always the narrator, both in the opera and then in the book. At some point, though, her character started to develop itself, and at some point she overtook the other main characters. I was glad about this – because I could see a lot of potential in Lucy, even if others don't like the way she finally turned out and what happened to her. She became real to me in the writing. I have tried to write the way that she felt about everything, and that has led to problems in the language I use.

There is always a difficulty with historical novels. Should the author stick only to words, expressions and turns of phrase that were used at the time? I have written this book for a twenty-first-century audience. I have tried to avoid modern slang or turns of phrase, but I have also tried to write an intelligible account that my modern audience could understand. I hope that I have succeeded in this. I have therefore avoided colloquial words of the time that today's audience would not follow, and I have a horrible feeling that some of the 'turns of phrase' would not be acceptable to historians. *Mea culpa.*

If I have missed any other mistakes, then I am sorry. There are a lot of words to check through! I had to add several words to the dictionary to avoid continual allegations of misspelling – the most notable problem with Microsoft Word being waggon – which I definitely wanted in rather than wagon.

This is the second full book that I have written. The first is written under a pseudonym, because I was concerned that the subject might be applied to me, and that would not be acceptable. This one is the first book that I have written that makes a serious attempt at being a proper historical novel – so I wanted to distance the other book from it for that reason – I didn't want comparisons. I have also written a short story (published on Kindle) and two playscripts.

I have a wife, a daughter and three cats. I live in Ilkley, West Yorkshire, and have lived here since 2010. I was/have been a music teacher for about thirty years, and worked for Oxford Bus Company for ten years before doing a degree in music. Then our history went Bangor (North Wales), Manchester, Stoke on Trent, Hitchin and Exeter, before Ilkley. I am chiefly known for composition, arrangement, teaching and performance of music: www.geoffcloke.com

Geoffrey Cloke, 2024

BIBLIOGRAPHY

Wikipedia: Timeline of the English Civil War. March 2015, June 2015, Jan 2023
https://www.google.com/search?q=english+civil+war+battles+in+order&oq=English+Civil+War+Battles+in+Order&gs_lcrp=EgZjaHJvbWUqBwgAEAAYgAQyBwgAEAAYgAQyCAgBEAAYFhgeMggIAhAAGBYYHjIICAMQABgWGB4yDQgEEAAYhgMYgAQYigUyDQgFEAAYhgMYgAQYigUyDQgGEAAYhgMYgAQigXSAQkxMjczOWo0ajE3qAIAsAIA&sourceid=chrome&ie=UTF-8

Wikipedia: https://en.wik ipedia.org/wiki/Helmdon General description of the village. Jan–April 2023

Helmdon Parish Council: https://www.helmdonparishcoun cil.gov. uk/ to locate other sources. Jan–April 2023

Google Maps: https://ww w.google.co.uk/maps/place/Helmdon,+Brackley/ @52.0891154,-1.1516512,15z/data=!3m1!4b1!4m6!3m5!1s0x487 71f39889c08 bd:0xaeec6b22f52e5616!8 m2!3d52.0884459!4d-1.1446513!16zL20v MDU5dDho?entry=ttu Consulted countless ti mes to check locations of roads, places in Helmd on, surrounding villages, etc. Helmdon's relation to Oxford/Northampton for distances: Jan–April 2023

Helmdon History Resources: http://www.helmdonhistory.com/history/ston e_article.htm An article by Edward Parry. For more information about what Helmdon was known for. February 2023

Helmdon History Resources: http://www.helmdonhistory.com/ parishchurch /church_history.htm Background information about the parish church in Helmdon – appearance, outstanding features, etc. Jan– April 2023

Helmdon History Resources: http://www.helmdonhistory.com/ hist ory/helm don_wills.htm An article by Edward Parry – used for surna mes of villagers, and to try to ascertain wealth and social brackets. January 2023

Google Search: Crime and Punishment in England: 1600s. https://www.google.com/search?q=crime+and+punishment+in+1 600s+england&oq=Crime+and+punishment+in+England&gs_ lcrp=EgZjaHJvbWUqCAgHEAAYFhgeMgcIABAAGIAEMgcIARA uGIAEMgcIAhAAGIAEMggIAxAAGBYYHjIICAQQABgWGB 4yCA gFE AAYFhg eMggIBhAAG BYYHjIICAcQABgWGB4yCAgI EAAYFhgeMggICRAAGBYYHtIBCTE3ODE0ajBqNKgCAL ACAA&sourceid=chro me&ie=UTF-8

I also read the opening paragraph: March 2023
Google Search: Policing in England: 1600s
https://www.google.com/search?q=policing+in+england+1600s& sca_esv=593252948&sxsrf=AM9HkKlYuDNviRtavvwkJD1nAi7I 0Lu0JQ%3A17033331028291&ei=1MSGZcy3EaSShbIP_ PSwuAQ&oq=Policing+in+England+1600&gs_lp=Egxnd3Mtd2l6L XNlcnAiGFBvbGljaW5IGluIEVuZ2xhbmQgMTYwM CoCCAAyBRAhGKABMggQIRgWGB4YHTII ECEYFhgeGB0yCBAhGBYYHhgdMggQIRgWGB4 YHTIIECEYFhgeGB1IhWdQAFigTnABeAGQAQCY AbIBoAGWE6oBBDE1Ljm4AQHIAQD4AQGoAhTCAgcQ IxjqAhg nwgI UEAAYgAQY4 wQY6QQY6gIYt ALYAQHCAh4QLhg DGI8BGOUCGKgDGJoDGOoCGLQCGAoYjAPYAQLCAhYQ ABgDGI8BGOUCGOoCGLQCGIwD2AEAEC wgIKECM YgAQYigUYJ8ICBBAjGCfCAgsQABiABBiKBRiRAsI CFBAuGIAEGIoFGJECGKIFGJ0DGKgDwgIKEA

AYgAQYigUYQ8ICFxAuGIAEGLEDGIMBGMcBGN
EDGKgDGNIDwgIUEC4YgAQYsQMYxwEY0QMY0g
MYqAPCAhQQLhiABBixAxiDARibAxioAxjSA8ICFBAuG
IAEGIoFGJECGKIFGKgDGJ0DwgIREAAYgAQYigUYkQIYs
QMYgwHCAhMQLhiABBiKBRhDGLEDGKgDGJ0Dwg
IIEAAYgAQYsQPCAg4QABiABBiKBRixAxiDAcICFxAuG
IAEGIoFGJECGMcBGNEDGNIDGKgDwgIFEAAYgA
TCAiYQLhiABBiKBRiRAhjHARjRAxjSAxioAxiXBRjcBBjeBBj
gBNgBA8ICChAAGIAEGBQYhwLCAgYQABgWGB7CAgg
QABgWGB4YD-IBBgAIEGIBgG6BgYIARABGAG6BgYIA
hABGAu6BgYIAxABGBQ&sclient =gws-wiz-serp

I also read the opening paragraph about p olicing pre-1829. March 2023